MURDER
AT THE
PAINTED
WINGS
CAFE

MURDER AT THE PAINTED WINGS CAFE

A SENECA JAMES MYSTERY

RUTH J HARTMAN

First published by Level Best Books 2024

This novel is entirely a work of fiction. The names, characters and incidents portrayed in it are the work of the author's imagination. Any resemblance to actual persons, living or dead, events or localities is entirely coincidental.

Ruth J. Hartman asserts the moral right to be identified as the author of this work.

Author Photo Credit: Iden Ford Photography

First edition

ISBN: 978-1-68512-810-4

Cover art by Level Best Designs

This book was professionally typeset on Reedsy.
Find out more at reedsy.com

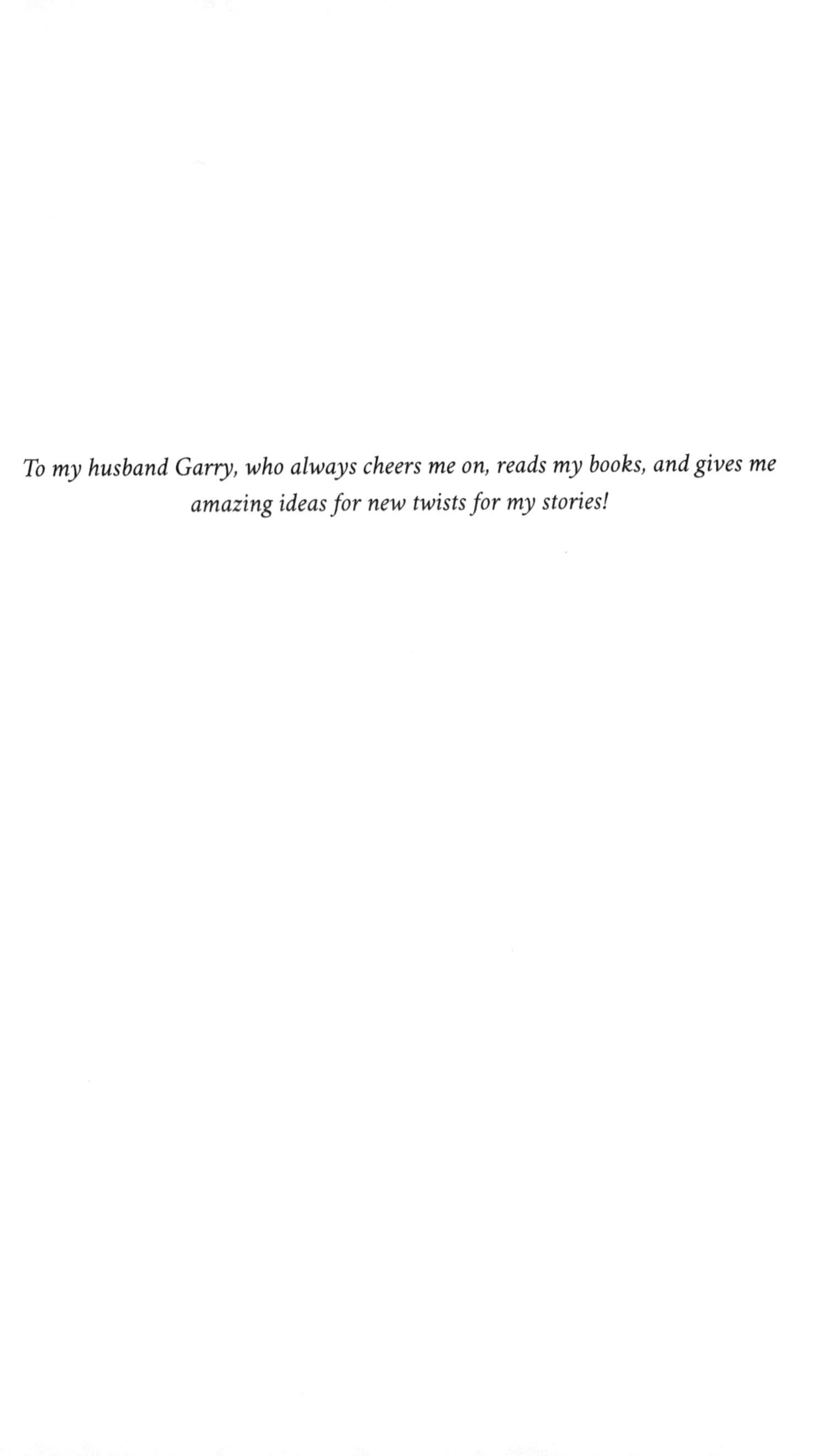

To my husband Garry, who always cheers me on, reads my books, and gives me amazing ideas for new twists for my stories!

Chapter One

At lunchtime, I headed toward my café, Painted Wings, which sat a short distance from my butterfly greenhouse and was run by my cousin, Evie. The first thing I noticed was that my cat, Winifred, wearing her monarch butterfly costume, had tagged along. This was a normal occurrence, her wearing a costume—yes, she liked it— and following me around, since my cat was so nosy. But then, she was a cat, so, that was to be expected.

When I entered the café, the second thing that caught my attention was that Evie, normally so on top of things and calm, was toe to toe with one of our regular customers, Burlington Snare, the manager of one of our two local banks in Maple Junction.

It was painfully obvious from their stiff body language, rigid jawlines, and Burlington's muttered insults, that this encounter was far from friendly. It was one of only a handful of times I'd seen Evie this upset. Something was up. And it was bad.

As I looked around the room, some customers were seated and others stood, but every single person was watching the current argument taking place. Who needed to bury themselves in looking at their phones when something more exciting than social media was unfolding right in front of them?

Just as I was ready to head across the café, Winifred pawed at my leg, wanting me to pick her up. What choice did I have since she, at least in her little mind, was royalty? Plus, the fact that she might start howling if I ignored her. Or place herself in the middle of whatever was going on with

Evie, and neither scenario was good. Evie and Burlington seemed to be having a catfight of their own, and didn't need any help from Winifred.

I grasped my cat under her tummy, careful not to wrinkle her costume, then pressed her close to my chest, glad when she let out a purr. I was grateful at least one of us was calm, because the scene taking place in Painted Wings looked to be anything but serene.

Burlington, a large man in his fifties with the worst comb over I'd ever seen, was frowning at Evie so hard, his forehead wrinkles had extension wrinkles of their own.

I moved closer. "Evie? Um, is there something I can do to help?"

My cousin jerked, startled by my words. Had she been so caught up in Burlington's tirade she hadn't noticed the room full of people who witnessed their encounter?

Her eyes, normally large anyway, were opened wider, as if she'd forgotten how to blink. "Seneca, I…" She indicated Burlington, glanced down at her finger pointing at him, then quickly lowered her hand.

It seemed Evie was at a loss for words at the moment. Maybe she'd used them up in trying to fend off Burlington. I knew for a fact my cousin wouldn't have started the fight. It just wasn't in her to do so. I normally wouldn't interfere in the way she ran the café, but today, it was obvious she needed assistance.

"Okay," I glanced first at Evie, then at Burlington, "why don't you tell me what happened here? Maybe we can get it sorted out and—"

Burlington stared at me. "I'll tell you what happened. And I'd like everyone in the café to hear it. That girl," he lifted his chin toward Evie, "had the audacity to ask me for a bank loan."

A few people mumbled from the crowd behind us. One man laughed.

Confused, I lowered my eyebrows as I studied Burlington. "Well, isn't that what you do at your bank? Give loans to customers when they need one?"

"She doesn't really need it, now, does she?" His hands landed on his hips.

I repositioned Winifred, who was now poking my shoulder with one of her claws. "I'm quite sure that if my cousin came to you for help, she really did need it."

Evie snapped out of her reverie. "Seneca's right, Burlington, er, Mr. Snare. I came to you at your office, at the appointed time you gave me, and respectfully requested a loan that, yes, I do desperately need. You said you'd definitely give me your answer within two days. And that was a week and a half ago. I thought that was ample time for you to have made your decision, considering the time frame you gave me."

Normally, we all called Burlington by his first name. But now I wondered if Evie had switched to calling him Mr. Snare out of respect for his position and title. More likely, she hoped it might cause him to be more inclined to help her out. Not that I blamed her. I would have done the same.

"The proper procedure is to call our office to inquire over the phone about your loan status, young lady," he said. "Not pounce on an innocent person the moment he steps into an eating establishment.

At the word pounce, Winifred meowed. I ran my fingers through the fur between her ears, trying to keep her calm. I leaned down to whisper, "He didn't mean you, kitty."

"I did call." Evie crossed her arms over her chest. "I left several messages, which is why I chose to say something when you arrived here today. I went through all the proper channels imposed by you, Mr. Snare. And once those didn't work, I felt I needed to take a different approach. I'm on a time crunch and needed to know as soon as possible what my options might be. Because if you can't help me, I'll need to come up with a different plan."

He waved his hand, indicating the café. "Yet you had to bring it up in a public venue, letting everyone know, like I was some sort of salesman out on a call. It's unseemly and frankly more than a little crass."

When she shook her head, her long turquoise earrings smacked against the sides of her neck beneath her short hair. "That's not at all how it was. And you know it. I whispered the question to you. I didn't trumpet it to the whole crowd like you did just now." Evie's face turned red, and tears threatened to spill down her cheeks.

I knew my cousin. She was normally a peace-loving woman, but right now, she was barely holding it together and ready to explode. Her frustration and embarrassment came off of her in waves. I wanted to go and hug her, but now wasn't the time. She was so rigid with anger, any kind of physical touch might send her careening over the edge.

A shuffling noise came from behind me. I peered over my shoulder to see Mable Kane heading toward me with her walker. People standing in the aisle between the tables moved aside to allow her to pass by safely. We adored our favorite octogenarian customer. I hoped she wouldn't become upset by the unwanted noise and tension in the room.

"Hello, Seneca." Then, as if there was nothing amiss in the café, she smiled at Evie and said, "Evie, dear, I'd like my usual, please." She then turned slowly, made her way to her favorite table, and took a seat. Her walker, who she'd named Wilbur, was positioned next to her.

Every time Mable visited Painted Wings, we all tried to accommodate her, and to keep her calm and unbothered. Apparently, due to Mable's hearing issues, she had missed the argument and bad vibes around the room. She smiled benignly at others in the café, then gave me a wave. That was okay. The happier she stayed, the better. I waved back, then turned toward Evie.

However, others in the café had no problem hearing the debate or taking in the scene before them with rapt attention. I knew for sure several of my regular customers had jobs to get back to soon, and normally got their orders to go. But not today. A lot of businesses would be put on hold with the number of people staying behind in the café.

Two older gentlemen, Sid Fairgate and Norman Gates, widowers who always seemed to hang out together, were watching the argument, eyes wide and enthralled, as if taking in an entertaining circus act. Their eyes sparkled in anticipation, and their smiles, beneath bushy mustaches, were wide. Those two always seemed to be in the middle of things, hoping for something to liven up their day. The trouble with that was, their entertainment often came at the expense of another person.

Also, Betty Rollings, who owned the local flower shop, stood nearby, holding a bouquet of pink carnations, no doubt to brighten our customers' day. She did this often, her habit placing them on our back counter, so everyone could enjoy them. However, today, she stood still, blinking at the scene in front of her and watching us intently. Then she switched her focus solely to Burlington, her eyes narrowed. Was she upset on Evie's behalf, or did she have another reason to be miffed at the bank manager?

And Mike Larsh, a young man in his twenties who worked at a local convenience store, sat at a nearby table. He clutched his ever-present paperback, his thumb marking open the pages as if he'd been interrupted while reading. With as loud as Evie and Burlington had been, I had no doubt Mike had indeed been transported out of his story and into the mayhem in front of him.

From the kitchen area of the café, Murray Grimes, our amazing café chef, appeared behind the counter, his eyes narrowed at Burlington, as his fingers absentmindedly brushed his long, white mustache into place, like some western gunslinger ready to draw his weapon on the bad guy. From the way he glared at the bank manager, maybe it was a good thing Murray wielded a spatula instead of a gun.

Suddenly, Winifred leaned away from me and reached out her paw toward Evie, tapping her arm. My cousin gave a tremulous smile, then lifted my cat from my arms. What was up with Winifred? She didn't often want to go to anyone besides me, or my best friend, Cody. But I was glad she'd made the offer, because Evie's shoulders relaxed a little as she snuggled the cat.

If Winifred could somehow summon up a purr, then we'd really have something. Her purrs had been known to relieve my headaches, stomach discomfort, and low moods, all from that little place inside her throat that vibrated out all kinds of happiness that only a cat could produce.

But Burlington's look of distaste when he saw Winifred was unmistakable. No surprise there, since he'd always made it plain he couldn't tolerate cats, or any animals for that matter. In my opinion, it was a pretty good bet that animals felt the same about him. Even though I longed to comment on his expression, it wouldn't do me, my cousin, or the café, any favors.

When Evie stood up straighter, she appeared to have gained back some of her courage. She looked straight at Burlington. "Mr. Snare, I'm… sorry for your negative experience in Painted Wings today."

I knew how hard it was for her to force out those words when the mantra, the customer is always right, didn't come anywhere close to being the truth this time.

His mouth formed a small smile, like he was winning the argument, and he liked it.

"So," said Evie, "that being said, I'd be, uh… happy to give you your meal today, on the house." When she uttered those words, I knew she meant she'd take the hit, paying for it herself, which I hated. But she was stubborn, a family trait I also possessed, and wouldn't change her mind once she decided on a course of action. In her shoes, I would have done exactly the same thing, and would have hated every second of giving Burlington any satisfaction.

But instead of Burlington thanking Evie, offering an apology of his own, or even giving her a pleasant expression, he let out a loud, obnoxious snort of laughter that reverberated around the room.

A communal gasp traveled around the crowd, including one from me. Winifred even hissed at the man, giving him her feline opinion of his snarkiness. I gave her a few extra pets for her support of Evie.

I shook my head. Evie had made the effort, extending the olive branch, and Burlington had, metaphorically speaking, chopped up the branch with a machete, tossed the pieces on the floor, and spit on them for good measure.

"Miss James," he said to Evie. "I'm a respected banker in this community. I'll not have it said that I was neglectful in paying my own bills, unlike some people I could mention." He gave her a meaningful glance. "Allow me to be the bigger person and pay for my meal, as meager and distasteful as it was."

My first instinct was to yell at him. Instead, I took a deep breath, let it out, and stood still, hoping to convey to my cousin that I was there for her, no matter what. I didn't even look in Murray's direction, sure he'd be livid at Burlington's slight about the quality of the food.

We waited as Burlington reached back into his pants pocket, then lowered his bushy eyebrows so his beady eyes were barely visible.

"Where is it?" he screeched, once again earning another hiss from my cat.

I was getting weary of his attitude and meanness. "Where is what?"

"My wallet!"

I lifted my hands in the I don't know gesture. "Maybe you left it at home?"

"No." He lowered his arms to his sides. "I had it when I entered this establishment. And now…. It's gone." He faced Evie, giving her a cold glare.

"Wait." Evie gasped. "You don't think…" She pressed Winifred closer to her chest. "You can't possibly think that I—"

"Oh yes, that is precisely what I think. No, it's what I know. Give it back. *Now.*" His last word was punctuated by a foot stomp, causing Winifred to narrow her eyes and growl.

"I don't have it. Why would I take your wallet?"

He glanced around the room at the ever-growing audience. "Isn't it obvious? You want to get back at me for not giving you the loan, for embarrassing you. So, you took my very own money from me, and tried to make me look like a laughingstock in front of the café customers. Well, it's not going to work. You'll give it back. And you'll do it now."

From my right, Murray rapped his fist, hard, on the counter to get everyone's attention. "Burlington, I can tell you right now that Evie didn't take your wallet. She never could or would."

"Why should I listen to you, Murray Grimes?" Burlington's sneer rivaled any good movie villain. "You're nothing but a glorified fry cook."

People grumbled from behind me, no doubt upset at Burlington's remarks. Murray's creations had no equal, and people loved them.

"I may be a fry cook, and proud of it, but I know the truth when it's right in front of me. Something aside from Evie taking it happened to your wallet. Besides, your money isn't wanted in this café anyway. I think it's time you left."

Burlington's mouth opened and closed in a pretty good guppy imitation. Finally, he held up his hand and declared, "I'll get justice, and I'll get my wallet back from you. Just wait and see. You haven't seen the last of me!" He stormed across the café, the crowd parting to allow his passage. The people cheered when he was outside of the building.

What in the world had just happened? Burlington wasn't known as a warm and fluffy guy, but to treat Evie like that was way out of line.

Just as I reached out to touch Evie's shoulder to comfort her, she slumped against Murray, who caught her before she slid to the floor. Winifred, appalled at the sudden change in her cuddle situation, growled, jumped to the floor, and, after dodging several pairs of human legs, scurried outside through the open doorway.

It took a few seconds for customers to realize the spectacle was over, but they soon began talking amongst themselves. Some found seats, others headed back outside to continue their workday, or migrated toward the order counter. Poor Evie. Would she even be able to work today?

"Honey," I said, "are you all right?"

She wiped her eyes, glanced toward the door where Burlington had taken his exit, then nodded. "I'll be fine, Seneca. Really."

I frowned, watching her, hoping what she said was true. "If you're sure. But I could stay and help you." She looked droopy and spent. Not good at any time, but especially at the beginning of her workday. "I don't mind staying."

"No. You go back to the greenhouse. You have a lot of work to do there."

And it was true, I did. But my concern for Evie was weighing heavily on me. I glanced at the doorway, wondering where Burlington had stormed off to. Part of me was afraid to know.

Burlington's warning about not seeing the last of him made me shudder. What mayhem was he planning for Evie next?

Chapter Two

The next day, I'd just gotten back to the greenhouse from checking the monarchs in my milkweed fields. The butterflies were all doing great, partly due to me acquiring the property adjacent to mine that was also full of milkweed for them to eat and lay their eggs on.

No matter how much time I spent with the painted orange beauties, I never got tired of seeing them, caring for them, or my favorite thing, when they deemed me safe enough to land on and rest for a bit. With the exception of Winifred's purr, I couldn't think of anything more relaxing than that.

As I spooned out Winifred's smelly salmon into a ceramic food dish sporting a cat's face on the front, my phone buzzed. The screen showed Evie's name.

I nudged Winifred's food dish with my foot, as I answered my phone. "Hey Evie, how's it—"

"Seneca!" she shouted. "You need to come to Painted Wings!"

I glanced down at my hands, which were covered in dirt and grime, and a little bit of cat food. "Um, sure, I'll be over in a—"

"No, right *now.*"

I frowned. It wasn't like Evie to yell. Something big was up. Was she still upset over her argument with Burlington? "I'll be right there," I said, but she'd already ended the call.

I stared at the dark phone screen. What in the world was going on over there? Evie's work ethic and wonderful way with customers usually meant business carried on without a hitch. I stuck my phone in my pocket, ready to see what Evie had going on.

I glanced down at Winifred, who had inhaled her lunch so fast, she had some food stuck to her whiskers. Assuming she'd need to wash her face for the next hour, I waved to her. "Okay, Evie needs me at the café, Winifred, so I'll be over at—"

My cat raced past me and then pawed at the closed screen door, her orange tail flipping in impatience of finding an obstacle barring her way.

"All right, then. I guess you can come with me."

I hurried toward her, opened the door to let her out, then jogged to the café. Evie's calls usually involved requests for me to go buy emergency ketchup or napkins, but this didn't sound like any normal call. The faster I went, the more concerned I became.

When I neared Painted Wings, it seemed like a repeat of yesterday. A crowd had formed right outside the open doors, the people pointing and whispering. Had Burlington come back so soon to make good on his threat? Why hadn't I insisted on staying with Evie and working with her yesterday and today? My duties would have gotten behind, but Evie's state of mind was more important.

However, my cousin wasn't with the onlookers. Maybe she was already inside. Then why were all these people standing out here? I could see that the double doors at the entrance were wide open, so the customers hadn't been mistakenly locked out. I noticed Connie Sellers standing nearby. "Hey, Connie, is Evie inside?"

Connie didn't answer, but her face had gone pale. She pointed to the café, opened her mouth as if to speak, but nothing came out.

When my polite excuse-me's didn't get me any farther through the doorway, I gently finagled my way inside. It took a few seconds before I focused on Evie, who stood near the front counter. Murray was there, with his arm around her shoulders. Since I'd assumed yesterday's comfort he'd given to Evie was an anomaly—the man usually came across as gruff and foreboding to those who didn't know him well—it was a shock to see him demonstrate physical kindness again today. Whatever was going on, it must have been a lot worse than having run out of ketchup.

And it was.

Because, as I made my way closer and could see past the tables and chairs that had blocked my view, I discovered what all the fuss was about. Make that a very messy fuss. I gasped.

Burlington was lying face down in a pool of dark blood. Unfortunately, that sight was something I knew all too well, from a previous murder, when I'd discovered my lawyer in the same predicament on my greenhouse floor. Since Burlington wasn't moving and couldn't possibly be breathing the way his face was pressed into the pool of coagulating red liquid, he had to be dead.

I was startled out of my thoughts when Evie's name was mentioned several times by the audience behind me. I grumbled. It was only natural for people to link this to what had happened yesterday with the argument between my cousin and the banker. But that was how rumors got started. And I didn't want that to happen to Evie.

When I took a few more steps toward the body, a glance at my feet showed Winifred skulking up beside me. In all the calamity of entering Painted Wings, I'd forgotten she'd followed me.

My cat's paw slowly edged out toward Burlington's prone form, ready to pat his face, or worse, check out the horrid red puddle. I bent down and snatched her up before she could get anything besides the normal foot traffic dirt on her fur.

I made eye contact with Murray. His mustache seemed to droop along with the rest of him. Even though most people thought of him as grumpy, he cared about Evie, me, and Winifred, as if we were his own family. Seeing Evie in such distress must be really hard for him, too.

"Murray, did you call Cody?"

"Yeah, he's on his way."

"Good. Thank you."

He glanced down at Evie. "Doing all right?"

Evie let out a sob, then collected herself somewhat, standing up straighter beneath Murray's arm. "Yes, I... um, yes."

Voices came from the crowd. From above the top of the people, I spotted Cody, my best friend, and our local sheriff, taller than the rest.

He waved his long arm toward the open doorway. "All right, everyone. Maybe it's best if you all go on home now."

A communal groan followed. No one liked to miss out on the latest happenings. Even, apparently, when a person had met his demise.

Cody stepped inside, spotted us, then made his way over. When he reached me, he touched my arm. "Seneca, were you here to discover the body?"

"Not this time." I lifted my chin in Evie's direction.

Cody pulled on disposable gloves, knelt, and examined Burlington. Afterward, he stood, made a quick call on his phone, then looked at my cousin. "Evie?"

Evie blinked, seemed to focus. "H-hey, Cody."

His brown eyes studied her. "Can you tell me what happened here?" His voice was gentle, as always.

She gave a slow nod, thanked Murray for his support, then moved closer to Cody. Murray, his help no longer necessary, crossed his arms over his large chest, frowning at the proceedings.

"Well," said Evie, "when I walked in to start preparing the place for the lunch crowd, he was already here."

Cody nodded. "Already dead, I assume?"

"Y-yes." Her voice faltered.

"Take your time. I know it's rough talking about it."

I stepped closer to my cousin, taking her hand in mine. I had to reposition Winifred to one side in order to have a hand free, earning me a growl from my cat. Evie smiled her thanks to me, then focused on Cody.

Evie took a deep breath, then let it out. "I unlocked the door and—"

"You're positive it was locked?"

"Yes, I'm sure. I turned on the lights, as usual, the switches by the main doors." She pointed toward the entrance.

"Obviously, Burlington got in another way. We'll check that out. And then… you noticed him here?"

"Not at first. Since he was in front of the counter, but behind the tables here, I couldn't see him until… until I nearly tripped over his legs." Evie blinked rapidly, as if she was going to cry.

"Don't worry about it," I said. "It's not your fault."

She frowned. "Of course, it's not my fault. I didn't kill him."

"I didn't mean that, Evie. I know you didn't. I meant, it's not your fault you nearly tripped over him, lying here."

"Oh." Her cheeks turned pink. "I'm sorry, I'm so upset. I don't know what I'm saying." She and I rarely had a cross word between us, but these weren't exactly normal circumstances.

I gave her hand a squeeze, then released it. I knew exactly how she felt. And it was the worst feeling ever. It broke my heart that she'd had to experience finding someone who'd died, someone she'd known, someone she'd recently argued with in front of an audience.

But wait…. Surely Cody wouldn't think Evie had anything to do with Burlington's death? However, after checking Cody's reaction, I relaxed. He was looking at Evie with compassion and sympathy for her current predicament.

I should never have thought he'd consider her guilty. When I was the one on the hot seat for my lawyer's murder, I'd been afraid Cody suspected me of that. But of course, he hadn't since he knew me so well. And he'd known Evie for just as long. No way he'd think she had anything to do with the man's death.

Cody glanced down at the body. "All right, so did you get close enough to check to see if Burlington was breathing, or…"

She stifled a sob. "I…I touched the side of his neck, where there wasn't any blood. But no pulse. Not that I expected there to be." She pointed to Burlington's position, facedown.

"You did the right thing, Evie."

I smiled at Cody, in appreciation for treating Evie with such kindness.

The crowd at the doorway, who obviously hadn't all heeded Cody's earlier words to vacate the café, parted. Right then, Arnold Wellings, Maple Junction's funeral director, entered, carrying a black body bag. The wiry, sixty-something man always appeared gloomy. Not only didn't he smile, but he didn't speak. For the longest time, I'd thought maybe he was mute, but when in his office during the investigation of my lawyer's murder, he'd uttered an audible phrase to me. The fact that Arnold had spoken had startled me so badly, I still jumped when I was around him.

Cody nodded to Arnold. After Arnold did his own brief examination of the body, he, with Cody's assistance, zipped Burlington into the bag, and carried him outside to Arnold's waiting hearse. Having witnessed this same scenario not too long ago, I'd be perfectly happy never seeing that sight again.

The body in a bag made me think of my monarch caterpillars in their cocoons. But what I looked at now was neither beautiful nor happy.

I glanced down at the puddle of blood left behind from Burlington's injuries. Had he fallen and hit his head? Or possibly slipped on something, landing hard on his way down? But why would he have been here in the middle of the night? And how had he gotten inside when the doors had been locked? I knew my cousin. She was a stickler for details and was extra careful. If she said the doors were locked, then they had been.

As I stared at the blood, it brought all my memories back from the previous murder, when my lawyer was lying in a similar dark red stain on my greenhouse floor, and I'd been the one to enter the building one morning, turn on the lights, and see him lying there.

But this wasn't about me. I gave myself a mental shake. Evie needed my support, and I'd do everything I could to help her. Maybe Burlington's death was just an accident. Although, my heart told me that probably wasn't the case. That he'd met with a much crueler fate. And that there was someone in Maple Junction who'd killed him. The previous killer had died, so couldn't possibly be guilty of this crime. What were the odds that a tiny town like ours would produce more than one murderer?

A fluffy orange tail whacked me in the chin as Winifred struggled in my arms. Her caramel eyes had a determined expression only present within felines. She wanted to use her natural nosiness to investigate, and she wanted to do it now.

"No, kitty, I can't let you down. It's not safe. You'll have to stay with me for a while longer, okay?"

She made a sound like a grumble, then hung her head over the side of my arm, pouting because she wasn't getting her way. I ran my other hand over her back, making the stiff fabric of her butterfly wings on her costume move as if she was flying.

Murray, watching the crowd still hovering at the doorway, gave a growl not unlike Winifred's, and headed in their direction. He waved his muscular arms. "All right, you people. Time to move on. We'll put a notice on the door when we can reopen."

The customers muttered and protested, but Murray wasn't going to change his mind. They'd been around him long enough to know that. He posted himself at the entrance, his hands on his hips, and stared down any who might dare to argue.

There were none. Everyone eventually wandered away.

Satisfied he'd done his duty, Murray returned to the rest of us.

"Thanks," said Cody. "Before I leave today, I'll put up some crime scene tape when I do a more thorough investigation of the café."

"It'll take more than yellow tape to keep them out."

"Yeah, I know." Cody rubbed his hand down his chin. "But it's worth a try, anyway."

Evie had gone pale and looked as if she might keel over.

"Hey," I said, "why don't we sit down?"

She nodded and found a chair close by, but still far enough away from the blood that we wouldn't have to look directly at it. I took the seat next to her, handing her Winifred, in hopes my cat would play nice and not growl, hiss, or struggle to jump down.

Winifred must have been ready to take a nap anyway because she settled down on Evie's lap, turning in a circle before contentedly washing her paws. It wouldn't last long, I knew that. But any comfort my fluffy feline could give my cousin right now would be a plus.

Murray opted to remain standing, watching all of us with an expression somewhere between anger and sadness.

After Cody grabbed a chair near us, he turned it to face in our direction. He leaned forward, his forearms on his knees. "First off, Evie, are you holding up okay under the circumstances?"

Her nod was shaky, but her eyes held a familiar determination she normally showed.

"Good." He smiled. "Now, as for Burlington,"—he pointed his thumb toward the scene of the crime—"it looks as if he was struck in the back of the head with something."

I leaned forward as well. "So, you don't think it could have been an accident?"

With a glance first at Evie, then back to me, he shook his head. "No, I don't think so. He was found lying on his front, but the injury was on the back of his skull. So, I don't see how he could have hit his head in the fall."

"I was afraid of that," said Murray. "Just like when Seneca found that lawyer guy in her greenhouse."

Cody nodded. "I'm afraid so."

"So…murder?" Evie squeaked out.

With a comforting pat on her arm, Cody said, "Yeah, I think that's what we're looking at."

"Look, Cody, I didn't do this. I didn't—"

"Yeah, I know."

"We all know." I reached over to pet Winifred, who was now purring with her eyes closed, still on Evie's lap. "Don't worry about that, Evie. Cody is on the case. So am I. And Winifred."

"Count me in, too," said Murray.

"Thanks, you guys." Evie wiped her eyes. "It's good to know I'm not alone in this."

"No," I said, "never alone."

There had to be an explanation of what happened to Burlington and who had done it. I was determined to find out and clear my sweet cousin's name. Even though Cody knew she was innocent, there was still the unofficial court of the town's gossip mill. And that, as I'd found out the hard way, could do quite a bit of damage on its own.

Chapter Three

Painted Wings was closed for a few hours while Cody and his deputy, Bud, finished their investigation. Once they were through, I'd help Evie clean up the mess. When my attorney had died and left a huge red stain on my greenhouse floor, I'd been the one to clean that up, too. Maple Junction was so small we didn't have people whose job it was to take care of matters like that. Cody and Bud were the extent of our police department. But people residing here were used to taking care of themselves. Even if it meant doing something as unpleasant and sad as cleaning up what a dead person had left behind.

After I checked on my caterpillars in their pens and the adult monarchs in their milkweed fields, I headed to the bank. I was running a little behind in my chores and errands for the day since my assistant, Annie, was now going to medical school, her lifelong dream.

We hadn't worked out the details yet of how much she'd be able to help me now, since her classes were an hour away. There'd been a mention of her possibly assisting me out on breaks and long weekends. That would help me out some, anyway. I hoped I didn't need to replace her, but that was a possibility. The girl was odd, but she was amazing with the caterpillars and loved working here.

But for now, I had some money to deposit from payments at Painted Wings, and also from recent sales I'd had from a wedding butterfly release, a similar one from a celebration of life, and from people who bought monarchs from me to supplement their own butterfly populations. Selling the monarchs to schools and museums also produced income at certain times of the year.

After I entered the bank's wide front door, which sat between short white pillars, I stepped into the small main lobby. There were no other customers, which wasn't unusual. Having three or four people ahead of me in line was considered a rush in our town.

As always, I headed straight to Karen Blain's station. I'd known her for years. We were more acquaintances than close friends, but I did like her. She'd actually been helpful in giving me information to find the real killer in the previous murder, even though I'd ended up bribing her with Murray's amazing cheesy fries to release her tendency to gossip. But she loved Murray's cooking so much, she hadn't seemed to mind.

If, for some reason, I ever went to the bank and didn't head straight to Karen's station, instead seeking help from Lawrence Goodman, the second-in-command teller, Karen would have a crying meltdown. It had happened before, and I had no desire to experience a loud, drippy repeat. She was a nice woman, though a tad dramatic.

But when I got to Karen's area, she wasn't her normal talkative, exuberant self. Instead, she was crying. Again.

Oh no.

Was it because I'd given Lawrence a friendly wave when I entered the bank lobby? He was a nice guy, after all, and deserved at least that. Had Karen taken offense to my wave, and thought I was ditching her for the other teller? I always hoped Lawrence didn't feel slighted that I seemed to favor Karen over him, even when there were times his line was obviously shorter than hers, and he appeared to be efficient and friendly to his customers.

Karen's eyes were red from weeping. She grabbed a tissue from a nearby dispenser and wiped her eyes. "Oh, Seneca. It's… well, you heard about Mr. Snare?" She shook her head. "Oh, of course you did, since it happened on your property, after all."

I grimaced. Even though Karen was correct about it being on my property, the fact that the only other murder happening in town was in my greenhouse wouldn't escape anyone's notice. The gossip train would travel full speed ahead, leaving me in its dusty wake, thoroughly talked about and pointed at.

But seeing how Karen was in such a sobbing state, and obviously upset over her boss' demise, I held in my thoughts of how the murder would affect me and instead gave her an encouraging smile.

"I'm sorry for what you're going through," I said. "If there's anything I can do to help, I'm here."

But she wasn't comforted. She gazed at me through bleary eyes, let out an owl-like screech, then turned and fled through a back door that I'd once been told led to a small employee lounge the size of a car trunk.

With a glance at the clock on the wall behind me, I grumbled. I'd hoped to accomplish my task here quickly, so I could get back to the café, spend time with Evie, and finish some work of my own. However, Karen running away wasn't making that likely to happen. She'd mentioned Mr. Snare. Had they been close? Maybe that was her reason for being distraught, which made sense. He had been her boss, after all. I tried to remember if she'd ever said anything about them being friends, but I came up empty.

I checked around the lobby. There was no one here except Lawrence and me. Gee, not awkward or anything. Now what? Did I breach Karen's unspoken rule and slide over to Lawrence's counter for assistance? I was in an uncomfortable spot here, not wanting to hurt Karen's feelings, yet hating that I might be offending Lawrence all the times I chose his coworker over him.

From my left, I heard a sigh, followed by soft-soled shoes stepping on the tile floor. The sounds soon produced Lawrence. He positioned himself at her counter, which might upset her, but under the circumstances, she'd left her post unattended.

"Sorry about that, Seneca. Can I help you today?"

I let out a relieved breath, glad he'd taken the initiative so I didn't have to. "Yes, please. I need to make a deposit." I grabbed the checks and deposit slip from the inside pocket of my purse and slid them to the middle of the counter toward Lawrence.

He typed something into the computer. Was he putting in his own code so the records would show he'd done the transaction? That might make Karen mad if she found out, but it couldn't be helped right now. And it might happen again, if customers came in for Karen, but waited at her station.

I tapped my fingers on the edge of the counter, impatient to get going. But when I realized how that might appear, I let my hand relax at my side. "Thanks for this, Lawrence. Um, is Karen"—I tilted my head toward the back area—"going to be all right?"

He lifted one shoulder up, then down. "She's been like that ever since Mr. Snare died. The bank board is trying to fill that position in a hurry, but in the meantime, it will be a little confusing around here, as you would expect. We've had auditors in here going through everything. I've been told it's something they do when a higher-up employee leaves." He blinked. "And he left in a big way, I guess you could say."

"Yes, unfortunately."

His eyes widened. "Wait, didn't I hear he was found in Painted Wings Café?"

"That's right."

"Gee…sorry. I wasn't thinking when I talked about Mr. Snare. It must be rough on you, having to go through all of that."

I waited for him to add the word 'again' at the end of his sentence but was relieved when he hadn't.

As Lawrence took my checks and deposit slip and began to type on the keyboard again, he stopped. "Actually, I take back what I said about Karen earlier, that she'd been upset since Mr. Snare died. Now that I think about it, Karen has been majorly out of sorts for a few days. She never said what the problem was and put out a vibe that she didn't want anyone to ask, so I didn't. She's a nice woman, but sometimes she can be…" His face reddened as if realizing he'd made that last comment out loud.

I smiled, wanting him to know I wasn't offended. As I waited for Lawrence to process my payments, I thought about Karen.

If her bad mood had started before her boss died, then her tears were for another reason, or an additional one, at least. I hadn't been to the bank for over a week, so I must have missed out on her moodiness. Maybe her tears weren't simply because of her boss' death. Was she having family trouble? Boyfriend problems? She hadn't mentioned seeing anyone lately, but it was hard to know since she kept it to herself. I felt bad for her, though, since whatever it was had made her so upset she ended up in tears. Crying that hard was bad enough, but doing it at work must be embarrassing.

I looked at the doorway Karen had fled through a bit ago. "Listen, Lawrence, I don't want to sound nosy, but I've never seen her this upset before." Okay, I was nosy, but he didn't need to know that. "Is there something else going on with her, since you mentioned she'd been upset for a while now?"

He waved away my comment. "You're not being nosy. Believe me, I've been concerned about her too. When you work right next to somebody day after day, you come to care about how they're doing."

"That's true." I thought of Murray, who'd become like a protective uncle in a way. And Evie. While it was true she and I were family, we were also friends. "But she never confided in you what might be wrong?"

"No. I assume it's about Mr. Snare, but I can't know that for sure. It's just been so stressful around here, as you can imagine. We've all been on edge." He finished my transaction and handed me my receipt. "Here you go."

"Thanks. I hope things get better here at the bank for you, with Mr. Snare being gone."

"Me too. I'm not looking forward to whatever transitions we might have in store for us. The board has made it clear there will be some changes."

With a wave, I turned and headed back toward the door. Maybe Cody and Bud were finished with their work at the café, and I could help Evie get it ready for customers again.

As soon as I stepped outside, I received a text from Evie. There were no words, just an emoji of what looked to be a frying pan.

I typed back with a question mark.

Her reply came with lots of exclamation marks, then, "It's a frying pan."

I shook my head. Maybe Evie needed a vacation from Painted Wings. She was obviously having trouble dealing with everyday things at the café. When I texted her that suggestion, her reply was immediate.

"No! Frying Pan! The murder weapon! Cody found it!"

My eyes widened as I read and re-read her answer. Having found the murder weapon made it seem all the more real. And there went any doubt of it being an accident, which had been wishful thinking on my part.

I drove faster than I legally should have, hoping with the sheriff as my best friend, I wouldn't get in trouble. Besides, I knew exactly where he and his deputy were at the moment, and I needed to get there fast.

And Evie, who was already traumatized from the argument with Burlington and discovering his body, would be frantic with worry about the murder weapon being found. Even though Cody had assured her he believed her to be innocent, I knew how it felt when the clues started rolling in and pointed toward the person everyone had already deemed guilty.

When I'd been concerned I'd be arrested for my attorney's murder, I'd made a wrong move and asked my ex-husband, our town's only remaining lawyer, for advice. That had opened up a whole lot of memories and new aggravations when Payne brought up us getting back together. Not only had I said no way, but Cody had been upset on my behalf, never having trusted Payne. I still wish I'd listened to my best friend about my boyfriend back in high school. If I had, I might have avoided lots of heartache, a crumbled marriage, and a broken heart.

A few minutes later, I was parked in front of my greenhouse. I grabbed my purse and ran to the café. The doors were shut, which was unusual for such a warm day, but I understood why. Left open, it would allow everyone and his uncle to step right on in and be in the middle of things they shouldn't see.

When I reached the doors, I also discovered they were locked, probably another smart move, so I took out my key and let myself in.

When Evie spotted me, she ran across the café, then threw her arms around me. "Seneca, it's terrible!"

I hugged her for a minute, then pulled away. "You mean the frying pan?"

"Now not only are people saying I did it because of my fight with Burlington the day before his death, now some have added the wrinkle that I occasionally use the frying pan when Murray needs an extra hand. And you know that's true."

"But hardly ever, right? I mean, it's usually just him."

"Right, but that doesn't matter. Not to some folks around here."

I glanced toward the front entrance. "Wait, if you just now found out about the frying pan, but the doors to the café have been locked, then how do people even know?"

Evie pointed to one of the side windows in the café. Several customers were standing out there, watching us. "I guess we were talking loud enough that they heard Cody's discovery."

"Okay, I get that, but how are people blaming you if they weren't even here? How did they let you know? Did they yell at you through the window glass?"

She shook her head, then reached into her pocket and tugged out her phone. After swiping her thumb across the screen, she held it up so I could see. Message after message was on her phone, pointing fingers—not literally, except for the one emoji that showed a cartoon character doing exactly that—saying she must be guilty.

I hugged her again, knowing how it felt to have people think the worst of someone. "Listen, I know it looks like there are tons of people sending you messages."

She waved the phone in front of me. "There are fourteen messages on here."

I glanced at the screen again. "True, but look, two are from Norman. And two are from Sid."

"All right, I'll give you that. But that's a lot of people who are thinking I'm capable of something I'm not." She shook the phone as if trying to empty the negative messages onto the floor.

"But Evie, think of all the loyal friends you have who would never in a million years believe anything bad about you."

"I know. I just can't get past the ones who do." She put her phone back in her pocket.

I got it. It was hard to focus on the positive when the negative was staring her right in the face. Difficult to keep up with everyday tasks when your future seemed scary and uncertain.

Footsteps came from my left. Bud walked toward us from the kitchen area carrying a large evidence bag, gave a nod, then passed us without a word.

I waited, knowing Cody wouldn't be far behind. And I was right. He stepped out from behind the counter, where he must have been crouched down since I hadn't noticed him before now. He gave me a sad smile. "I guess Evie told you we found the murder weapon."

"Yep." I rubbed Evie's shoulder.

She looked at Cody. "If you're finished, can I start cleaning up now?"

"Yes, I'm finished. Do you want me to help you?" His eyes were kind, showing how much he cared about Evie.

"No, but thank you."

I knew what she'd say, because it was the words I'd used when in the same situation. She might get Cody to leave, but no way she was getting rid of me. "I'll be here to help."

Evie's eyebrows shot up. "But I just said…"

"Listen, I know how you feel, since I've been there before. But think about it. There are people clamoring to get back in here, and you know how impatient some of our regulars can be. The longer the café stays closed, the more outrageous stories they'll be passing around out there. If I help you, it will get done that much faster, and we can both get back to work, right?"

She pointed toward the entrance. "But you have things to do and—"

"My dear cousin, I'm not leaving."

"Okay. Thanks."

Cody chuckled. "Now that you two have that settled, I'll be on my way. I have all the evidence we need. Want me to take down the crime scene tape by the door?"

I thought about it, then shook my head. "I'll do it after everything is ready. Otherwise, people will take it as an invitation to come on in."

"Good point. I'll go then. Call if you need me." He went to the front door, shooing away some people who arrived after I came inside.

After he'd closed the door behind him, I hurried to relock it. No sense making it easy for people to walk right in. As I studied the café, I groaned. It really was a mess. Cody and Bud couldn't help that, with checking out everything, digging for clues in tiny corners, and dusting for prints, but seeing the place, which Evie normally kept so tidy was disheartening.

Even though I volunteered to help, and I knew where all the cleaning supplies were kept, I waited for Evie to give me instruction on how she wanted to proceed. While it was true that I owned Painted Wings, the rest was all Evie. She was in charge, and that was how we both wanted it.

Once she had a plan of action, we both got to work.

Evie took charge of the floors, and I scrubbed off the tables and chairs. She got the worst of the deal, having to clean the spot where Burlington had left some of his blood. I offered to do it, but she refused, grimacing the entire time she cleaned and bleached the area. I had to give her credit. When I'd done that same task in my greenhouse, I'd had a bout of nausea and nearly couldn't finish, but I finally had. She toughed it out, giving a sigh of relief when the spot was gone, and the floor was back to normal. I knew that now, at least, she could move on, get back to taking care of the café she loved, instead of stepping around the dreaded spot that had been a constant reminder of a dead body, and all that it entailed.

Once we'd finished cleaning everything in sight and several places that were hidden from view, we opened up the windows to let in some fresh air and to get out some of the strong bleach smell. I knew there'd be some customers who'd complain if the place where they ate smelled like a swimming pool, but they'd be missing the bigger picture, that the alternative was leaving the awful red stain right in front of the ordering counter.

When I reached the window beside the doors, something moved right outside. I shrieked.

"Seneca?" Evie came running. "Are you all right?"

I swallowed hard. "I…. There was someone out there." My heart raced. I took a few deep breaths as I tried to calm down.

Evie looked through the glass. "I don't see anyone close to the window. Let's go ahead and open the doors for more fresh air. Besides, people will be wanting to come in soon."

She unlocked the doors, shoved them open, and waved at a small group of people standing outside a few feet away from the building. Murray was out there, too. He'd offered to help clean up as well, but Evie said he needed a break from the mayhem. It shocked me that he'd done as she asked, but he did have a soft spot for both of us. His customary frown was there as he stepped inside, and he passed us without speaking, heading right to the kitchen prep area.

I stuck my head out the door, seeing the waiting customers. Several were sitting on the low stone wall a few yards from the entrance. One woman, maybe forty with short dark hair, someone I didn't recognize, was staring right at me. Her glare was so fierce, I took a step back. But just as quickly, she turned away, acting as if she hadn't just freaked me out.

Then who had been right outside the window and had scared the stuffing out of me? Did it have anything to do with what had happened to Burlington?

When I stepped out into the sunshine, I heard a sound from the direction of the ground. It was a sneeze. A tiny one. And there sat Winifred, her expression all innocence and sweetness.

"Ah." I put my hands on my hips. "So it was you who scared me, huh?"

She glanced up at me and blinked. It wouldn't have been the first time she'd jumped to the wide windowsill outside of that window. She liked to sit there and enjoy the sunbeams.

I picked her up, then turned, giving a nod to each person who entered Painted Wings. Was one of these customers, possibly one of my friends, responsible for the gruesome murder that had happened here?

Chapter Four

That evening, I invited Evie and Cody to my house for pizza. And no, I didn't make it from scratch like Murray would have. I was either a put it in the stove, or microwave, girl. But no one seemed to mind. Besides, Cody was always hungry and would eat anything.

While we ate our food in the living room, Winifred chowed down on some dry kitty treats in her bowl in the kitchen. As I watched her through the open doorway, I shook my head. Winifred might eat as fast as Cody did, but she certainly wouldn't eat just anything. Most cats were picky, but my kitty took it to a whole other level. In true form, she ate her treats so fast, she was soon sitting at my feet, pawing at my knee as she begged for my food. "Sorry, kitty. You don't need pizza."

"Neither do I," said Evie, who was tiny, but always talked about watching her weight, "But it tastes good, so I'll just enjoy it."

Winifred looked at Evie and gave her a wide-eyed stare as is she, too, couldn't imagine why Evie worried about her appearance.

Startled, Evie coughed and set her plate down on the coffee table. "Sorry, Winifred. Didn't mean to upset you." Evie glanced up at me. "What did I say?"

I took the last bite of my pizza, wiped my hands on a napkin, then picked up my cat. She growled at first, but soon must have decided it wouldn't be so bad to nap on Mama's lap for a bit. Once she had curled into a fluffy ball of paws, ears, and whiskers, I held her close, then looked at Evie. "You know how"—I covered Winifred's ears—"high-strung my cat is." And I didn't lie. Winifred was wired so tight, sometimes I was surprised she didn't spring to the ceiling when she heard a loud noise.

Evie gave me a faint smile. "Yeah, I do. But I love her anyway."

Not wanting to bring down the pleasant mood in the room of food and companionship, I nevertheless knew we should get down to business. "Well, I guess we should talk about the fun time we've all been having lately at Painted Wings."

Cody finished a piece of pizza, then set his plate on the coffee table. "Yeah, we should. But first of all, how are you holding up, Evie?"

She let out a sigh as her shoulders slumped. "About as okay as I can be right now. I can't believe this has all happened. And that a man is dead."

"Evie," I said, "I know this may not help now, but it will get better. I promise."

"How can you know?" She swallowed hard. "What if I'm arrested, or..."

"Hey," said Cody. "Don't think for a second that you're a suspect, okay?" He watched her closely, concern evident on his face.

"Yes, okay." She nodded. I hoped she believed him. Because I knew he was telling the truth. Cody didn't say things he didn't mean.

I ran my hand through Winifred's fur, causing her to let out a low purr. "Evie, maybe you could fill Cody in on the reason for your loan request from Burlington. I'm sure having more information will help him investigate the crime." We'd been so consumed with the actual murder and cleanup, Evie and I had both forgotten to bring that up to Cody.

"Yeah, if you don't mind," he said. "It would help me out."

"Sure, that makes sense." Evie wiped her hands on a napkin, then tossed it on her plate. "It does seem to be the whole reason he was mad at me the day before he... died." Her face paled. Was she reliving the argument they'd had, or finding him lying there the next day, not breathing and covered in blood? Probably both.

Cody sat forward, forearms on his knees and hands clasped together, ready to listen.

Evie glanced at me, then at him. "You see, my apartment building is being sold. And I need a place to live. Fast."

He tilted his head. "I hadn't heard about the building closing."

"Yeah, it happened so quickly, there wasn't even a mention of it on social media. I thought that was weird, too. Like they didn't want anyone but the tenants to know until it was a done deal."

"Who's the owner? Somebody local?"

She shook her head. "I'm not sure. It's in a corporation's name."

"Okay. I'll see what I can find out about that. What's the reason for the corporation's sudden decision?"

"The owner didn't give a reason. He, or she, also hasn't given us much time to find other arrangements. I can't believe this is happening. It was such a shock when they informed me and the other tenants by sticking notes under our doors and telling us we only had a short time to get out. I'm going to have to rent a storage unit as it is, for all my stuff while I look for a new apartment. Boy, the thought of doing all that over again is depressing."

I didn't blame her. I'd lived in an apartment before our grandmother died and I'd moved in here. It was a pain to find one and to have to abide by all the rules the owners and managers had set up. I hated that my grandmother was gone—I missed her every day—but so very thankful I got to live in this house.

"Are there other apartments you could rent? Any openings?" he asked.

I knew why he'd mentioned that. Maple Junction didn't have much in the way of places to rent. Most homes were owned by the inhabitants, some having been in the families for generations, like my old farmhouse.

Evie looked at me again. Her mouth turned down at the corners.

I reached over and touched her arm. Then I turned to Cody. "What's happening with Evie is that she's been saving up for a down payment for a house for a long time now and just needs a bank loan to cover the rest. Having her own home has been a dream of hers." I smiled at her. "I have, of course, offered more than once to have Evie move in with me."

She brushed some moisture from her cheeks. "Thank you, but you know how I feel about taking handouts."

"There's tons of room here in this house. And it's not a handout if it's family."

"Still..." Evie crossed her arms over her chest, appearing stubborn and defiant.

Cody looked at Evie, then pointedly at me. "Gee, reminds me of someone else I know."

I ignored his comment as I snuggled Winifred closer. "As you remember, Cody, that when our grandma left me Majestic Monarchs and the house and land that went along with it, she left Evie a lump sum of money."

Evie smiled. "She sure did. What an amazing gift that was. I used part of it to save up for a future house, but had used the rest for college, to get my management degree."

I winked. "And see how wonderful that turned out. For you, me, and our customers. You're the most awesome manager I could ever imagine."

"You don't have to say that just because we're related." Her cheeks turned pink.

"Believe me, I'm not." I repositioned Winifred, who was lying with her back half hanging off my legs.

"I can promise you she's not, Evie," added Cody. "Seneca brags about you all the time."

"Well, thanks." She grinned at me.

Cody watched her for a few seconds. "But Mr. Snare wouldn't help you with a loan? And wouldn't give you a reason?"

"Nope." Her smile fell. "He left me hanging after I'd followed their rules and had called at the appropriate time. When I never heard back, I decided to approach him quietly at the café. I was running out of options by then and needed an answer. And oh, yes, he gave me an answer. He flat out refused."

I got mad all over again on her behalf. "And he laughed at her in front of a full café about it." The way he'd spoken to her had been mortifying. And I couldn't blame Evie for having been upset that day. No one should have to put up with that sort of treatment. Especially someone as sweet and thoughtful as my cousin.

Evie huffed out a breath. "And then, of course, after he insulted Murray's cooking and said he, himself, always paid his bills, he went to get his wallet. He insinuated that I was some sort of loser because I'd come to him for a loan and because I didn't have loads of money of my own, like he does. But when he couldn't find his wallet, he accused me of stealing it, which was the icing on the cake."

"Not a very good cake," said Cody.

I shook my head. "Not good cake at all."

When I said the word 'cake,' Winifred woke suddenly, stood on her hind legs, pawed at my shoulders, and meowed.

I looked her straight in the eyes. "No. We've had this discussion. Cats don't get dessert."

Cody held up his hand. "That's right. Cats get—"

I pointed at him. "Don't you dare say the 's' word."

"I was going to spell out s-a-l-m-o n."

Winifred meowed.

"Seneca." Evie's eyebrows rose. "Does Winifred know how to spell now?"

My cat sat back on her haunches and stared at us, one at a time, her whiskers twitching and her eyes bright. She even licked her lips.

"I honestly don't know, Evie, and sometimes, I'm afraid to find out."

Cody appeared to be deep in thought, then focused on Evie. "So, back to the investigation. You said Burlington accused you of stealing?"

"Yeah, it was awful. I still can't believe he did that. And every person in the place would have heard it, too. He was yelling, waving his arms around. Saying I'd done it to get back at him for not giving me the loan. I was so embarrassed. I wanted to crawl under a table and disappear."

Poor Evie, being accused like that. It hurt and hurt deeply. I knew that all too well. And she was such a gentle soul. For Burlington to have done that was so very wrong. "I'm so sorry you had to listen to him speak to you that way. You didn't deserve that and don't deserve any of what's happened since."

"Thanks. Just glad it's over and done." She blinked. "Um, that came out wrong, considering he's dead now. I didn't mean—"

"I knew what you meant." Wanting to lessen her burden, to soften the painful feelings she was having, I turned Winifred so she was facing Evie, then moved the cat's paw in a tiny wave. It got the desired reaction when Evie laughed, even though Winifred was still so sleepy, she barely registered being moved. Maybe it was a good thing, since her sharp claws had been known to make an appearance if I dared touch her without permission when she was in certain moods.

Cody tapped his finger absentmindedly on the coffee table, something he did when trying to solve a problem. "And Burlington accusing you. This happened the day before he died?"

"Yes, that's right."

"What a prince of a guy, speaking to you that way. Embarrassing you publicly." Cody ran his hand through his short hair. "As I've said, I know you're innocent of Burlington's murder. But unfortunately, there are bank board members who are all over me to find the killer and fast. They don't want the name of their bank dragged through the mud by being connected to a murder. I need to get to the bottom of this, as soon as possible."

I could understand the people in charge of the bank being concerned about business, but honestly, a man had been murdered. Couldn't they at least give it a little time for the guy to be buried, and for Cody to have the opportunity to do a thorough investigation? Having observed Cody figuring out the identity of the previous murderer, I remembered how meticulously he had to search everything in order to find the truth. That wasn't something to be rushed or hurried through, even though he must have felt like he was being pushed to do just that.

"Yeah," said Evie, "and unfortunately, a couple of those members were in the café when Burlington accused me of stealing, and were also there waiting outside the open doors when I was standing there over the body."

"I'm thinking about the frying pan," he said.

Evie and I made eye contact at his change of direction. "Okay," I said, "what about the pan?"

"We all know Evie uses Murray's cookware, but only occasionally, right?" She and I nodded.

Then Evie held up her index finger. "But some of the people I'm getting texts from are saying they know I use it sometimes. That I had convenient access to that frying pan in the kitchen area to use it as a weapon. If they've seen me helping him out with the cooking once or twice, it's possible they assume it happens more frequently."

"Can I read the texts?" he asked.

"Sure." She reached into her pocket, got her phone, and scrolled to the right page of messages.

Cody read them, then handed back her phone. "Can you forward those to my number?"

"Yes." She quickly copied them and then hit send.

He glanced at his phone, then slid it into his shirt pocket. "Thanks. All right, so here's what I'm thinking."

I sat forward and noticed Evie had done the same. Winifred growled at being repositioned, but soon calmed down on my lap again. She wasn't getting a full nap, a sure sign she'd be grumpy at bedtime. Good thing I kept kitty treats in my bedside table for just such moody emergencies. It was also the reason I kept small pieces of chocolate in there. But those were for me. I figured that if my cat could have snacks in bed, I should be able to as well. At least, that's what I told myself when I felt guilty about eating after brushing my teeth.

"See," Cody said, "even though some people were pointing out that you use the pans and other things on occasion, and believe me, I'm not ruling them out as suspects, there's this little thought niggling the back of my brain."

"Uh-oh," I said, "when the niggling starts, stand back."

He rolled his eyes but laughed. "All right, that's enough out of you, Seneca."

It was good to talk about something not so serious, at least for a few seconds.

"What do you mean about the thought you had, Cody?" asked Evie. Apparently, she wasn't able to enjoy the mirth along with us. But I understood. Even though Cody didn't blame her, she still had to endure the gossip of people she saw every day. And that wasn't easy. Or pleasant.

Cody crossed his arms over his chest. "I'm wondering if the person who did this, the one who, I really believe now, is setting you up, might not know that you don't ordinarily work in the kitchen area. But thinks that using a frying pan to kill Burlington would make you look more guilty."

"Well, it worked."

"Maybe. Or it just might be that this particular clue might eventually point straight to the killer."

"I sure hope so," she said. "I'm sort of dreading when the café reopens and having to endure people whispering about me as I walk by."

"I know it's hard, believe me," I said. "But the weirdos who sent you messages and whispered about the murder are a small minority. It seems like more now because they're the ones at the forefront, the ones you're hearing. Give it a little time to settle down, and your true friends will show you that you have tons of support."

"Thanks, Seneca. I'll try to keep that in mind."

"When the previous murder happened, remember how there were some people in town who talked about me, who thought I was guilty?"

"Yeah, I do. I felt terrible for you and what you went through. It made me so mad on your behalf."

"Thank you. And I feel the same for you." I tapped her arm. "They might think you did it. But don't worry. You have Cody, Murray, and me, to help figure it all out."

Winifred meowed.

"Yes, and Winifred, too."

Chapter Five

To alleviate some of Evie's stress, I made it a point to head to the café more often than normal. Evie was the manager and always made it a point to do all that she could on her own. But she didn't squawk at me this time. I couldn't blame her. Having found a dead body in her workplace was bad enough. Having people point fingers and whisper about her likely being the murderer? Nearly unbearable. It made everything harder, and even though Evie wasn't guilty, the things people said could make her feel like she'd done something wrong anyway.

As I walked into the café, waving at several customers, I noticed that Mike Larsh was there, wearing full Civil War garb. And he was visibly upset. Normally, he was friendly and approachable. Today, however, he seemed to have a proverbial burr under his saddle— a frown on his face, and his hand knocked against his paperback book that sat on the table in front of him.

Something was definitely wrong. The people who came into Painted Wings were here so often, Evie, Murray, and I knew when something was off. Deciding to find out what was up, I headed to where he sat at a table near the back of the café.

"Hey, Mike. Doing okay?"

He wouldn't meet my eye. "No, definitely not okay." His palm continued to lightly hit his beloved book.

"I'm sorry." Knowing he might rebuff my efforts, I plunged ahead anyway. "Mind some company? I could get us both some drinks. On the house." Often, an offer of something free got people's attention.

He watched me from beneath lowered eyebrows, then gave a nod. "Um, all right."

"Great. Want your usual?"

"Sure."

As I left the table, I could still hear him rapping against his poor, defenseless book. And as much as Mike loved to read, he'd have to be terribly upset to treat a paperback that way.

I walked the short distance to the counter, put in the drink order with Murray, then made my way back to Mike. I took a seat across from him and propped my elbows on the table. "So, why are you not okay? Anything I can help with?"

"Not sure there's anything you can do, Seneca."

"Maybe you could tell me what's happening, and I could at least listen. Sometimes, just saying things out loud can make it clearer for the person going through it."

After watching me for a few seconds, he nodded. "Well, I guess it can't make it any worse, right?" He finally gave me his normal lopsided grin, even though it didn't last long, and he went back to frowning.

"You're right." I gave him what I hoped was an encouraging smile and clasped my hands together as I waited.

"It's like this." He placed both hands on the table, palms flat. "You know how I like to help out with the local historical club's yearly reenactment?"

"Sure. You seem to love doing that." I edged my chair closer to the table when a customer had trouble squeezing past me.

Mike's face lit up. "I do. It's one of life's highlights for me."

I had no doubt that was true. Mike talked about their yearly presentations often, and when they weren't actively preparing for their event, he was busy reading historical books. I glanced at his now battered paperback. Hopefully, that course of action wouldn't continue. Books weren't cheap. And even more than that, I happened to love reading too and took great care with my own copies.

"You might think this is silly, Seneca, but I actually have dreams about history. Like I'm living in a past time, fighting for my country."

"I don't think that's silly at all. I dream I can fly."

His eyebrows rose.

"Think about it. I do spend a lot of time around things that have wings. Like the monarchs."

"And your cat, with her wings."

I laughed. "Yes, that's true. So, about your reenactment. Are they having it this year? Is that what bothers you, that it won't take place?" I glanced at his uniform, wondering why he'd dress that way if that were the case. Most guys in their twenties that I knew of would balk at wearing a uniform like that even if someone forced them to.

"They're having it all right. But it's going to be different this year. Way different." Mike's scowl was an expression I wasn't used to seeing on his sweet face.

Evie brought our drinks, gave me a wink, and left to check on other customers. I was glad to see she was holding up okay with everything that had gone on. Murray's expression was a different story. He was glowering and gruff, but that was nothing new.

"How is it different this year?" I took a sip from the straw in my drink.

Mike glanced right, then left, like he was worried someone might overhear. "Some people who are involved this year want to change the script."

"You mean, have different dialogue than you usually do? Like a scene that's not like it has been in years past?"

He swirled his straw in his drink. "It's more than that. Not only do they want us to use modern phrases and pronunciation—which I find appalling— I was also hoping to use my part in this year's reenactment to finally get into my desired history major at college that I've been saving up for by working at the convenience store. If our production is not historically accurate, it will affect my chances of acceptance. The professors are very particular about who they accept for the program. Seneca, I've wanted this my whole life, and this is my chance."

"I'm sorry you're having so much trouble with this. That must be awful for you." My heart was heavy for him. It also brought to mind my assistant, Annie. Her only dream being attending medical school. It almost hadn't happened, but thankfully, things turned around for her. Hopefully, Mike would have a good outcome for his dream as well. Not doing what your heart longed for could crush a person's spirit.

"Yeah, and we were just informed that some of the actual history reenactment will be changed as well."

"But that doesn't make any sense. How can they change history if it already happened?"

Mike huffed out a breath. "See? That's my point exactly. It's not right." He smacked his palm down on his book, causing a woman walking by to stare. "Why would anyone want to alter the play my fellow historians and I have performed for the last several years? We've gone to great lengths to make sure our production is accurate and professionally done." He sat up ramrod straight as if in the middle of his performance, standing at attention in a line of fellow soldiers.

Having seen their performance in the past, I wasn't sure I could agree with the term professional, but in their defense, they were amateur actors. However, it was obvious they were passionate about the subject and always gave it their all. I nudged his drink closer to him, hoping he'd pay more attention to it and leave the poor paperback alone. "Do they want to change anything besides the word usage?"

"Oh yeah. Like"—he pointed to his chest—"our uniforms."

Again, I checked out his jacket. It was obviously not new. Mike had been doing this reenactment for several years, and the cuffs and edges looked frayed. Actually, right now, his clothes were so wrinkled they looked as if he might have slept in them.

Was he so upset about the latest turn of events that he'd given up on his normal daily habits of taking care of himself? "Maybe they want you to have new sets of the same thing, to look, I don't know, fresher, somehow?" I hoped he hadn't taken offense to my comment, thinking I was putting down his appearance.

"No. They want to change them completely. As in, they won't resemble the actual Civil War uniforms any longer."

I propped my elbow on the table and my chin in my hand. "This doesn't make any sense. I can see why you're upset."

"No, it doesn't make any sense at all." He started to beat up on his book again, glanced around him and, instead picked up his drink. "Uh, thanks for this"—he held up his cup—"that's really nice of you."

"You're welcome." I wanted to find out more about the background of the changes for the reenactment. Mike was so upset about it. I'd never seen him act this way before. "So, as far as the ones wanting to change everything, is it a group of people who are doing this or…"

Mike's eyes narrowed. "It was the idea of one person. But it snowballed to several people from there who agreed with that person to change it."

I watched him, hoping he'd supply more information.

"Listen, Seneca, I'd rather not say who it is. Don't want to cause any more trouble for my group."

"No problem." I sat back and shrugged. "You don't need to say who's behind this. I'm just sorry it's happening to you."

I'd envisioned Mike upset because a naysayer wasn't happy with the way history actually happened and wanted to rewrite it. While the uniforms and word usage didn't seem as huge to me, I could see he was having a hard time dealing with the changes. Besides, what did I know since history had never been my strong suit?

Mike glanced at his watch. "I didn't realize how late it was. I have a group meeting in twenty minutes." He downed the rest of his drink and stood. "Thanks again for the drink. And for listening."

He turned and hurried to the door. He was already gone when I glanced down and saw his paperback lying on the table. I never would have imagined him going off and leaving his reading material behind. He'd always been so careful with his possessions and carried a book with him wherever he was. But he'd be back soon, since he came into Painted Wings so often. I could give it back to him then.

I stood and reached for the paperback. A torn piece of paper slipped out onto the table. It wasn't a page of the book, although it wouldn't have been surprising if a page had come loose the way Mike had been smacking it, but it looked like some sort of note.

Steps approached from behind me. I assumed it was Evie coming to clear the table, but to my surprise, it was Cody.

"Hey," I said. "Come in for a snack?"

He patted his flat midsection. "While that does always sound good, and yes, knowing me, I'll get something before I leave, I wanted to check in on Evie, you, and Murray. Are you guys holding up all right?"

"Thanks. Yeah, so far we are. Evie is rushing around, and Murray is scowling but making the world's yummiest food."

"So, a normal day, then."

"Yep."

"And you?"

I glanced toward the order counter. "I just want everything to be okay for Evie."

"I know you do. It's one of the things we all love about you."

When he said the word love, I jerked. But he hadn't meant it in a romantic way. Or that it was just his feelings he talked about. He'd included Evie and Murray. Was all the gossip from townspeople making me think about Cody in a different way than I should?

I grinned. "You're just trying to butter up the café's owner for free food."

"Is it working?"

I smacked his shoulder.

"Hurt your hand, didn't you?"

"A little." I made a face. "But of course, it's working. You know you can come in here anytime and get anything you want, on the house."

He crossed his arms over his chest. "I appreciate the offer, as always, but you know I always—"

"—pay your own way, I know."

He stood up straighter and gave me a salute. "Civil servant, and all that it entails."

"Good grief, it's getting deep in here."

"Fine, I'll quit." His smile dropped when he saw the book on the table. "Was Mike here? That looks like the kind he usually carries around with him."

I picked it up. "Yeah, he was just here. We had a heart-to-heart about his troubles."

"Is he all right?"

"Well, he's concerned about the current historical reenactment."

"What's going on with it? Is he not going to be in it?" Cody frowned. "I can't imagine that."

"He's still doing it, but apparently, there are some who want to change a lot about it this time. The uniforms, manner of speech, and the one that really confused me, they want to change some of the facts of what actually happened."

His eyebrows rose. "Why?"

"I don't know. And neither does Mike. I feel sorry for him. He's so upset about it; he was pounding his fist on his book."

"Mike? Wow, that's something else hard to imagine."

"I agree, and I actually saw him do it."

He pointed to the piece of torn paper. "What's that?"

"It fell out of Mike's book. He left in such a hurry, he went off without it." I opened the folded paper and gasped.

"Seneca? What is it?"

I showed it to him. I could tell when he read the words on the paper because both of his eyebrows shot up.

"Yeah, I see why you gasped. 'The evil-doer must die' does raise some questions of its own, doesn't it?"

"Yeah, it does. And the fact that Burlington's name and phone number with a drawing of a man lying on the floor surrounded by a pool of blood makes it pretty clear what Mike had been thinking."

Chapter Six

Later that afternoon, the screen door to my greenhouse opened with a squeak. Not many people walked in without at least knocking on the doorframe first. My heart raced just as it did every time this happened. Ever since a murder had been committed almost precisely where I stood, Cody had been after me to keep my doors locked, but I had to admit, I'd become a little lax since the previous murderer was caught and put out of commission.

When I turned around, I relaxed, pleased to see it was Annie, my assistant.

"Hey, boss." Her wild, curly red hair was as uncontrolled as ever. With a sigh, she reached into her shirt pocket, retrieved her ever-ready hair band, and wrangled as much of it as she could. The remaining curls bounced and waved, like balloons in a light breeze.

"Annie," I smiled, then hugged her. "Glad to see you. Does this mean you're on a break and coming to help me out?"

"I wish." She looked longingly at the cocoons. She'd always loved working with the caterpillars, keeping their pens clean. She was also in the habit of talking to them, asking if they'd slept well the previous night. "My studies take up so much of my time, it's hard even getting the chance for a quick trip back home to see my mom."

"Oh, darn. You know I miss you around here."

"I know. I miss you too. But Seneca, medical school is amazing." Her already large eyes widened behind the lenses of her wireframed glasses. "It's so wonderful. Magical even."

"Magical?"

"To be with other people who are as excited about diseases and issues with the human body as I am."

"I'm glad it's going well for you." Even though I was sad she wouldn't be around much, the fact that she was getting to pursue her lifelong dream was the most important thing. If I couldn't work with my monarch butterflies, I'd feel lost, like my life was incomplete.

A scratching noise came from my left. Winifred, who'd been napping in the back room, strolled out. She sat down, washed her paw, then caught sight of Annie. Except for a brief period when Annie was having a rough time, and Winifred had allowed the girl to pet her, Winifred never acted very fond of my assistant and gave a not-so-polite hiss in Annie's direction.

Annie, however, didn't seem to notice. Instead, she stopped suddenly and moved closer to me.

"What's the matter?" I asked, because with Annie, you never knew.

Her brow furrowed. "Have you had a checkup recently?"

"Uh…" I tried to remember my last one. Nothing was coming to me. When was the last time? I thought some more. Nope, couldn't come up with the month. Or year? I should probably do something about that. In my spare time, between taking care of my butterfly farm minus my assistant, helping Evie in the café when needed, and, oh yeah, trying to figure out who killed Burlington and was framing my cousin for the murder.

"Never mind. I can see by your expression that you've been neglectful in that area." She grabbed my wrist, placed her fingers over my vein, and checked her watch.

I opened my mouth to say something, but she shook her head, causing more strands of red hair to pull out of the confines of the hair band. So, I waited, trying to hold still and not squirm, so I wouldn't act like Winifred when it was time for me to trim her claws. I looked at my cat, who was watching us with interest. Her whiskers twitched, and her tail quivered against the floor.

Wait, was Winifred smirking? Maybe she thought it was about time I got treated to being held down, having someone hold onto my paw, er, hand, against my wishes.

My cat squinted up and me, gave a loud purr, then sauntered away, tail stuck high in the air. No doubt about it, she seemed pleased at my comeuppance.

Annie released my wrist. "Your heart rate was a little high, Seneca."

"Maybe because I hadn't been expecting to have my pulse taken right then?" I rubbed my wrist with my other hand.

She brushed some hair from her eyes. "If you're not careful, you could be at risk for a heart attack, or stroke or—"

"Hey, I'm not even thirty yet."

"It can happen. Or you could just drop dead, right here on the floor. Right where we're standing." She glanced down and frowned. Was she remembering that it was the spot where my lawyer's body had been discovered before? "Just promise me you'll get a checkup soon?"

"I will." I made a mental note to make a written reminder to maybe, someday, make an appointment. I had so many things to do right now than to go to the doctor's office. "Anyway, I'm glad things are going well for you. How's your mom? I haven't seen her for a while."

Annie's mom, Dana, worked for Cody, but I didn't often run into her. She had been on the hot seat for a while, as had Annie, for my lawyer's murder. Unfortunately, I'd seen a lot of Dana then when my ex-husband, the only other lawyer in town now, had gotten involved in trying to get Annie legal help.

"She's good. She misses me, though."

"I bet you miss her too."

"Yeah, I do. Since she and I are the only family we have, I know she gets lonely. At least since I'm so busy, I don't think about it as much."

"Medical school won't be forever, you know. Maybe when you're through, you can come back to Maple Junction to set up a practice."

My eyes widened. Had I really just suggested that? Annie always had a habit of trying to diagnose everyone she came in contact with, even before she started med school. I lost track of the number of people who'd visited my greenhouse or the café who left in a panic because Annie had told them they were on the brink of death, or had some terrible disease that would leave them disfigured and hideous for the rest of their lives and they'd never be allowed to set foot outside of their houses ever again.

But maybe actual medical training would help her to have a calmer, gentler bedside manner. At least, I hoped so. Now, I was resigning myself to most likely giving up Annie as my assistant, at least my permanent one. Hopefully, she could still help out a little if she wanted to on longer school breaks.

"Well," she said, "I just wanted to drop in and say hi." She started to go, then jerked to a stop. "Oh, by the way, I heard there's been another body found here at Majestic Monarchs."

"Uh, yeah." Boy, news sure did travel at lightning speed around here.

"Might want to figure out how to stop people from dropping dead on your property. Well, bye!" She waved and left the greenhouse.

Yeah, it would be great to not have this keep happening at my farm. Maybe I could put an ad on social media, or even just spread the word through the many gossips who lived in town, to please go die someplace else.

No, probably not.

I had just retrieved my broom from the corner to sweep the floor area beneath the cocoon pens when I heard a car door outside. I hadn't heard one from Annie before she arrived, so she must have ridden her bike over here. But who could it be now?

Footsteps sounded outside the screen door. "Seneca?"

It was Cody.

"Come on in," I called.

"It's unlocked?" He opened the door and stepped inside. "Why wasn't it locked?"

Shoot. I could have avoided this scolding if I'd only locked the door. What would that have taken me, a whole ten seconds to do? "Um… well, Annie was just here for a quick visit. And… I hadn't locked it behind her yet."

He watched me for a few seconds. "Okay. But you're being careful, right?"

"Yes. Of course. Careful."

Cody's shoulders relaxed, as if he'd been worried something might have happened to me. Of course, it might have, not that I dwelled on it too much, but I had to give Cody credit for caring so much about my well-being.

"How is Annie doing anyway?" he asked. "I kind of miss her around here. And Dana misses her like crazy. You should see all the photos she has of Annie on her bulletin board at work. It's like a mini-art gallery in there. Annie in scrubs, looking into a microscope, holding a thermometer."

I smiled at Dana's devotion to her only daughter. Those two women definitely were close. "She's good. Busy, as you can imagine."

"I'm so glad it all worked out for her to go since it's all she ever talked about."

"I agree. I'm glad, too. Annie even talked about medical school to the monarchs. Not that they ever answered."

"You're frowning." He studied my face. "That doesn't seem glad to me. Wait. Are you all right? Did something happen?"

"No, nothing happened. But as happy as I am for her, now I need to find a new assistant."

"Right. And that might take a while. It's such a unique job and will take just the right person."

"True. But as goofy as the girl had been, she was awesome working around here for me. How am I going to find someone like her? And from where? And quickly?" I tapped my foot on the floor as I glanced around the greenhouse at the cages filled with caterpillars lying inside their cocoons, ready to make their grand appearances when the time was right.

He stepped closer. "It will work out."

"I know. But I can't think of anybody off the top of my head who might be a good replacement for her." I waved my hand at the room. "And I really need some help, like, right away. Annie, having been gone even the last few weeks, has put me behind. When she left, I was so delighted for her that she'd get to chase her dream. I didn't fully comprehend what that might mean for me and Majestic Monarchs."

Cody glanced around. "Does it have to be permanent right now?"

"What do you mean?"

"Maybe you could get somebody to help you out temporarily. You know, part-time, and just for a short while until you find the right person. Like maybe that right person might be out there, but not quite ready for you yet.

Does that make sense?"

"I hadn't thought of that. Maybe I could make do with temporary help for now, just to help me get by for the time being. As long as I made it clear that this would be temporary. And I guess it's possible that a temp might turn into permanent if it went well." I tilted my head and looked up at him, which took some effort with our vast height difference. "You know something, Sheriff? That might not be such a bad idea."

He couldn't hold back his smile as he faked trying to look hurt. "Don't look so surprised that I might come up with something brilliant."

"Who said anything about brilliant?" I laughed and smacked his arm.

"I thought it was implied."

"Now you're being nonsensical."

Cody placed his hands on his hips. "Oh, come on. You always drag out the big words when you want to win a disagreement."

"And it usually works, doesn't it?"

"Yeah, you got me there." He grinned.

"Okay, seriously, thank you for the idea."

He lifted one eyebrow.

"Yes, all right. Your brilliant idea."

"You are quite welcome. Any other wisdom I can impart today? I have a little time. I could probably come up with something else amazing to help you out of your desperation."

"Stop. Now it's getting deep in here, Cody. Time for you to catch some bad guys."

"Yeah, there is that." His smile faltered. "Too bad the wildest thing in Maple Junction wasn't once again chasing Philly Greenfield through the town square."

"Once again? Wait, when was this?"

"This morning."

"I guess I missed hearing about that one. Didn't she just have her ninety-third birthday last week?"

"That's right." He rubbed the back of his neck.

"And was she wearing her hot pink thong like last time?"

"Unfortunately." He closed his eyes. Was he trying not to picture Philly in her skimpy attire?

"You poor man. Even though I'm sure it wasn't a pleasant experience for you…"

He shook his head.

"…I'm sorry too that it's not the worst thing about your job lately. Any leads on who killed Burlington?" I crossed my arms over my chest but avoided eye contact.

"Not yet. It's early still. I know that look, Seneca."

"Which look? I can't see what I look like." I focused on his ear.

"Your mind is spinning with ideas about how you can help find Burlington's killer."

"What's wrong with that?" I shrugged, as if everyone, everywhere, did that all the time. Like doing laundry or driving their car.

Cody grasped me lightly by my shoulders, forcing me to fully face him. "The big thing is that last time, you were nearly killed by the murderer."

"You were nearly killed too, Cody." This time, I stared right at him, holding his gaze.

He swallowed hard. "That was a bad day."

"But with a good outcome for us, right?"

"Right." He gave me a quick hug.

"And maybe makes you the tiniest bit grateful that chasing Philly was the worst thing to happen today."

"Yeah, well, so far, anyway." He stepped back. "All right, I'll go back to work, taking your advice. But only if you take mine."

"About…"

"Finding some temporary help for your business."

"Oh, that. Yes. It is a good idea." I tapped my finger against my chin. "Any thoughts on the best way to advertise that?"

"Your café is always filled with people. Maybe if you put up a sign at the door or where customers give their orders, you might get a bite."

I made a face. "Not a physical bite, I hope."

"Why would you think that would happen?"

"You have to admit, some of our customers are pretty weird."

"You have a point there." He chuckled. "Well, I'm headed out. Let me know if you get any bites, um, any responses to your sign."

"Sure. See ya later."

I desperately hoped Cody was right, that maybe I could get some temporary help until I found just the right person to replace Annie. Because if I didn't get someone soon, I was in deep trouble.

Chapter Seven

I was out of twine. Not something every girl would be worried about, but as a butterfly farmer, it was a staple of life, helping me maintain cocoon pens, bent stalks of milkweed, or a rusted-out piece of fence at the back of my property near Pines Park.

Our grocery store was small enough that it didn't carry much beyond the four basic food groups, along with lots of snacks that were so yummy they deserved a group of their own. So, anything outside of edibles I usually had to venture out to our town's only hardware store, run by Mr. O'Hurley.

He was a nice man, a little chatty about things I might not want to know, like his wife's hysterectomy, or the creepy surprise the plumber found in their kitchen pipes, but I could always depend on him for friendly service and reliable results of whatever I needed to buy.

Today, however, when I checked the usual spot for the sought-after twine, the space was empty. I groaned. It wouldn't be so bad if I could buy it some other place in town, but O'Hurley's was the only choice.

When he saw me walk up the aisle toward him, he grinned. "Let me guess, Seneca. Today, you either need…duct tape, garden stakes, or glue."

I smiled and shook my head, even though duct tape was a good guess since I tended to go through a ton of that, too.

"Shoot." He snapped his fingers. "Thought I had it right this time."

It was a little game he liked to play when his regular customers came into his store to see how close he could come to guessing their reason for showing up.

Life's little pleasures.

"So, how can I help you today?" He placed his hands on his narrow hips.

"I'm out of twine."

He gave a mock gasp and clasped his hands to his chest. "My goodness, how will we go on without twine?"

I laughed. "Sometimes we do not go on. Until we make a visit to see you. Unfortunately, I didn't see any back in the aisle. Any chance you might have some in your storage area?"

"Maybe, let me see if I have some in the back." He pointed behind him. "Pretty sure I do."

"Great, thanks." I took a few steps to my right, checking out the latest Farmers' Almanac. Sometimes they were right about weather forecasts, other times, not. While I found them interesting, I didn't often purchase them. It seemed a better use of my time to simply wait and see what each day was like. Besides, my mudroom was always equipped with a sunhat, rain gear, boots, or a parka and gloves for whatever that day brought.

A scuffling noise came from my left. I hadn't realized anyone else was in the store except for me. With nothing else to do while I waited for Mr. O'Hurley, and to be honest, I was simply being nosy, I sidled in that direction, keeping my steps light. No sense in startling someone who might be just around the next aisle endcap. Especially if it was someone like Mable Kane. I couldn't imagine what she might buy at the hardware store, but who knew? Maybe bling to decorate her cane?

But when I got closer to the sound, I also heard a voice. After I listened for a few seconds, I realized it was Devan Keller, Mr. O'Hurley's stock boy. Since I only heard him talking and no one else, he must have been on his phone.

A quick glance back at the front counter showed that Mr. O'Hurley wasn't back yet. I hoped he could find that twine, otherwise, I might have to improvise with the duct tape or glue he'd mentioned, as a last resort. And the results wouldn't be pretty. Or very sturdy.

In the meantime, Devan's tone had taken that of a desperate plea, the intensity of his voice drawing me closer. What would a twenty-year-old guy have to be so morose about?

I shuffled a few more steps in his direction, hoping he wouldn't hear me. "But sweetie, you can't do this."

Sweetie? Did Devan have a girlfriend? Not that it would be so unusual at his age, but I'd never seen him around with anyone. With the small number of places to eat in town, our café often saw young couples coming in for their dates. But Devan either wandered in alone, or sometimes with friends.

"I'll die, just die," he whimpered.

My eyes widened. Either this was serious, or Devan was being melodramatic. Hopefully, the latter. I knew how painful a broken heart could be.

"How can I convince you not to do this?" He sounded so desperate, like talking someone out of jumping from a four-story window. What was going on with the other person?

In my haste to get closer and not miss a word, my hand brushed against a display of yard chimes, causing a small ripple of tinny sounds. I held my breath, hoping Devan wouldn't come around the corner to find me there.

"Wait," he said.

My heart thudded hard. What would I say if he found me here, obviously eavesdropping on his very private conversation? I took one step back, checking behind me that I wouldn't run into something else noisy, like the huge display of those metal keychains that have everybody's name available, except mine.

A few seconds went by, then Devan said, "Never mind. I thought my boss was checking up on me, but I don't hear him walking this way. He tends to clomp his feet."

Letting out a long, silent breath, I waited for my heart to stop racing, then I crept closer again, this time narrowing my eyes at the chimes, willing them to stay quiet. Stupid noisemakers.

"Listen, sweetie, there has to be a way for us to…." He gasped. "What? She hung up! On me! The love of her life!" Something rustled, then shoes hit the wooden planks. Had he been sitting on the floor as he talked to his sweetie?

I let out a squeak, then scurried to the counter, just as Mr. O'Hurley appeared from the back area. I ended up in a full-out run the last few steps.

Had he or Devan heard my loud footsteps?

"Good news, Seneca. After much searching, I found the shipment box that had the twine. Isn't that wonderful?"

I took a deep breath and let it out, trying not to hyperventilate. "Truly amazing. I can't thank you enough."

Loud foot stomps approached from behind me. Apparently, Mr. O'Hurley wasn't the only noisy walker. "Oh. Hi, Seneca."

"Hey Devan, how's it going?" There was no indication that he knew what I'd been up to. It was just as well. How in the world would I have explained it?

He lifted one shoulder in a shrug. "I've had better days." He frowned and leaned to the side, looking behind me. "Hey, boss?"

"Yeah?"

"Can I take my break early?"

Mr. O'Hurley's eyebrows lowered as he glanced up at the clock. "Sure, I guess. Be back in half an hour. There's lots of boxes of new shipment that need unloading."

"Yeah, okay." Devan left the shop, allowing the door to slam on his way out.

"Sorry about that, Seneca. Devan is normally a good, even-tempered kid, but…." He lifted his hands in a helpless gesture.

"But he's still a kid?"

"Yep, that's it exactly. He's twenty, but not very mature yet."

I tilted my head toward the door. "He seemed…moody. Is he okay?"

With a glance toward the entrance door, Mr. O'Hurley said, "From what I've gathered from Devan's mumbling as of late, there's something going on with his girlfriend."

"Things aren't going well?"

"I'm afraid not. Trouble in paradise and all that."

I knew from experience that what you thought would be paradise could sometimes turn out to be a small, swampy island full of hungry mosquitoes and nothing to wear but itchy underwear. "Well, maybe things will turn around for him. I hope so. It's tough being in love sometimes."

He gave a dreamy smile. "You know, my wife and I have been married for over forty years."

"That's wonderful." It would take a very special person to stay together happily for that long. Payne, my ex-husband, and I had only made it a couple of years. Suddenly, I thought of Cody. What kind of husband would he make? Then, I mentally shook myself. I had to quit thinking of him in those terms. We were just friends, after all.

He bobbed his head. "Thank you. Yes, I think so too. Life has its ups and downs, but mostly up, at least for us. Say, did I ever tell you about my wife's hysterectomy?"

"Why, yes, as a matter of fact, you did." Several times, in fact.

"Well, anyway, that was one of the not-so-great times, as you can imagine."

I waited, hoping he'd move on to a different subject.

"Say, speaking of love…"

When he didn't add anything else, I said, "Um, yes?"

He leaned toward me, and his eyebrows wiggled up and down. "Didn't I hear something about you having a passionate kiss with our very own town sheriff?"

I clenched my teeth together. "No. Not passionate…" When would people stop bringing this up?

"So, there *was* a kiss."

"Actually, no."

"That's not what I heard." He put his hands on his hips and watched me.

I'd be so glad when this subject died down. "I can promise you, there was no kiss."

"Shoot. And that's what I've been telling everybody."

Just great. I forced a smile. "Well, now that you know the truth, maybe you could help me out and pass along the facts?"

"Absolutely. Glad to do it."

I was sure that was true. He was always happy to gab. The subject matter wasn't important. I was just relieved he didn't have anything about me to say besides a kiss.

Even though that episode had been a close call, the locking of lips hadn't actually occurred with Cody. There were times I almost wished it had, only if it was under different circumstances. Without half the town in attendance while we were at an auction.

I pointed to the twine Mr. O'Hurley had laid on the counter. "Thanks so much for checking your stock room. I appreciate it. My milkweed stalks will thank you, too."

"No problem, Seneca. Always like to help out my best customer."

I grinned. It was a sweet thing to say, but I'd heard him say those exact words to other customers many times. But he was a nice man and genuinely liked people. Even though he did like to discuss his family members' medical procedures in great, gory, colorful detail.

He rang up my purchase, and after I paid him, he placed the twine in a small sack. "There you go. Hope it does what you need it to." He gave me an exaggerated wink, then smiled.

"Yes, thanks so much." Wait. Why had he winked? What did he think I needed twine for? Tying up someone? Making sure they couldn't get away from me? Then I thought of Cody, encased in twine, and me kissing him. My face heated.

"You all right, Seneca? You look a little flushed."

"Uh, fine." I waved my hand in front of my face. "Just warm in here."

He scratched his chin. "Is it? I can't always tell. But then, after my wife's hysterectomy, she has hot flashes, so you never know."

"Um, yeah…okay." I picked up the tiny sack and stuffed it in my bag, ready to leave the store before he asked about my medical history. "Thanks for this, and I hope Devan gets things straightened out with his girlfriend."

Another customer entered, and Mr. O'Hurley turned to them with a smile. "Hello. Let me guess. You need fertilizer today."

I rushed out the door, glad when a breeze felt cool against my skin. What in the world had caused me to have that ridiculous thought about Cody? One thing was for sure, even though he and I told each other pretty much everything, I wouldn't be sharing that with him. Because if I did, the teasing would never end.

Chapter Eight

The next morning, I needed to get some flea-prevention medicine for Winifred, so I stopped by the vet's office. I loved Dr. Cummings but wondered how long he'd keep practicing. He had to be past eighty. As I stepped inside the small lobby, I spied Penny, his daughter, who was nearly retirement age herself. She'd been her dad's receptionist for as long as I could remember.

"Hi, Penny." I waved and walked toward her.

Normally, she had a big, friendly smile for everyone who entered the office. But today, her lips were downturned. As I got closer, I noticed her lashes were wet, as if she'd been crying.

"Penny? Are you all right?"

She reached for a nearby tissue and wiped her eyes. "I…I'm afraid not."

"I'm sorry. Is there anything I can do for you?" It struck me that something might be going on with Dr. Cummings. "Or for your dad? Is he—"

"No, Dad is okay. I'm worried about him. I wish…." She waved the thought away with her hand.

"I don't want to pry, but it's obvious something has you very upset. I'd like to help, if I can."

"You're so sweet, Seneca. And I truly do appreciate it. I—" A sound came from the back area, causing Penny to jerk suddenly. "I need to get back to work."

I nodded but felt helpless. This wasn't normal behavior for Penny. And her dad was amazingly healthy, especially for an older gentleman, but that could change, like it did for my grandmother. She was always so active and involved in everything. Then, in a matter of months, she got sick and passed away. I jerked out of my thoughts when the wheels of Penny's chair squeaked.

"So, how can I help you today?" She forced a smile. "Is Winifred all right?"

I truly did love these people. They genuinely cared for their clients and pet parents, knowing our furry children were our family. "Yes, she's fine. I just need to pick up her flea-prevention meds."

"Sure." Penny typed something on her keyboard, read the words on the screen, then gave a nod. She stood. "I'll be right back with that."

"Thanks." There was something wrong going on with Penny. What in the world could have made her so upset?

As I glanced around the room at the cute wallpaper with images of frolicking kittens and puppies, the door to the office opened. A man stepped in, someone I didn't know. He was around thirty or so, dressed in khakis and a button-down shirt. In one hand was a large brown satchel. Maybe he was a drug rep or something. Surely, a vet's office had to order new supplies like everyplace else did.

"Hello," he said, but didn't offer anything more. Did he think I worked here?

"Hi. I'm not waiting for an appointment, so you can go ahead of me if you want." I waved my hand toward Penny's empty chair.

"No, thank you." He gave a shy smile. "I don't have an appointment. I actually work here."

I blinked. He worked here? Since when? There had never been anyone working in this office except the doctor and Penny. Maybe there was something wrong with Dr. Cummings, after all. I gave a confused smile. "Nice to meet you. I'm Seneca James."

He came forward and tentatively put out his hand to shake mine. "Nice to meet you, too. I'm Drew Paulson. The new veterinarian."

It took all of my will not to let my mouth drop open. When he said he worked in the office, I assumed in a smaller role, like maybe an assistant or some kind of salesman who stopped by often. But another veterinarian? When had this happened? I hadn't been in for a while since the last time I'd brought in Winifred for her dreaded exam—she always made it clear that the invasion of her personal space and having that man poke at her private areas was unacceptable. How had I not heard of this other guy working in the office?

"I can see by your expression you didn't know anyone new was here."

"Um, right. No, I didn't." I glanced behind me. Penny must still be in the back area. Was Dr. Cummings here, too? Or had he retired and not told anyone? My heart sank at the thought of him leaving.

As if sensing my thoughts, Drew said, "Don't worry, Dr Cummings is still working. I'm sure he's here today since their schedule has been busy lately."

"Their schedule? But you said you work here too."

"I do. Sorry. It's still all new to me. I do work here, but sort of as an interim." He set his briefcase next to his feet.

"Oh. So, Dr. Cummings is going to leave soon?"

He held up his hand. "Not right now. But he wanted someone else to come into the practice and get settled, get to know the clients and pet parents well before he officially left. He didn't want to leave his patients without proper care, since he's the only veterinarian in town."

That made sense. But it was still hard to take. I sure would miss seeing Winifred's doctor. Even though she wouldn't mind a bit. But wait until she found out there was a new guy she'd have to get used to on top of still having to endure the atrocities of having someone aside from me or Cody getting up close and personal with her furry sense of royalty.

Steps came from behind the counter, then halted. Penny stood there holding a small sack that I assumed held Winifred's medicine. "Hello, Drew."

"Hi, Penny. How are you today?"

"Fine." She darted a gaze in my direction. I knew good and well she wasn't fine, but other than it was something to do with her dad, I had no clue as to why. Did it have something to do with the new doctor now present in the office where it had always been just her dad as the veterinarian? I could see how that might upset her. It would be a huge change to have to get used to.

Drew pointed down to his leather case. "Thought I'd give you guys a hand today."

"Thanks. That would be great. Dad's in the back with a Great Dane, who's quite a handful."

"Sure, glad to help." He grabbed his bag and nodded in my direction.

As soon as he'd walked past the reception area and down a side hallway, Penny turned to me. "I guess you know we have a new employee now."

"Yeah, he seems nice." I leaned to one side and watched as Drew stepped into a room off the main hallway. "Although it might take Winifred some time to get used to someone new."

The corners of her mouth turned down. "It will be an adjustment for all of us."

"I'm sure. It's just been the two of you all this time, right?"

"Yes." She clasped her fingers together at her waist, acting fidgety. "Always just Dad and me. It's been my whole life. And I've loved it."

Then, I had another thought. "Penny, you're not leaving the practice, are you?"

"No, I'll still be here. I still need to work, and the office will need me to keep running the front area and doing all the billing and paperwork. It just won't be the same." She blinked rapidly as she glanced down at her desk. I couldn't imagine how difficult this change would be for her.

"No, of course not. Change is hard." When she didn't say anything more, I pointed to the sack she'd placed on her desk. "How much do I owe you for Winifred's meds today?"

She gave me the amount. I handed her my credit card, waiting until she returned it with my receipt and the bag. "Here you go, Seneca."

"Thanks. Um, listen, I know you'd said you were fine, but you still seem kind of sad. I'm worried about you."

She blinked hard again and sniffed. "I'm afraid I can't talk about it. I'm sorry. But thank you for caring. I really mean that."

I nodded, even though I wasn't sure what she meant. Was she prohibited for some reason to discuss office business? Or was she still obviously upset about the new veterinarian coming to work in probably the only office she'd ever known?

Drew called from the back room, and Penny gave me her apologies and headed in that direction.

I was ready to leave when the front door opened again, and a woman in her forties entered, carrying the tiniest dog I'd ever seen, more like a large rat wearing a collar. It had long fur that needed a trim. The woman and the dog were both frowning. I could imagine the dog might be uncomfortable with all that hair but had no clue about the woman's reason for seeming annoyed. When I studied her closer, I realized it was the same woman I'd seen outside Painted Wings. The one who had glared at me for no apparent reason and had freaked me out.

"Are you in line?" Her voice came out a little gruff.

"Uh, me?"

"Who else is standing there?"

Wow, a little surly, this one. "No, I'm not in line."

She stared down at the space where my feet were, and I got the point. I moved a couple of paces to the side, watching as she came closer. She looked me up and down. "Where's your dog?"

"I don't have a dog."

"Why not?" Her free hand landed on her hip.

"I...um..."

She studied me. "You're one of those cat people, aren't you? I can always spot them."

What in the world did that mean? It wasn't like I had long whiskers or a tail. "I do happen to have a cat, yes. Her name's Winifred, and she's—"

"What's your name?"

I jerked, having to switch mental direction at her question. "I'm Seneca James. Nice... to meet you."

"I'm Nora." No last name. No other information.

She stared at me. Was I supposed to tell her more than my name?

"Where do you work?" she asked.

This lady was out there. Obviously, she had no filter and whatever popped into her brain immediately flowed out from her lips. "I own Majestic Monarchs."

"What in the world is that?" Her words came out so loud, her little dog yipped.

"It's a butterfly farm."

Her brow furrowed. "Never heard of one. Sounds odd. What do people do there?"

I grabbed the strap of my purse right at my shoulder, as if it could protect me from the verbal barrage coming from this stranger. "Sometimes people come for tours."

Her expression looked like she'd eaten a banana peel covered in vinegar and tobacco with rotten sour cream on the side.

"Or, there's also a café there. It's called Painted Wings." I didn't know why I kept answering her questions. But somehow, I felt the need to defend who I was, who my cat was, and what I did for a living.

She gave a quick nod. "That's more like it. Might have to check it out."

I knew for a fact she'd already been at Painted Wings since I saw her outside before, glaring at me. Why would she act as if she didn't know about it?

More silence followed. She stared at me again. What a strange lady she was.

I wasn't sure if I should say more, but was relieved when Penny came back, and I didn't have to continue the conversation. I waved to Penny and walked toward the door. Maybe the other lady was just passing through town and needed something quick from the vet. I hoped I wouldn't run into her again.

Chapter Nine

Later that morning, I finished cleaning out the larvae pens in the greenhouse, then headed over to check on things at Painted Wings. I glanced around, hoping there wouldn't be any drama today, aside from the norm, since our town was never drama-free, and was relieved to see that the customers seemed calm. No one was pointing or whispering about anyone else, and thankfully, no dead bodies were lying around, either.

Murray stood behind his counter, and Evie flitted around much like the two butterflies that had drifted inside through the open doors, wings flapping gently.

Just the butterflies. Evie didn't have wings. However, speaking of those, Winifred followed me again. Today, my cat wore a swallowtail butterfly costume, as she sauntered into the café, tail in the air, head held high, surveying her kingdom as she often did.

When Winifred reached me, I bent down. "So you followed me again, did you?" I picked her up, then smiled when she let out a booming purr. I just never knew with her since she was often moody, but if she chose today to be pleasant, I'd gladly take it.

With the people, butterflies, and Winifred seeming relaxed and at ease, I happily made my way toward Murray to get my daily drink order.

But as soon as Winifred spotted Murray, who happened to resemble her a bit with his fluffy mustache and bushy eyebrows, my cat scrambled to get down. She dove beneath a nearby chair, apparently not caring that there was a person sitting directly above her.

So much for Winifred's good mood. I rolled my eyes, then gave Murray a smile, which he did not return. I didn't take it personally, that was just my chef's nature. But he was a good man, and took care of Evie and me, and even Winifred, though she didn't always show her gratitude with more than a flip of her tail or an ear twitch.

"Afternoon, Seneca." He handed me my drink, not having to ask what I wanted, since it was the same one I'd been getting since the café first opened.

"Thanks." I took a quick sip from the cup. "How are things going here?"

He tilted his head toward two ladies in their forties. "That's Nora, on the left, and Flora Jaminsky, who had only moved here a couple weeks ago. They're twin sisters, as you can see, and both work in the same pharmacy, as technicians."

When I turned to view them, I held in a gasp. There were two versions of the strange lady who'd been in the vet's office. Was the sister as annoying as the one I'd met? And I still couldn't figure out why Nora had acted as if she hadn't been here before, when she had.

Murray leaned closer. "They've been having quite the debate."

"What about?"

"The newest thing everyone is talking about." He nodded toward the floor where Burlington's body had been found. It was just a couple of feet from where I now stood. I tried not to think about it every time I entered the café but wasn't always successful. Especially not when people were actively discussing it, pointing to it, or walking over the place where the man had taken his last breath.

But getting all the information I could from people would hopefully help me clear Evie's name, because I never knew what a person might have seen or heard. Maybe saying an innocent hello to the women would be in order. Even though at least one of them wasn't the friendliest. After observing them for a couple of minutes it was evident they were talkers, for sure.

If I walked over to see them, it might be all it took for them to spout off their latest observations. And if it could help Evie get off the hot seat by possibly gleaning new information, I was all for it.

They were seated at a table close to where Murray stood behind the counter. And they weren't keeping their voices down. No wonder he'd heard what they'd been talking about.

As I stirred my drink again, I approached their table. "Hi, ladies. How are you doing today?"

Nora had been leaning toward her sister, but at my words, straightened in her chair. "Oh, hello, Seneca. I guess I should ask how things are going for you." At least she'd remembered my name from meeting at the vet's office. Much like Murray had done, Nora angled her chin toward the place of Burlington's demise.

As Murray had told me, they'd already heard about the murder. Maybe someone in the café had been talking about it. I didn't even know these women, and they were ready to jump into it.

Not wanting to, but unable to stop myself, I looked at the spot too. "Oh, well, we're hanging in there. Thanks for asking."

"You're quite welcome." Nora eyed me up and down. She appeared to be the more formal of the two, making me feel like I was being scolded simply by her indignant tone.

Flora, who came across as gentler than her sister as she gave me a friendly smile, waved to an empty seat beside her. "Won't you join us?"

I couldn't tell if Nora was annoyed by the invitation or not. She seemed like Murray in that way, coming across as miffed. A thought sparked in my mind. If Nora and Murray were somewhat alike, both single, and close in age, maybe I could suggest...

No, maybe not. They might be too much alike to get along well, like two cats suddenly thrust into the same home against their will.

Realizing I hadn't answered Flora, I grinned at her. "Yes, thanks, that'd be great."

There hadn't been any other comment or facial expression from Nora, so I took that as a plus and sat down. "Can I get either of you anything to go with your drinks? Murray's cheesy fries are to die for."

Why had I said 'die' when we sat so close to what I now thought of as the death spot, on the floor?

"No, thank you," said Nora. "We're fine."

Flora blinked and stared at her sister. Maybe she would have liked a snack but was too used to her twin getting her own way. I'd have to keep that in mind the next time I saw Flora in here and offer her something when Nora wasn't in earshot.

Wanting to get right to the matter at hand, and taking advantage of Nora's question about how I was doing, I said, "Thanks for asking about me. Like I said, we're trudging along. It's been hard for Evie, though, when some people are accusing her of killing Burlington. Have you met her yet? She's my cousin."

"Well..." Nora's left eyebrow rose. "I know she's your relation and all, but can you blame people for their opinions? From what I've gleaned listening to customers in here, there might be a reason."

Flora's eyes widened. "Nora, honestly."

It wouldn't do me any good to get in the middle of what was obviously a disagreement between the sisters about who might have done Burlington in. But since they'd already been discussing the matter, I didn't mind taking advantage of what they'd seen or heard. Plus, I wanted to defend Evie since she wasn't standing here to do it herself.

I took a sip of my drink, then set it aside. "I guess I could see why a person who didn't know my cousin well would take it at face value, that Evie and Burlington's harsh words the day before the murder, made her seem guilty. But trust me when I say, she had nothing to do with Burlington's death."

Nora watched me carefully, but said nothing, even though my reference to a person had been about her.

Flora grabbed a napkin from the dispenser on the table and immediately began wiping her hands over and over. She hadn't had any food to clean off, so why did she need the napkin? As I watched, she began to tear it into tiny little bits, as if she was nervous.

Nervous about what?

Quickly, Nora's hand snaked out, snatching the pile of white bits and brushing them toward her side of the table. When she shook her head at her sister, like a disappointed spinster aunt, Flora's face reddened. Obviously, this wasn't the first time Flora might have done this, or something like it. But why did she seem so flustered?

Nora gave a sharp nod. "I, for one, believe only what I see and hear."

Evie rounded the corner from the kitchen area and came our way. "Hi Seneca, I see you've met Maple Junction's newest citizens."

"Yes." I gave the ladies a smile.

Evie slung the hand towel she was carrying over her shoulder. "Can I get either of you anything?"

"No," said Nora.

Again, Flora frowned.

"Okay, then. I'll be floating around if you change your mind." Evie walked to a table near the front door when a man waved his arm in the air to get her attention.

"Your Evie person acts skittish and guilty," said Nora.

My Evie person?

Flora's finger tapped on the table. "I…" Her face was still red. "I, um…"

"Spit it out, sister," said Nora. "What are you mumbling about?"

"I happen to think," she sat up a little straighter, "that perhaps Evie isn't…"

Nora narrowed her eyes. "Isn't what?"

"Well, um, guilty."

"How can you possibly say that?" Nora's voice took on a screechy quality, causing Winifred to dart out from beneath her latest hiding place and take refuge behind a potted fern in the front corner.

I observed the twins as they volleyed words back and forth across the table. Was this what Murray had heard them talking about before? If he'd heard Nora make disparaging remarks about Evie, then no wonder he was especially grumpy today.

Wanting to see what the sisters might have heard otherwise about the murder, I turned to Flora. "Thank you for saying Evie might be innocent. I really appreciate your support."

"You're quite welcome." Even though Flora said the same phrase that Nora had uttered when I'd first sat down, Flora's gentle tone and small smile softened the sentiment.

I looked at Nora, then back at her sister. "Have either of you two heard anything about possibilities of who else"—I glanced at Nora—"might have committed Burlington's murder?"

Flora reached for a second napkin, but her sister tugged it away from her. Why did that question set Flora off again?

With nothing to tear to bits, she grasped her hands together on the table, then glanced at her sister, swallowed hard, and turned in her chair to face me directly. "There is something..."

Nora huffed out a breath, but waved her hand, as if giving her twin permission to continue.

"What is it?" I asked.

"See, I, uh, we, did hear something." Flora looked around the café. Was she afraid someone might overhear her? But with all the other customers talking, laughing, and moving around in the place, I highly doubted that was a problem. An orange blur zoomed across the floor, making its butterfly-costumed way toward the entrance. Winifred hated loud noises and had obviously had enough disruption, so I doubted I would see her again for a while.

When Flora still hadn't replied to my question, I glanced at the clock on the wall above the front counter. Usually, by this time of day, I was checking on my adult butterflies in their milkweed fields. I hated getting behind in my routine. But this was for Evie. I forced myself to be patient and waited for Flora to continue.

She peered down at the napkin dispenser again, and her fingers flinched, but she gave a small shake of her head and let out a sigh. "Well, Seneca, what we heard was this. Um, you know that woman who works at the bank."

"You mean Karen Blain?"

"That's the one. When my sister and I were in there the other day to take in the deposit for the pharmacy..."

It took both women to run that errand? It seemed odd, but who was I to judge? They were twins, after all, and even worked at the same job in the same place of business. Maybe their time together in the womb made them want to be together?

"...Karen was away from her station."

"Okay."

"And that man, what's his name?" asked Nora.

"Lawrence Goodman," supplied Flora.

"Yes, he wasn't around either. Is that any way to run a reputable bank?" She held up her hands in question.

"Anyhow," said Flora, "after Karen came back…I think she might have been in the ladies' room"—her face reddened—"she still didn't have time to help us."

Even though Karen was flighty, and with the exception of me needing to avail Lawrence of his kindness to help me out the other day, Karen was normally all about the job, dressing professionally, and was kind and courteous to customers. What was going on with her lately?

"That's right," added Nora. "Miss Karen had to take a phone call. A phone call! I ask you, when she should have been doing her financial duty and taking care of our banking needs, why was she doing that?"

I reached for my cup and took a drink. "What was special about the call? Did Karen seem upset afterward when she came back?"

"Oh," said Nora, "yes, but we heard her part of the conversation, didn't we, Flora?"

"Yes, even though I felt guilty about eavesdropping."

"Why would you feel guilty?" Nora frowned. "We weren't doing anything wrong. Just standing at the counter, waiting a long time, I might add, for Karen to do her job and help us. The fact that she talked loud enough and stood close enough to us that we heard her side of the conversation wasn't any of our doing."

Flora nodded. "She's right."

"Of course I'm right."

Watching the two of them bicker made me all the gladder for my friendship and closeness with not only Evie, but with Cody as well. I could tell those two anything and know they'd have my best interest at heart. Knowing I had limited time to sit here, I held up my hand. "What was her conversation about?"

Flora glanced at her sister. "Karen told the person on the phone that she didn't get the job at the bank she'd been hoping for."

"Oh?" I sat up straighter.

"That's right," added Nora. "Miss Karen thought she'd get a huge promotion since Mr. Snare was no longer there. That she'd counted on getting the job." She eyed me pointedly.

Flora gasped, then seemed to compose herself. "What my sister isn't saying is that Karen might have been the one to have killed her boss. To get his job."

"That's very interesting." Especially since a few minutes ago, she verbally tossed my cousin under the bus for the very same crime.

Nora nodded. "Of course it is."

Flora slowly reached for another papery victim, only to be hissed at by her sister. The sound was so cat-like, even Winifred would have applauded her efforts. "Sorry," said Flora.

I frowned. "Sorry for what?" Did she think I'd be upset that she had a nervous compulsion to destroy innocent paper products? We all had our quirks, after all.

"For spreading gossip."

I hoped the smile I gave her would make her feel a little less guilty. "Listen, I know it's not the polite thing to do either, but I need all the information I can get to clear Evie's name for Burlington's murder. So, thank you."

If Nora's disgruntled harrumph had been any louder, Winifred's fear of loud noises would have had my cat halfway to Ohio by now.

Nora tapped the table much like her twin had just done, but I was sure wouldn't admit to doing anything like her sister. "Even though I think that Karen woman was acting fishy, I still haven't let your cousin off the hook yet."

Since there wasn't anything I could do to stop Nora's negative opinion about Evie, I shrugged and hoped my attempt at a noncommittal expression was successful. With a smile for Flora, I stood and picked up my drink. "Thanks for letting me join you, ladies. I need to get back to work. Have a nice day."

I waved at Evie, who was speaking to Murray at the front counter, then I turned to leave.

From behind me, Flora said, "Sister, I wish you wouldn't be so mean about

Seneca's cousin."

"Why should I be nice? What did that ever get anybody? You, of all people, should know that by now."

Chapter Ten

My help wanted sign had garnered exactly three interested applicants. But I wasn't sure how two of them would work out. Still, I had no choice until I found someone permanent who I thought would be great for the job since Annie was currently out of the running.

I opened the greenhouse screen door to allow two of my new employees to enter.

It was Sid and Norman.

I let out a breath. What had I done? If this experiment went way south, I could sarcastically thank Cody for his brilliant suggestion. But for now, I needed to keep positive thoughts. Nothing good would come from me starting this venture with only doubts.

I couldn't imagine why the two crotchety old guys would even want to help me out. Maybe they were bored and needed something to occupy their time. During the previous murder, they'd both very loudly announced to passersby that not only did they think I had killed my attorney in the greenhouse, but I was most likely out at night, stalking people to hunt them down and maim or murder them. They'd spread that nugget of news gleefully to anybody who'd listen. But again, they were all I had at the present.

My other interested party was Lawrence Goodman. He, of course, would only be able to give a few hours a week since he worked full time at the bank, but he'd told me that he didn't usually have much to do after his bank working hours since he was single and didn't have a social life. Gosh, that could be me, too, so I totally got it.

He also said he could use the extra cash, wanting to build a small nest egg in case things didn't go well with his bank job. Ever since Burlington had died and the bank board was scrambling to find solutions to the upheaval, Lawrence felt on edge about the security of his position there.

But for today, Sid and Norman were my willing participants, so the ornery men were all I had for the time being. I'd make it work. What other choice did I have?

Before I could begin preliminary instruction on even the simplest of tasks, Sid pointed to a tree outside the greenhouse. "Betty Rollings."

Norman blinked. "What are you babbling about?"

"Don't you remember?"

"How can I answer that if you don't tell me anything more?"

"Fine, if you're going to make me remind you, like I do nearly everything, then I guess I'll have to."

Norman huffed out a loud breath. "Just tell me, will you? I'm not getting any younger, as you know, since we're the same age." He slipped his thumbs beneath his red suspenders, which clashed glaringly with his bright orange shirt. I'd told them to wear older clothes to work in but had seen this same ensemble many other times. Maybe all they had was old clothes. I glanced down at my outfit. But then, who was I to judge?

"I pointed to the tree, because it made me think of Betty Rollings, who works at the flower shop."

"What about her?" Norman's eyebrows had lowered, covering the top half of his eyes.

"You really don't remember stuff, do ya?"

Norman rolled his eyes at me, as if to say, 'this is what I have to put up with every day.'

"Anyhow," continued Sid, "that Betty woman has a very interesting past."

When Norman didn't seem inclined to comment, I went ahead and asked, wanting to know if he truly had information about Betty. "Interesting, how?"

He wiggled his eyebrows. "Back in the day, when she was a youngster, she did some wild things."

I bit my lip, trying not to smile. To the eighty-year-olds, would "youngster" normally mean someone in their sixties? Betty was only in her thirties. In their minds, maybe an infant?

"Why was her past interesting?" I wanted to get the conversation over so we could get to the real reason they were here. And also, I wondered what his definition of wild would be. Probably went out past her curfew when she was a kid, or something.

"According to my sources," said Sid.

"Sources?" Norman barked out a laugh. "I'm the one you usually talk to. And I don't remember anything in Betty's past that was off. So, who is your source?"

He crossed his arms. "I refuse to divulge that information."

"Fine. Don't tell me who. Just get on with what Betty did that has you so hyped up."

"I'm not hyped up, I—"

I held up my hand. "It doesn't matter. Why don't you tell us what Betty did? Then, I can start to train you guys on what help I need around here." Maybe the mention of the reason they'd come today would hurry them along.

Sid leaned over to Norman and, in a supposed whisper that came out more like a trumpet blast, said, "This young whipper snapper wants to train us on something?" Then he snickered.

I could already see how nonproductive this day was going to be. Why couldn't I have found the right person right away to take over for Annie? Was that too much to ask? Surely, there was someone around town who'd love to take over the job she'd done at the farm. My problem was that I didn't have the luxury of waiting around for that to happen.

I observed Sid and Norman. How long until the men had stopped poking each other in the arm and giggling like girls at their first dance? I crossed my arms over my chest and tapped my foot in a rapid rhythm.

It must have worked, because they stopped snickering and faced me like Winifred did when she'd knocked over something valuable, with me standing right there to see it.

"Fine," said Sid, having finally composed himself and gave only the occasional residual snort. "What I heard was, when Betty Rollings was young, she used to chain herself to trees."

My mouth dropped open. "She did what?" That was definitely more in the wild category than I'd imagined.

Norman snapped his fingers. "Oh, I remember that now."

"Finally, he gets it," said Sid.

"Why would Betty have done that?" I asked.

"Don't know why. Just that she did. Chained herself, used a padlock, then tossed the key far enough away that she wouldn't be able to reach it in case she changed her mind at the last minute."

I had a difficult time putting the tidy, sensible woman who owned a lovely flower shop and routinely brought flowers to the café just to brighten everyone's day with a younger version of herself who was chained to a tree. I checked out the two men, who were now standing back-to-back, trying to see which of them was taller. But then, anything coming from those two had to be tempered with a dose of common sense, of which they seemed to contain very little.

Still, I was intrigued that if it was true about Betty, she did indeed have a very interesting past. Maybe I could check into that more later. In my spare time, dealing with an employee shortage, Evie's plight in having to tolerate people whispering about her and pointing, and the dead body that very recently turned up on Majestic Monarch property.

But for now, I really needed to get some work done for the butterflies. Dreading the task ahead of me, I held in my sigh. "Okay, ready to get to work?"

The men glanced at each other. Norman raised his eyebrows at his friend. Sid gave a shrug in return, then said, "Might as well. Got nothing else going on today."

I wanted to say, Great, thanks for that endorsement. Instead, I forced a pleasant expression. "Fine, let's get started."

I motioned them to follow me to the back area, where some of the cages were filled with cocoons.

From behind me, Sid muttered, "Think we'll have to actually touch those critters in there?"

I peered over my shoulder at him. "Yes, you will, but you can wear disposable gloves, if you'd like."

Sid's eyes widened. "You heard that?"

My hands landed on my hips. "Of course, I heard that. It's a tiny space."

Norman looked at his friend and shrugged. "Guess she has the ears of a bat."

"Guess so. Hey, do bats even have ears?"

This time, I made no effort to hold my sigh in, and it came out loud and proud.

With a scowl for his friend, Norman said, "Great. Now you've made her mad."

"Me? What about you? Besides, I didn't do it on purpose. Who could have known she could hear that nearly silent whisper I just used."

What he thought was nearly silent, came out sounding like a sonic boom in the close confines of my greenhouse. I kept my back to them, biting my lip against a laugh. I couldn't let that out like I had the sigh, because what longed to escape was a snorty guffaw that the men would be telling everyone about for the next few months.

And I could already imagine what they'd say about their time with me here today. Their stories might have me cracking a literal whip, yelling at them to work harder, or it was the guillotine for them.

Biting my lip harder, I closed my eyes for a second. *Must contain my mirth.* Finally, I opened my eyes.

And jumped.

Norman and Sid had moved—how had I not heard them this time? Were they able to control their noise level at will?—and were now standing in front of me, openly staring. Sid elbowed his friend. "Ah, there she is. Thought for a minute she was asleep."

"I'd wondered if she was dead."

"Guess it's good she's not. Otherwise, that would make three people total who'd expired at this bug farm."

"That's right. And if she was dead, we wouldn't get paid for today. And I have better things to do with my time. How about you?"

"Darn tootin, I do."

I rubbed my temples hard. How had I gotten myself into this predicament?

A tap came from the greenhouse door. Evie stepped in. She glanced at the men who no longer seemed interested in working, not that they ever were, but were totally focused on Evie.

"Hey," said Sid, "did you happen to bring over some of those cheesy fries Murray makes?" He glanced down at her hands, which were obviously empty. Did he think she'd stashed a large sack of food in her back pocket?

Her eyebrows rose. "Sorry, uh, no. Just came to see Seneca for a minute."

Norman let out a long, loud moan. "That's a shame. Now, what will we do?"

I pressed my fingertips against my temples, hoping I could keep it together around those two. Time would tell. I looked at Evie. "Hey, you wanted to see me? How about outside?"

Sid tugged on my arm. "What about us?"

Yes, what about them? I didn't want to turn them loose with either the adult monarchs or the ones in cocoons. I glanced to a corner where I kept tools I used often. I walked over there, grabbed a couple of brooms, and returned.

With skepticism written on his face, Norman asked, "What should we do with those?"

What did he think? That I wanted them to fly around the room on them? "How about you guys sweep the floor in there while I talk to Evie?"

The men glanced at each other, gave shrugs, then reluctantly took the offered brooms.

I watched them for a few seconds as they conferred on exactly the right way to use them. How had I thought this would work? But what choice did I have?

I followed Evie outside into the partly cloudy day, the sun playing tag with the clouds. We walked to a place partway to the café, halfway between her workplace and mine. "What's up, Evie? Are you okay?"

It was unusual for her to leave the café unless she was on break.

She wrapped her arms around her middle. "It's... I just needed to step outside for a minute. Murray told me to go ahead since everyone in there has been served and seems content for the time being."

I rubbed her arm. "Do you need to talk about it?"

"It's nothing different than before, just people whispering about me as I walk by, thinking I can't hear them. Or maybe they know I can hear, but just don't care if they upset me."

"I'm so sorry you're going through this. You know I understand."

"Yeah, you sure do. More than anyone. When people talked about you like that, how did you handle it?"

"Not very well."

One side of her mouth rose in a half-smile. "Yeah, I get that. But from what I saw, you took it much better than I did."

"I really didn't. Maybe it just appeared that way. But inside, I was seething. Mine came out as sassiness and irritation."

"Mine just feels like worry and sadness."

I hugged her. "And that's where you handle it better than I do."

"Why would you say that?"

"Because you're so sweet, you just walk away from it. Where I sometimes, okay, often, scolded people when they said things about me."

"I don't remember you doing that."

I pointed over my shoulder with my thumb. "Well, it was mainly Norman and Sid."

"That's right. I forgot how those two talked about you in the café, coming up with weird ways you might have committed the murder. They suggested some whoppers."

"They sure spread the word. And didn't care if I knew it, or who they told. Or what they said about me, for that matter, true or not. Mostly not."

Evie nodded. "And the whole town was placing bets on what happened. I even heard one about your lawyer having been abducted by aliens. Although, how they thought that had happened when the poor guy's body was lying on your greenhouse floor was beyond me." She laughed.

"That's a nice sound, Evie."

A blush crept up her cheeks. "Sorry, didn't mean to insult you."

"You didn't." I giggled. "Now looking back, it's hilarious the things people came up with about me. At the time, though, it was hurtful and harsh."

"Thanks, Seneca."

"For what?"

"For being willing to listen to me. You always make me feel better."

"What are cousin-sisters for?"

"You've got that right." She glanced at the greenhouse. "I guess I should get back to the café, And you probably need to supervise your new men."

"I do. But I'm glad you came over so I could have a few seconds to relax before I go in there and get frustrated all over again."

"If anyone can whip those guys into shape, it's you."

My eyes widened in mock horror. "Don't say 'whipped' too loud, or they may tell people that's what I did to them."

I needed to get back to work before a solid visual of that scenario got stuck in my head.

Chapter Eleven

The next day, I took a quick break from checking my monarchs to do a favor for Murray. He sent me a text that only said 'SOS.' Ordinarily, that text from Evie would mean disaster or needing immediate help. For Murray, however, it meant women in low-cut dresses wearing bustles.

My chef had an affinity for historical romances. He voraciously read the books as quickly as Winifred devoured award-winning salmon that I could rarely afford. However, Murray couldn't always order the books online he so desperately wanted to read and sometimes needed to get the aid of Linda Princeton from her bookstore, Bodacious Books.

When that occurred, Murray begged me to go pick up his newest novel. He couldn't bear the thought of walking into the store and having to admit he wanted the latest historical tale with the woman on the front in the long dress, clinging to the man who would eventually save her from her plight.

As I entered the shop, I stopped to admire the décor, the cute way she had displayed the newest releases near the front door, and the easy-to-find sections with signs directing the shopper to whatever genre he or she might want to peruse.

Linda stepped out from the back area. She set down a small stack of books she'd been carrying onto the counter, then waved. "Hi, Seneca. How are you?"

"I'm doing fine, thanks."

"Good to hear. Um, I mean after what happened in the café." She lowered her eyebrows.

"Yeah, that wasn't a good day."

"I'm sure it wasn't. I was actually standing in the crowd outside, waiting to get in for lunch. You didn't seem to notice me, but then, you had other things on your mind."

When I'd come upon the crowd standing outside Painted Wings, it hadn't made any sense. But when I finally wedged my way in and had gotten closer to the counter, it made perfect, yet horrible sense. "Yes. I hate what happened to Burlington, of course. What a horrible way to die. But I'm also concerned for Evie. You should hear some of the things people are insinuating about her."

I remembered Nora's words, how she wasn't letting my cousin "off the hook" so easily. But then, she and Flora had practically accused Karen of shady behavior in the bank. Why were the sisters making others look as if they were guilty of something? Were they possibly covering up for themselves?

Linda shook her head. "Poor girl. It sounded like she was getting questioned pretty thoroughly. Although I have no doubt that Cody was thorough, yet gentle with her."

"You're right. He was. I'm afraid it was comments from bystanders that were more painful to hear."

"Unfortunately, I heard several when standing outside the café. Lots of speculation. Finger pointing." She tilted her head. "But I'm guessing you're here today for a different reason than to revisit that."

"Yep, picking up a book."

"Ah, for a certain chef we both know and love?"

I laughed. "That's right. Bless his heart, as big and gruff as he is, the thought of going out in public to buy a book he's been looking forward to intimidated the stuffing out of him."

She smiled, "Yeah, it seems to. I love Murray."

"Me too."

"It's so nice of you to do this for him."

"I don't mind. He, along with Evie, are the backbone of Painted Wings. It literally wouldn't run without their talent and expertise."

She angled her thumb toward her chest. "I, for one, am thrilled that Painted Wings exists. It's always a pick-me-up when I want a snack, or just to get out and see my friends. Let me go back to get Murray's treasured story for you. It was in the shipment we just got in. It may take me a few minutes to find that box."

"Great. Thanks." I shook my head and chuckled. Why wouldn't Murray just admit he liked romances and picked them up himself? I seriously doubted Linda would make fun of him for it. She loved it when anyone was a reader. The more, the merrier, no matter what they chose to read.

As I glanced around the shop, I realized I was nearly finished with the latest mystery I was reading. Although I was busy with the monarchs and helping out at the café when I could, I somehow found a few minutes each night before bed to read something fun.

Once Winifred had gotten her nighttime snack, she was happy to lay beside me in bed, purring her encouragement as I read the stories aloud to her—yes, I actually did so she could know who the killer in the stories turned out to be. She and I both slept better once the mystery had been solved. Too bad Burlington's murderer couldn't be found as easily as in a mystery novel.

While I was in the bookstore, it was a perfect chance to browse. When I didn't see any brand-new releases that grabbed my attention, I headed to a back corner where I knew the mysteries were shelved.

One of the authors I liked had several books that were older, that I hadn't had a chance to read yet. I caught her name on the spine of the books on the bottom row. I crouched down to read the titles, hoping one would jump out at me. Not literally, like Winifred would, but from the angle I was looking at the books, it wasn't the easiest to reach.

The last time I'd been to this section, the author I'd wanted was conveniently shelved on the top row. That had been nice. But I was still glad Linda's store was stocked with great mysteries. Who was I to be picky about where she chose to place her books?

The bell on the door rang, but I didn't bother to stand to see who had entered the shop. In a town as small as ours, it was probably someone I knew, and had seen or spoken to recently. Besides, if I could rise from my awkward position, I wasn't sure I could get back down to the bottom row easily again.

From the back, Linda called out, "Be out in a second!"

"No problem," called back a woman's voice. It sounded like Penny Cummings.

As I finally discovered a title that I hadn't read yet, I heard a phone ring.

Penny answered, "Hello? Who's calling, please?" There was silence, then, "Wait a second. What are you saying?"

My leg was starting to cramp, but at this point, I didn't want to spring up, have her see me, and think I was eavesdropping. Which I was. In my defense, how was I not supposed to hear her when the bookshop was so small?

"You can't mean that," said Penny. "I don't believe you."

I rubbed my calf, hoping the cramp would go away once I was allowed to stand and stretch out my legs.

A gasp came from Penny. "But you can't! Please, don't do this."

The sound of crying came from Penny's direction. Whoever she talked to really upset her. Maybe I should offer to help.

Ignoring my cramp, I attempted to stand. Now, my other foot was asleep. Perfect. I grabbed onto an upper shelf I could reach and tried to pull myself up. It wasn't going well. The asleep portion of my body protested, sending those painful, annoying needle-like sensations as the blood was forced back into the area. I gritted my teeth together, trying not to yelp loudly, which would definitely call attention to where I was stationed.

Footsteps came from the back area. "Hi, Penny," said Linda. "How can I help you today?"

"I…" snuffled Penny, "I need to go."

I frowned. But she'd just gotten here. And I happened to know that Penny loved to read as much as I did.

"Oh," said Linda. "Are you all right? Do you need—"

"Sorry. Need to go." Penny's words came out in a jumble, like she couldn't get them out fast enough.

The bell jingled on the door. Had Penny left the shop?

Silence. Then, "Um, Seneca? Are you still here? I have Murray's book."

With effort and not a little pain, I clung to the shelf and hoisted myself to stand. "I'm here." My labored breath came out in a whoosh.

Her eyes widened when she spotted me. She hurried over, "My goodness. What happened?"

I forced out a laugh. "I was looking at a mystery on the bottom shelf and got a leg cramp."

"Ouch, those cramps are awful. Sorry about that."

"It's not your fault."

"Yes, it kind of is. Rearranging those books has been on the list of things to do for some time now. And I haven't gotten to it yet. Obviously. I'm so sorry it took this happening to remind me to fix the problem. Are you going to be all right?"

I rubbed my calf, glad when the pain subsided to nearly non-existent. A few stomps of my other foot got rid of the awful tingles as the feeling flowed back into my foot. "Don't worry about it. And believe me, I have a list like you do. It's so long, I may never get it all done."

"Thanks for understanding." She held up the book. "I have the book you came in for. Murray had already paid for it online, so it's all ready to go."

"Great. Thank you."

"Did you find what you were looking for down there?" She pointed to the spot where I'd been crouched down.

"I did. But…" I grimaced as I glanced at the book, really wanting to buy it but not looking forward to repeating my acrobatics in order to get it.

"You don't want to go through all that again?"

"Right. The title is 'Murder and Meltdown'. Bottom shelf."

She winked. "Like me to get it for you?"

"If you wouldn't mind."

"No problem." And it was indeed no problem for Linda, as she deftly bent over, twisted a little to one side, and snagged the novel, like when Winifred had batted her favorite catnip mouse under the edge of the couch and turned herself into a furry pretzel in order to rescue it.

"Nicely done."

She laughed. "I've been over every inch of this place and have developed a way of reaching everything. I'm guessing it's the same for you in your greenhouse and milkweed fields."

I thought of all the acrobatics I sometimes had to perform to see into the back of my caterpillar pens and check on the health of adult monarchs who were hidden in the depths of the milkweed. "Yes, definitely. Thanks so much."

"Glad to help." She headed toward the checkout counter, and I followed. "Is there anything else I can get for you today?"

"No, that should do it." I reached into my purse and got out my credit card, looking forward to diving into the newest story as I read it to Winifred. I handed Linda the card.

"By the way, I'm guessing you heard Penny in here earlier."

"Yeah. I did. Hard not to have heard her. But I couldn't stand up."

Linda's brow furrowed. "She seemed upset. That wasn't like her at all. Usually, when she comes in, she spends her whole meal break just browsing and enjoying her time here. I hope she's all right. Do you have any idea what happened?"

"I did actually overhear her phone conversation."

"Really?" She glanced at me as she typed in something on her computer.

"And yes, she was upset about something." I shrugged. "Not sure what."

"That's too bad. I like Penny. She's so sweet."

"Yes, she is. I like her too." I wished now I could have stood up and checked on her, even if it would have been an awkward situation, since I would have already heard her side of the conversation without her knowing, and my leg felt like it was on fire.

"I wonder if it had to do with her dad?" Linda printed out a receipt for my purchase.

Alarmed, I asked, "Is he okay? No health issues, I hope?" Penny had said he was fine, but with hiring a vet to come in, there might actually be something wrong. At his age, it wouldn't be surprising if he did have an issue or two.

I was glad he was still able to treat Winifred in his vet's office, but sometimes wondered how long he might be able to practice. Winifred didn't like him much, but who could blame her when her only exposure to the guy was him giving her shots and poking around her personal, private areas.

Linda put Murray's book and mine in separate sacks and set them on the counter in front of me, then handed me back my card and receipt. "I don't know of any health problems, but with the new vet that just started working there, it must be stressful for both Penny and her dad. It's fairly recent. Drew Paulson is here to eventually take over the practice when Dr. Cummings is ready to retire. Drew seems nice, but a little quiet. Not the sort to make a big splash and venture out to see a lot of people yet. I think maybe he's more comfortable around animals than people. I only met him because he came in here to pick up a couple of books."

"I just met him too." I smirked. "Were his books Romances, like Murray likes?"

"Ha, no. More like you. Mysteries."

With a wave for Linda, I left the bookstore and headed back to Majestic Monarchs.

After I'd worked with the larvae in the cages and cleaned up in the greenhouse, I dropped off Murray's newest book. Although a tiny part of me wanted to tease him a little about being too bashful to get his own book, I didn't. He did so much for me, Evie, and Painted Wings, that if all he asked was for me to occasionally run a secret errand for him, I was glad to comply.

When the afternoon was nearly over, Lawrence pulled up into the lot outside my greenhouse. He got out of his car wearing faded jeans and an old T-shirt. With a glance at my own outfit for the day, which nearly matched his, I nodded. What he'd chosen was the perfect attire for the type of work I did around here.

I stepped from the greenhouse, feeling something brush past my leg. Winifred darted outside, tail high in the air as if looking forward to seeing someone. Had she thought it was Cody stopping by? Since he did most days, I could see why she might have assumed it. But my cat slammed on her paw brakes when she spotted Lawrence instead.

Winifred took a sharp right turn at his vehicle and hightailed it over to

Painted Wings. It was just as well she'd hang out over there since she was locked out of the house at the moment and didn't have a pocket in which to carry a key, or even have thumbs with which to use one.

"Hey Lawrence, glad you could make it."

He glanced down at his clothes. "Hope this is okay. Not something I'd normally wear."

"Yours is perfect." I pointed to my own T-shirt.

"Great. Looking forward to helping you out and learning something new."

"I'm glad you're here. Just want to make sure you know it's temporary until I find a permanent replacement?"

He held up his hand. "Yes, and that's just what I want. It works out great for me."

"Wonderful. Want to get started?"

He nodded, looked over his shoulder, then back at me. "I hope I wasn't seeing things, but was that cat dressed like a butterfly?"

I laughed. "Welcome to Majestic Monarchs."

Chapter Twelve

As I stepped outside from the greenhouse, I waved at Johnny Overmeyer, one of our senior customers, who stood outside the café, checking his ever-present pocket watch. He waved back, but the gesture wasn't so much, 'Hey how are ya', as 'Come over here right now.'

With a glance over my shoulder at the greenhouse, I held in a sigh, knowing I still had tons of work to do with the caterpillars. I'd only ventured out there to get a little sunshine, but Johnny was a friend and a loyal café customer. How could I ignore his now more exuberant arm movements?

When I reached him, I smiled, couldn't help it. The man was adorable with his thick white hair and lively blue eyes. "Hey, Johnny. How are you?"

"I'm great." He put his thumbs under his suspender straps and gave them a loud snap. I couldn't fathom how men his age liked suspenders. Were they as reliable as a belt?

I hoped there was more of a reason than that for his insistence that I come see him. "Glad you're having a good day. Anything in particular going on?"

He smoothed down his white mustache. "Why yes, now that you ask. I just had the most superb cheeseburger a man could ever experience."

So, this was about food. "That's great. Glad you like Murray's culinary skills as much as I do. He's the best, isn't he?"

He patted his tummy. "You made a wise choice in hiring him. He's a credit to his craft."

"I agree." Something pressed against my ankle. Winifred now sat behind me, staring up at me with round caramel eyes. Her whiskers twitched, and her orange fur shifted in the light breeze.

"Hey," Johnny pointed down at the cat. "I see your little friend has tagged along. What kind of butterfly costume is she wearing today?"

"It's a Painted Lady."

Every morning, Winifred and I went to her little chest of drawers, and she placed her paw on the butterfly costume choice for the day. Sometimes, when she'd worn the same one several days in a row, I insisted she choose something else. She did it, but under duress. Although, since I was the one who dressed her, what could she say? At night, she chose a different one to go to bed in. Cat's pajamas.

Johnny nodded his head, glanced behind him, then said, "I understand now. *Painted*, like that café. How marvelous."

"Painted is one of her favorites."

"Mine too."

It took me a second to realize that while I'd meant her favorite costume, he'd meant his affinity for the café. And the thought of him possibly liking to wear a butterfly costume made me nearly giggle. How would the wings fit beneath his suspenders? Did the costumes come in extra-large? That would take a lot of glued-on glitter for those giant wings.

"Does she follow you around a lot?" he asked.

I startled, realizing I'd allowed my imagination to go off the rails again. "Yeah, she never wants to miss what's going on."

He chuckled. "I know the feeling. It makes my day more interesting if I hear tidbits of this or that to share with someone else."

That's when I remembered that one of Johnny's favorite places to hang out was the hardware store. Maybe he'd know something about Devan that could be useful.

"You said you like to share things. You could always tell me, if you wanted."

"What a splendid idea, Seneca." He grinned.

If the idea was so splendid, why hadn't he blurted out the news without making me work for it? Or before I'd had to imagine the guy in a giant, sparkly, winged costume where he'd leap and frolic among the milkweed?

Winifred meowed and pawed at my leg. I picked her up, cuddling her against my chest.

Johnny reached out slowly, then ran his arthritic fingers along the cat's whiskered cheek. Amazingly, Winifred closed her eyes in pleasure and actually gave a tiny purr. I never knew how she'd react, so I was proud of her for being sweet. This time. If she were in a different sort of mood, it wouldn't have surprised me if she'd tried to bat at his suspenders.

"Hey, I know you like to hang out with Mr. O'Hurley at the hardware store."

His eyes sparkled. "True enough."

"Anything interesting happen there lately?"

"I'm guessing you have something specific in mind?"

"Yeah, I do. I was wondering how Devan was doing. Do you know?"

He squinted in concentration. "Devan…."

"Mr. O'Hurley's stockboy."

He snapped his fingers. "Of course. While I was in the hardware store yesterday, I heard something."

"Okay…." I waited so long for him to continue that Winifred must have gotten my annoyance vibe. She turned her head and stared at him, too.

"See, I needed a new hammer, because the head of my own one kept falling off. Did you know that duct tape only holds a hammerhead for one swing onto a nail, then falls back off?"

"I didn't know that." Not that I'd ever tried. But it did make sense.

"And also, that you should always wear hard-soled shoes when using a faulty hammer in case the heavy metal piece tries to make friends with your big toe?" He peered down at his foot, lifting the toe of his left shoe as if I might be able to view a possible bruise on his foot.

I stared at his shoe. "That couldn't have felt good."

"You're absolutely right. It didn't feel pleasant in the least." He blinked. "Anyhow, I was checking out the hammer section. Did you know Mr. O'Hurley has nine different types of hammers? How is a customer, a weekend warrior do-it-yourselfer guy like me, supposed to choose the appropriate one?"

"I actually didn't know there were so many hammer styles to choose from. I'll keep the information in mind, though." I put an emphasis on the word information, hoping I'd get more than hammer talk in my very near future.

Johnny petted Winifred again, but she'd dozed off, so I doubted she even knew it. "When I'd finally chosen my hammer, with much trepidation that I'd chosen wisely, I took it to the counter."

Winifred was in deep sleep mode now. And drooling. A warm, wet patch developed on my shirt right above my breast. Perfect. Now, I looked like a nursing mother. Maybe no one would notice. I nodded at Johnny, encouraging him to continue, willing my shirt to dry extra fast.

"See, I'm usually checked out by Mr. O'Hurley. But apparently, he'd had an emergency call of nature and was in the restroom."

Though I wanted information, that wasn't exactly what I'd intended. "So you just had to wait on him to return?"

Johnny waved his hand. "No, that other fella, Devan, he helped me that time. He did his job adequately, I suppose, but…"

"Did something happen?"

"He was whining about some girl. Of all things." He shook his head, as if every young person on earth needed to benefit from his advice and experience.

"He has a girlfriend?" Even though I knew there was someone Devan was interested in after hearing his conversation on the phone at the hardware store, I wanted to see if Johnny had anything else to add.

"Not anymore, it seems."

Disappointed this was all Johnny had heard, I tried to seem upbeat and forced a smile. "Ah, well, young love, right? Always some drama."

"True." He rubbed his chin. "This seemed over the top, though."

"How so?" I could feel dampness from Winifred's drool on my skin. It had gone through my shirt and bra.

"Young Devan's love interest had experienced some bad news, I'm afraid."

Maybe there was something to learn here, after all. "That's not good."

"No, it wasn't. Apparently, things were fine between them, all hearts and flowers, with singing birds and rainbows thrown in for good measure."

Somehow, I doubted a guy around twenty years old would use those terms when talking about his girlfriend, but I let it slide. "What happened to change that?"

"According to Devan—who cried, dripping actual tears on my new hammer as he told me his tale—his girlfriend was related to the guy who was found deceased right in there." He pointed toward the café.

"She was related to Burlington?"

"That's right."

Before the other day, I hadn't been aware that Devan had a love interest. But then, even though I went into the hardware store from time to time, yes, even for hammers, like Johnny, I was usually waited on by Mr. O'Hurley, and didn't have a huge reason to speak to his stockboy all that often. "What was his girlfriend's name?"

Johnny brushed some thick white bangs from his forehead. "He didn't say. But from his snuffling and sobbing, his life was probably over."

I nodded, remembering those days when losing a boyfriend did seem like my whole future had just been wrecked. I could feel for Devan. Thank goodness, he hadn't gone through an awful divorce, like I had with my ex, Payne. Twice the anguish, with monetary woes added in.

Johnny gave a sigh of his own. "In my case, of course, it's been a very long time, but I haven't forgotten the heartache of losing my first love. She was a Democrat. I'm a Republican. It never would have worked out."

"That's too bad. Sometimes, things are just not meant to be. But maybe it led you to better things after that?"

"Yes. My late wife was my soulmate. My best friend. I can't imagine not having had all those years with her."

Right then, Cody's face popped into my mind. He was my very best friend, always had been, but recently, at an auction where I was elated to get my neighbor's milkweed-filled property, I'd jumped into Cody's arms, taking him by surprise. The near-kiss was witnessed by half of Maple Junction.

As if he'd known my thoughts, Johnny's eyes opened wide as he focused on me. "Say, didn't I hear something about you having a romance of your own?"

"Um, I..."

He studied me intently, as if trying to pry loose my secret. Then he snapped his fingers. "Yes, I have it now. Sheriff Bales. Seems to me what I heard was a very, uh, shall we say, descriptive version of a long, drawn out, titillating kiss."

Titillating? That was a new one. Time to nip this in the bud. "First of all, it wasn't titillating."

His face fell. "What a shame. Those kisses are always the best. Why, when my wife and I were courting, we used to—"

Good grief, I didn't want to hear whatever came next. I held up my hand. "So, anyway, uh, it wasn't, you know, that, or long, or drawn out."

"Now you're spoiling the whole story. I've been telling people that version for weeks."

Just great. "Maybe tell them it's not true? In all honesty, there wasn't a kiss."

"None? Nothing at all?"

"No."

He reached out and placed his hand on my shoulder, as if in consolation. "My dear girl, I'm terribly sorry. How bereft you must be that your knight in shining armor has rejected you."

"What? No. I wasn't rejected. It's not like that at all."

He shook his head. "It does no good to deny the truth, my dear. And sometimes, it's to a person's benefit to have a good cry and get it all out of your system." His eyes lit up. "Maybe if you asked Mr. O'Hurley nicely, he'd let you take a cue from his stockboy and allow you to weep openly over one of his hammers. Perhaps Devan could give you some weeping tips."

He gave Winifred one last head pat. "See you girls later. Chin up, Seneca, you are a bright, attractive, intelligent woman. Your day will come. And by the way, might want to do something about that, uh, problem happening on your…" He pointed vaguely in the direction of my chest, where the drool spot had grown larger. "That could be why your man decided to give you the heave-ho."

As he strolled away, he whistled a tune I was pretty sure was from a fifties romantic musical.

I shook my head. When would people learn to mind their own business about Cody and me? As I looked behind me at the doorway to Painted Wings, I knew the answer. People would forever be curious about what others were doing. And right now, figuring out for Evie who killed Burlington Snare was much more important than what people were saying about some long, drawn-out titillating….

Nope, not going down that road. Immersing myself in those kinds of thoughts about Cody wouldn't get me anywhere except in trouble.

"Come on, Winifred. Let's go to the greenhouse and get some work done."

She opened one eye and yawned.

"Great, I can see how much help you're going to be."

She murmured something in cat-speak, then turned in my arms, getting comfy for a long nap. Now, I just had to figure out how to get my work done and not wake up my extra spoiled feline.

Chapter Thirteen

When I stopped in to the local library that evening, I was pleased to see Mable Kane behind the main counter. I so admired her, that in her eighties, she was still willing and able to donate her time to help others. I'd heard that the library didn't always have funds to pay for full time employees, so often relied on people like Mable to fill the gaps.

I also knew that Betty Rollings often stopped in here on Tuesdays. If anyone would know the latest scuttlebutt about her, it was Mable.

"Why hello, Seneca James. How lovely to see you outside of your café and your greenhouse."

"Good to see you. How are you today, Mable?"

"I am well." With the aid of her walker, Mable stood up to her fullest height, which I guessed wasn't as much as it used to be.

"Has it been busy today?"

"Oh, certainly."

"Anyone I might know come in?" I glanced down at a couple of new titles lying on the counter as if I wasn't too interested in knowing the answer.

"Betty Rollings was just in." She pushed her walker to one side, then sat on a stool right next to her.

Bingo. This could be helpful. Mable would know if something weird had happened with Betty or if Norman and Sid had been just blowing smoke.

"How is Betty doing?"

"It was actually very odd." When Mable shook her head, a glimmer from the fluorescent lights reflected off of her glasses.

I placed my purse on the counter, hoping to hear something interesting.

With Mable, it was a toss-up. Her news could be fascinating, or it could be about a new piece of gravel she acquired to add to her rock collection.

"Miss Rollings checked out books on plants and trees." Mable gave a terse nod to emphasize her point. The easy way Mable spouted off what reading material another library patron had borrowed made me glad she didn't work at a doctor's office where she could inform people what ailments other patients had.

"That doesn't sound that strange. I mean, that is her business, after all."

"Normally, young lady, I'd agree with you. But these books were vastly different from generic, everyday ones about flowers and arborvitae."

'Vastly different' sounded like it might be more interesting than rocks. "How so?" I rested my forearms on the tall counter.

Mabel checked behind her, then glanced around the room. She must have been satisfied we were alone because she stood, moved the stool closer to the counter, and sat back down. I leaned in as well, ready to hear whatever it was she wanted to tell me.

"Well," she whispered, as any good library worker should, "When Betty was in here earlier, what a commotion she caused."

"She did?" I whispered back.

"What was that?" Mable placed her hand behind her ear.

"A commotion?"

"You'll have to speak up, dear."

Apparently, my whispering in return to hers wasn't going to work. Hoping I wouldn't disturb anyone who was in another part of the building, I amped up my volume as I asked, "What was the commotion you mentioned about Betty?"

"At first, when she wandered in, I thought it would be business as usual. You know, checking out the new arrivals, perhaps finding a book that looked interesting and sitting down to read a bit of it to decide if she wanted to check it out."

"But she didn't?"

"What was that?" Her hand went to her other ear.

I cleared my throat and tried again. "She didn't do that this time?"

"No, certainly not. I was so embarrassed, for me and for her." Mable waved her hand in front of her face, as if cooling hot cheeks.

"I'm sorry you were embarrassed. What happened?"

"You really will have to speak up, Seneca. Not all of us have the ears of ten-year-olds."

I was pretty sure mine wasn't as sharp as when I'd been in fifth grade, either, but poor Mable was really having an issue with my voice. I tried again, determined to help her hear me. "I said, I'm sorry you were embarrassed."

From behind me, footsteps sounded on the tile floor. I turned to see who it was. A little girl tugged on a woman's hand and said, "Mommy, why is that lady yelling at that nice older lady?"

The mom stared at me. "I don't know, honey, maybe the younger one is crazy. Walk faster, okay?" They rushed past me through the lobby and out the doorway.

Perfect. Now, I was crazy as well as the person who kept finding bodies on her property. Not the greatest attributes anyone would want to endorse.

Mable tapped the counter with her fingernail, the sound reverberating around the quiet room. "Seneca, if you want to hear what I have to say, please give me your full attention. It's common courtesy, something you should know about since you run your own business."

My face heated. "Yes, ma'am." I said it loud enough that not only could Mable hear me, the mom and little girl outside probably did, too.

"That's better." She nodded in satisfaction, causing her dangly pink earrings to bob. "Now, as I was saying about Betty. She marched straight to the counter, set her purse on the floor beside her, and began to weep."

"Weep?"

"That's correct. Loudly and with lots of wet, drippy tears. I had to clean the countertop after she left for fear of getting the next person's books wet."

First of all, Betty's sobbing must have been loud for Mable to hear it. And secondly, the image of books nearly drowning in a person's tears made me flinch. Maybe I should get Betty together with Devan so they could shed tears together. "Did you find out why she was so upset?"

"I did indeed. She was heartbroken that something would happen to the trees."

"Which trees?"

Mable tapped her chin as she thought. "Something about near where she lives. A man wanted to cut them all down, taking away her serenity and feeling of security of being surrounded by living, breathing, leafy friends."

"I never realized Betty's descriptions of trees sounded so poetic."

Mable pressed her hand to her chest. "Those were my words, dear."

I grinned. "I'm impressed. Nicely done."

She gave me a wink. "This old gal still has a few tricks up her sleeve."

I nodded. "Yes. You do."

"There's more."

I raised my eyebrows. This really was better than hearing about gravel.

"When Betty's weeping had diminished, she went into a sort of tirade about saving trees, how people should care more about them, and be better guardians of the earth and our planet."

"That sounds rather involved."

"Oh, trust me, it was." She patted her silver hair back into place.

"Was there anything else?"

"Of course. Then Betty asked me if we had any books on people who were passionate about trees. Especially ones where a person might have gone to great lengths to save them. And perhaps books about one of those passionate tree people risking their lives to save their beloved green friends."

My eyebrows shot up. "Risking their lives?" That sounded like a radical idea to me. "And were there any of those books?"

Her eyes widened behind her glasses. "Seneca, of course there are. Don't you know there are books about most anything you could ever want to read?"

"I guess I never thought about it."

Mable pointed to her left. "I personally stepped from behind the counter, grabbed my walker, and had her follow me to aisle number seven, where she could indeed find the sort of book she was looking for. The only thing that encouraged me in that situation was that instead of scrolling through mindless drivel on the internet, Betty had at least come to the library to search for answers and quench her thirst for knowledge."

Even though I'd heard every word she'd said, my mind snagged on the fact that aisle number seven might help me figure out more what Betty was looking for.

She placed both hands on her hips, something I'd seen her do in Painted Wings if her order wasn't being delivered as quickly as she thought it should. "Speaking of thirst for knowledge, Seneca, what brought you in here today? I haven't seen you in here for quite some time. At this rate, your library card is going to get moldy."

I jerked, realizing I'd been glancing away from Mable again. I really would rather not be scolded for inattention for a second time, so I focused on her and tried to sound reasonably intelligent. "I doubt my library card would actually mold."

"It was a figure of speech. You young people, always taking things literally."

I could see this was not getting me anywhere but in more hot water. Hoping to divert her current critical view of me, I said, "Actually, I've been reading a lot from my Kindle lately."

She made a tut-tutting sound. "Kindle? One of those newfangled gadgets. Mark my words, that kind of warped technology won't last into the new year."

"Well," I said, hoping to placate her, even though I didn't agree, "You might be right."

"Of course I'm right." She huffed out a loud breath. "Now, you never answered my question about why you stopped in here today."

I blinked, trying to focus. Her news about Betty had caught me off guard. It took a second to remember my reason for showing up. "I actually came in for books."

She pressed the fingers of one hand to her chest. "Goodness gracious. Am I to assume you're giving up those Kindle things that supposedly pass for books?"

I moved from foot to foot, feeling like a scolded kid in class. "Yes. I need some actual books printed on paper."

"Wonderful." She clasped her hands together. "And what can I help you find today?"

Not sure how she'd take my request, I didn't make eye contact. "Children's books."

She peered over the counter to view my midsection. "Do you have a bun in the oven, dear? Is it Sheriff Bales' baby? I heard about the passionate kiss at the auction."

My face heated as it had that day when I'd jumped into Cody's arms. "No, not passionate. It wasn't even a kiss. It was a near kiss."

She continued to gaze at my middle. "Miss James, I may be old, but I still remember that it takes more than a near-anything to create a baby."

I shook my head as I pointed to my stomach. "And there's no bun. Not even a biscuit. Cody and I are just friends."

Her expression was that of skepticism, but she shrugged. "If you say so." She flipped her hand in apparent annoyance. "Why, then, do you need children's books if you don't have any children? Or biscuits?"

I glanced behind me, then muttered, "It's for Winifred."

"Speak up, please."

"Winifred," I said as loud as I could.

Her eyebrows scrunched together. "Isn't that the name of your cat who follows you around in those little tutus?"

This wasn't going well. Maybe it wasn't a good thing Mable was on duty today. Would another library worker have questioned me about what I wanted to borrow? And about possible buns in the oven? "They're butterfly costumes, actually, and yes, that's Winifred."

Mable leaned forward, placing both forearms on the counter. "Are you telling me your cat can read? Maybe she should join the circus."

"No, of course, she can't read. And she hates the circus." I found out the hard way one time when a traveling circus was in town. One of the clowns had stopped by the café, wanting to place some fliers for the circus on our bulletin board. Even as a kid, clowns had never been my favorite. And obviously, they weren't Winifred's either, the way she hissed, ran in place, then shot out of the café like a man out of a cannon.

"Then why do you need books for her?" Mable's gaze was unwavering, making me feel like a bug under a magnifying glass.

I blew out a breath. When I'd come here, I hadn't envisioned this being so complicated. But it seemed that in order to get what I wanted, I'd have to spell it out for Mable. "See, before bed every night, Winifred lies down beside me and likes me to read to her."

She placed her chin in her hand. "Fascinating. Go on."

Heat rose up my neck to my cheeks as I realized I wasn't getting out of here with the books until I told Mable things I hadn't planned to. "She likes to hear cozy mysteries, you know, the ones with no gore or bad language. But I had been reading her a newly released suspense book, and it scared her. It kept her up all night."

"I thought cats were nocturnal." Mable's eyes narrowed. Was she trying to catch me in a lie?

"They are, but they do sleep part of the night. But since she was afraid to go to sleep, she kept me up. Then I was tired during the day when I needed to take care of the monarchs and—"

She reached out and patted my hand. "Dear, it's all right. I don't judge a person on what they choose to read, or who they read it to." She glanced down again. "Or what they may have in their oven."

"Um, thanks." Even though it seemed she hadn't bought my explanation of the near kiss and not having a bun, I was nevertheless grateful that now, perhaps, I'd get the books I wanted for my cat.

She pointed to her right. "If you walk in that direction, you'll find the children's section. I happen to know there are several books with the main characters as cats. I'm sure Winifred would enjoy those."

I nodded, ready to rush away from the counter, when I noticed two women standing a few feet behind us, openly gawking at me. How long had they been listening to my conversation with Mable? How much had they heard?

Perfect. Now, town gossips could add that I read books to my feline. So would I now have a crazy cat lady label attached to my name as well? Wasn't being teased about the non-existent kiss enough for people? Or the fact that a second murder had been committed on my property? Or that I might be housing a biscuit?

By the smirks on the ladies' faces, and the way they elbowed each other and snickered, apparently not.

As quick as I could without all-out running, I rushed past the women, then made it to the children's area. It took a while to wade through the sections—dragons, wizards, llamas, before I found the pets section. After passing by dogs, rabbits, and parrots, I finally came to the feline section. I hurriedly grabbed several books—yes, with cats on the covers—but I didn't go directly to the counter to check out. I placed the books on a nearby bench and would pick them up on my way out. Maybe by that time, the redness from my embarrassed face would have faded.

Instead, I crept a few aisles over to see what titles Betty might have been looking for.

When I turned the corner, I was confused. The books weren't necessarily about trees, but about people who'd died, defending the honor of others, or their homes, or their possessions. Would Betty really had given up her own life for the sake of saving trees? But if what Norman and Sid had told me was true, she'd chained herself to a tree to save it. What if whoever was on the other end of a giant tree saw wasn't a compassionate person? Hadn't cared if Betty was injured or worse?

Sure, that person would have committed a crime if they'd allowed her to be injured or killed, and it was likely that scenario wouldn't have happened; then the police would have been called, and Betty would have been in trouble for trying to hold up a service that the owner had chosen to have done.

But there was always the risk that the person in charge wouldn't be the kind who would try to keep a crazy tree-hugging young woman from harm.

Was Betty setting herself up for future trouble if she hadn't given up her quest to protect the trees of Maple Junction?

Chapter Fourteen

The next morning when I checked the cabinet where I kept Winifred's canned food, it was empty. Again. I was a terrible mom. Sure, things had been hectic, with having no reliable help at the farm and my cousin being accused of murdering a man in my café, but, at least according to Winifred, I needed to get my priorities straight.

My angry cat sat on the kitchen counter. Her tail lashed so hard when I only gave her dry food in her bowl, she knocked over my salt and pepper shakers. That created a whole different mess, but I didn't take the time to clean it up. A trip to the grocery store was in order, and fast.

I made it there in record time, my truck's tires squealing in the parking lot when I turned too sharply and nearly took out a large trash dispenser located by the cart return area.

After grabbing my keys and purse, I jogged to the main entrance. When I entered the store, cool air hit my sweaty skin, giving me a moment of relief. I took a few seconds to stand still as I caught my breath and allowed the blowing air to hopefully dry what was now my too-dewy complexion.

There were no customers near the front of the store, but Tonda was standing at her cashier station, checking out her manicure and looking bored, as she normally did. I grabbed a plastic basket from just inside the door and gave her a wave.

Since I always bought the same kind of canned food and this was the only grocery store in town, I knew exactly down to the number of steps it took me to reach the coveted cat aisle. No one else was there, so I practically flung myself at the shelves and loaded up my basket with as many cans as it would hold. In the quiet of the store, I made quite the sensation as the metal cans clanged one on top of another as I pitched them into the basket.

As I was ready to leave, I turned, and the toe of my shoe caught on something lying on the floor, partially hidden beneath the edge of the lowest shelf. Intrigued, I set the basket down and bent over to see it better.

Whatever it was sparkled in the overhead florescent lighting. It was a piece of jewelry. Beautiful gold filigree with small rubies placed all around the edges and a large one in the center. When I picked it up, something poked my skin. I flipped it over—I could now see it was a brooch—and the clasp on the back was broken. It was no wonder whoever had been wearing it had lost it.

When I glanced around, I didn't see anyone. Maybe I could leave the brooch with Tonda. Surely the store would have a lost and found like we did at the café. I hurried to the checkout counter, glad that no other customers were standing there. With the few cars, there had to be some other people in the store. I was just glad they weren't all in line now, so I wouldn't have to wait.

Tonda, still looking bored, studied the contents of my basket. "Ah, run out of cat food again, Seneca?"

My eyebrows shot up. "Uh, yeah. It happens."

"Seems to happen to you a lot." She grinned, obviously taking great delight in my misfortune.

She scanned the individual cans, taking her sweet time about it. I wanted to shout at her to hurry up, but knew from experience it wouldn't do any good and might just entice her to move even slower.

"Gee," she said, "I guess I could add that finding dead bodies on your property happens a lot too. What is it with you?"

If this wasn't the only grocery store in town, and Tonda wasn't the main, and often the only, cashier on duty, I might not put up with her rudeness. But I needed the cat food, and she knew it, so I put up with her.

Finally, Tonda dropped the last can into a grocery bag and told me how much I owed. "Does that do it for you today, Seneca?"

Just as I was ready to say yes, I remembered the brooch, which I'd stashed in my pocket so it wouldn't get smashed in the basket with all of the cans. "Wait. I found something back in the cat food aisle."

She smirked. "Let me guess. Cat food?"

I rolled my eyes. "No, I found this." I gingerly removed the brooch from my pocket, and, being careful to avoid another stab from the broken latch, I held it out in my palm for Tonda to see.

She frowned. "Uh, okay. It's a… pin or something?"

"A brooch, actually."

"Right." She rubbed her chin. "I think my great-granny used to wear one of those. That thing must be ancient, just like she was."

Although her description of her great-grandmother hadn't sounded flattering, Tonda was right about the brooch looking old.

"So, are you going to keep it?" she asked.

"No, of course not." I held it out so it was closer to her.

Tonda put up her hands, palms out. "Don't give it to me."

"Why not?"

"I don't want it. Can you imagine the teasing I'd get from my friends if I wore that old thing pinned to my clothes? My best friend would never let me live it down."

Her best friend, Gretchen, worked for Arnold, our funeral director. Tonda and Gretchen were equally good, or would that be bad, at gossiping and had gotten me in trouble by spreading things about me that weren't true during the previous murder. At least for now, I only had to deal with one of them.

"Tonda, I didn't mean for you to keep it or wear it."

She relaxed. "Well, that's good. Because I won't."

"What I meant was, doesn't the store have a lost and found? Whoever it belongs to has been in the store, since I found it in the cat food aisle. They're going to want it back."

She was shaking her head before I'd finished. "No, I won't take it."

"Why not?"

"I don't want the responsibility. That thing looks expensive." Her eyes widened. "I mean, do you think those gems are real?"

I glanced down at the brooch. I wasn't an expert by any means, but the craftsmanship and artistry of the brooch and apparent age of it, sure did make it appear authentic. "Yes, I'd guess they're real, but—"

"Listen, Seneca, my boss is on vacation and I'm in charge for the next week. What if something happened to that pin thingy—"

"It's a brooch."

"—while it was in the store, and I'm in charge?" She crossed her arms. "No. I won't do it. I need this job, and this week on my own is my time to prove my worth as a reputable cash register associate. I do have ambitions of moving up to store manager before I'm thirty, you know."

"But I can't just walk out with it. It doesn't belong to me." With my luck, Bud would somehow see me with it and question me about where it came from and whose it was. Cody would nip any investigations in the bud—no pun intended—but who wanted to go through the hassle of trying to explain how I'd ended up with it?

Tonda frowned. "Since I can't have it stay here, what if I took a picture of it with my phone and had you sign something saying it was in your possession until you found the owner?" Her eyes grew large and pleading.

It seemed there was no way I'd talk her into keeping the brooch with her, or in lost and found, and I wasn't going to just leave it where I found it on the floor. This appeared to be the only way I'd get out of the store any time soon. "Fine," I said from between my clenched teeth. "Take your picture, and I'll sign whatever you say."

She whipped out her phone, snapped a photo before I realized she'd done it, then grabbed a pen and piece of paper from below her cash register. She handed them to me.

"Wait, I thought you were going to write something and I'd sign."

She shrugged. "I wouldn't know what to write. You do it, okay?"

I took the pen, jotted down my name, phone number, address, and dress size—no, not really the last one, but it felt like I should have. Then I wrote a description of the brooch, where I'd found it, where it would be for the time being until the owner was found, and added that Tonda had a picture of the brooch as well. After I scribbled my name at the bottom, I handed it to her. I would also take a picture of the brooch to have on my phone in case

I misplaced it, or Winifred decided to steal it and bury in the depths of her litter box.

Tonda squinted as she read it. "Wow, your handwriting is awful."

"I know it's not great, but can you at least make out what I wrote?"

More squinting, then she finally nodded. "Yep, this should do."

An elderly man hobbled up behind me in line. Tonda greeted him, looked at me, tilted her head toward the exit, and then began to ring up the gentleman's purchases.

I'd been given the royal summons, and it was time to go. Fine by me. I'd been gone much longer than I'd intended anyway. I'd take the brooch to the café and have Murray guard it.

But first, time to head home. I raced equally as fast as my ride to the store, practically feeling Winifred's stare the closer I got to my house.

Once there, I stuck the key in the door and heard kitty paws scratching frantically on the other side.

"I'm coming, kitty. Hold on!"

I unlocked and opened the door and was assailed with a furry orange body who attached herself to the front of my shirt.

"Okay, little one, Mama's finally here." I gently peeled her claws from my shirt and set her on the floor.

I'd only gotten half the wet food into Winifred's dish before she shoved her face into the bowl, snuffling and snarfing down the smelly food.

As I watched her and tried to catch my breath, I remembered the brooch. I gingerly tugged it from my pocket, glad that I hadn't been impaled or that the broken latch hadn't torn my pants.

I studied the piece of jewelry, which was easier in my kitchen, with a shaft of bright sunlight streaming through the wide window over my kitchen sink. The brooch was beautiful, and yes, as I'd told Tonda earlier, looked to be authentic. It had dark red stones, possibly rubies, in the middle, surrounded by a gold filigree design with swirls that formed into a tiny heart at each corner.

It appeared to be something an older, possibly wealthy woman might wear. Like somebody who'd be at least my grandmother's age. Mable Kane came to mind. But why would she have been in the cat food aisle? As far as I knew, she didn't have any pets. At least, she never mentioned them.

Why would the owner have been wearing something like this at the grocery store anyway? Of course, people could wear what they wanted. But in tiny Maple Junction, a rural community where dressing up was putting on your newest pair of jeans, it seemed out of place to find something so fancy and expensive lying on the floor beneath the shelf of kitty treats and catnip.

I'd have to ask Mable the next time I saw her in case it did actually belong to her. Or she might know who did own it, since she seemed to know everyone in town and what they were up to.

Once Winifred had finished chowing down on her meal, she sauntered over to her pillow positioned between the refrigerator and stove, plopped down on it, and began her hour-long ritual of tongue-bathing her orange fur from the tips of her ears to the end of her tail.

I waved at her. "I need to check in at the café. See you later."

She lifted her head and stared at me. It was all I could do not to laugh, because, having caught her in mid-lick, her tongue stuck out at me as it she was giving me her not-so-nice opinion.

I carried the brooch loosely in my hand as I walked to the café. The doors were open, allowing the bright sunlight to filter into the room. Several people were already there, feasting on Murray's edible delights, drinking coffee, and filling the room with individual conversations among various groups.

Evie was speaking to Dana Hastings, Annie's mom, at a nearby table, so she only had time to give me a quick wave before turning back to her customers. Murray stood at the counter, holding out a cup toward me. Usually, when I came in at my normal time, he was so good to have my favorite drink ready to go. But this wasn't my usual time. How had he known?

I walked toward the counter and smiled. "Hey, thanks. Wow, you go above and beyond. Are you also a mind-reader?"

He blinked. "I saw you through the front window as you drove past the café. Figured you'd be in any minute."

"Oh, well, that works too. Thanks!"

He placed the drink on the counter. "What do you have there?" He angled his chin toward my partially closed hand.

I opened my fingers so he could see it. "Believe it or not, I found this in the grocery store and…"

"Ran out of Winifred's food again?"

"Why does everyone always know that?"

"Maybe because it happens often."

"Well, anyway…"

Footsteps came closer from behind me. It was Evie. "Hey, Seneca." She peered down at my hand. "Ooooh, how pretty. Is it yours?"

I opened my mouth to speak, but Murray beat me to it.

He pointed to the brooch. "She found it at the grocery just now."

"Ah, run out of Winifred's cat food again?"

I pressed my hand to my chest. "Am I so predictable?"

Evie laughed and gave my shoulder a pat. "Yes, sorry, but you are. But no more than I am. And than Murray is."

He grunted something I couldn't quite catch, but might not have wanted to hear it anyway.

I did my best to ignore their comments, then held the brooch out to Evie. "Careful, the latch is broken, and it's sharp."

She gingerly picked it up and studied it. "That is gorgeous. And I bet expensive. Will you take it to a jeweler to get repaired and appraised?"

"No, I was thinking maybe asking Mable Kane if it was hers, or if she might have a friend it belonged to. Other than that, we'll keep it here in lost and found."

"Why didn't they do that in the grocery where you found it?"

"Tonda didn't want any part of the responsibility."

Evie studied the brooch again. "We'll do our best to help find the owner. Right, Murray?"

"Yeah. Want me to make a sign saying it's here?"

With as expensive as it appeared to be, I'd hate for someone to claim it falsely and simply sell it for the money they'd get from a pawn shop. "Yes, let's do a sign, but make it more generic. Like, we've found something, but not be specific what it is. That way, whoever the owner is will have to prove in some way that it's theirs."

"Good idea," said Evie.

"I agree." Murray looked down at the object in Evie's hand. "Do you want me to put it in our safe in the office until then?"

"Yes," I said. "Perfect."

Evie handed the brooch to Murray, who curled his large fingers gently around it as if it were a fragile butterfly.

And thinking of that, I needed to get back to my monarchs. With a wave to my friends, I left the café and headed out to my milkweed fields to check on their progress.

Chapter Fifteen

inifred and I had just come from paying a short visit to Cody. Once in a while, he liked me to bring her in. I kept telling him he should get a cat, but he said that sharing mine was what he wanted. As we drove past the quilt shop, I saw Mike stepping inside. What would he want in a fabric store?

It might be a great opportunity to gain more information. Plus, Angel had called me recently about some new butterfly costumes they'd sewn for Winifred.

"Winifred, we have one more stop to make. I think you're going to like this one. Angel and Connie made you some new outfits. Want to check them out now?"

She blinked at me, then looked out the front windshield as I pulled into a space not far from the shop.

When we arrived, with me carrying Winifred under one arm, the loud bell that sounded overhead the door startled her. She hissed at the offensive musical instrument and hid her face in my armpit. Not the most comfortable position for either of us, but I had to admit, the bell was super loud.

"Hey there," said Angel, giving us a wave. "Oh, you brought Winifred, yay!"

Angel was a tad dramatic, but I loved her. With Cody being my best friend, it was almost like Angel was also a cousin of mine.

Mike was standing off to the side, holding a sack and looking uncomfortable.

I waved. "Hey, Mike. Go ahead. You were here first."

"No, Seneca. Ladies first."

Connie tapped the counter. "We can do both. Mike, I'll help you down here." She waved him a few feet toward the other end of the counter.

"Great." He moved in that direction.

Angel smiled. "That leaves you two girls with me."

"Yes, thank you for making her some new outfits. What a nice surprise."

"You know how much we love Winifred." She giggled. "And creating those costumes is so much fun." She reached beneath the counter and pulled out two tiny sets of clothing. "I used a shimmery fabric for the edges of the wings of this one. See what you think."

"Aww. Those are amazing. When do you two have the time?"

"Are you kidding? We love our work so much; we don't stop creating things when we close the shop."

I placed Winifred on the wide counter and carefully removed her tiny tunic. The wings shimmered from the overhead fluorescent lights.

Winifred looked up at me and meowed.

"Yes, I realize you're naked, but give Angel just a second so you can try on one of your new costumes."

As I had hoped, the costume fit Winifred perfectly, earning Angel a slow kitty blink in acceptance.

"Great," said Angel. "Can we try the other one, too, to make sure it fits?"

I ran my hand under Winifred's chin. "I know you just got this one on, but there's one more to try on. Okay?"

The cat let out a sigh, then nuzzled my hand with her nose.

"Thank you," I said. "Okay. She's ready."

Angel took the yellow one, replacing the beige one over Winifred's orange fur. The effect was stunning. My cat pawed at the beige one.

"Hey." Angel laughed. "You can't wear both at once."

"She might try."

From the other end of the counter, Connie held out her hand toward Mike.

Mike reached into a sack and tugged out a folded navy blue shirt. "I was out, um, trimming bushes the other day and got a rip in one of my favorite shirts. Wondered if you could repair it?"

"Let me have a look." Connie studied the shirt Mike had given her, staring closely at the torn area. "Yes, that shouldn't be a problem."

"Great. Thanks. Was hoping you'd be able to help." He ran his finger around the neck of the yellow shirt he wore beneath his Civil War jacket, as if the collar was too tight. He'd had the jacket on the day before, too. Was he wearing it to make a statement about whoever it was that wanted to change the way their play was presented?

From in front of me, Angel shifted against the counter. I turned, hoping I hadn't seemed rude for appearing to ignore her. "Winifred looks amazing in both. Thank you so much. How much do I owe you?"

Angel shook her head and grinned. "You don't owe us anything. You're family."

"Wow, thanks so much. I'm sure Winifred will love wearing each of them."

A cell phone lying on the counter buzzed, and Angel picked it up. After reading the text, she said, "Excuse me." Then she stepped away.

I took advantage of her absence to take another look at the shirt Mike wore. Yellow didn't seem to look right with the rest of his ensemble. A glance at the torn navy one now lying on the counter made me wonder—was that the shirt he normally wore with his Civil War garb?

When I lifted my head, Mike was watching me. Had he seen my interest in his two shirts? His face reddened, and he averted his gaze to the floor. Why would it bother him that I noticed what he wore?

Connie tapped her finger on the navy shirt. "We can have this ready for you by tomorrow afternoon."

"Thank you," said Mike. "I want to have it in time for the meeting."

Why would a shirt that he wanted especially to wear to a certain venue have been one he'd trimmed bushes in? And just now, he'd stumbled over his words a little when he'd said that about wearing it to do outdoor work.

"No problem," said Connie. "How does three o'clock tomorrow sound for you to pick it up?"

"Perfect."

He gave us a wave and walked out.

Angel returned from her text. Connie glanced down at Mike's shirt, then picked it up and walked toward me. "Seems like a dressy shirt to wear trimming bushes."

I nodded. "That's what I thought. When you two do outdoor work with power tools, don't you normally wear something old? Something you don't care if it gets torn or stained?"

"Power tools?" Connie snickered. "The closest Angel and I get to that is our sewing machines."

"That's true," agreed Angel. "I'm afraid I'm not very outdoorsy."

Connie's eyebrows lowered. "I was also surprised to see Mike in the jacket."

"What do you mean?" I asked. "He always likes to for their historical reenactment."

"True, but he's had it on for…what would you say, Angel, three days?"

"Yep, I'd say so. And the reenactment hasn't started yet. It's like he doesn't want to part with it."

I thought for a minute. "Now that you mention it, I have seen him in the café more than once lately wearing it."

"Do you think it's some sort of statement?" asked Angel.

"Could be." I shrugged. "He did tell me something odd is going on with the committee that oversees the reenactment every year. That they want to change something about it. He seemed very upset when he told me."

"I can understand why that would make somebody want to take a stand," said Connie. "Maybe that's what he's doing by not removing his jacket."

"And," said Angel, "did you happen to notice that tiny mustard stain above his left jacket pocket?"

Connie nodded. "I sure did. I was afraid I'd blurt something out about it while he was here. Glad I didn't. I wouldn't want to embarrass him."

"There was something else," said Angel. "When I saw Mike in the convenience store yesterday, he was on his phone, talking to somebody. It was about Burlington."

"Really?" I smoothed my hand over Winifred's new outfit, then picked her up. "Do you remember what he said?"

She furrowed her brow. "Let's see…the words 'cad,' 'scoundrel,' and 'liar' come to mind."

Connie and I exchanged glances. "As we all know," I said, "Mike uses words most twenty-somethings might not. But those are inflammatory terms, all right."

"True," said Connie, "and it's like he's got the mind of someone sixty years older with some of his words. I do like him, though."

"Me too." I hoisted Winifred a little higher against me. She'd begun to wilt.

Angel nodded her agreement. "I'm almost positive he'd said those things about Burlington, since he used his name a few times in the conversation right before he said them."

Connie raised one eyebrow. "Eavesdropping, were we?"

Her face turned pink. "Hey, you know what a tiny store that is. How can you not hear what someone is saying?"

"Did Mike know you were eaves—uh, listening to him?" I asked.

"I don't think so," said Angel. "I was a few aisles over. But, honestly, it's hard to tell. He was so upset. I was shocked to hear him so angry. Usually, he's kind and sweet."

"Something's really gotten him keyed up." Winifred pawed at my arm. Was she ready to go back home?

"Hey," said Connie, "I heard you have some temporary help out your way."

"Yeah, I do. You wouldn't happen to know anyone who wants a permanent job, do you?"

"Sorry, no, but I'll keep my ears open."

"Great. Thanks."

"So, how are your new workers doing? I would imagine Lawrence is a good employee, at least he strikes me as being that way from when he waits on me at the bank."

"Yes, he does a good job. It's just too bad he doesn't have more hours to give me, but I appreciate what he does give, considering he works full-time somewhere else."

Angel and Connie shared a glance.

"What?" I looked from one to the other.

"Well," said Connie, "we'd been wondering most of all how things were going with Norman and Sid."

"Those two…" I chuckled. "They keep me on my toes, that's for sure."

They laughed. "We were trying to imagine what would happen if they worked here for us."

"Right. I can imagine them trying to help with some of your skeins of yarn, both of them tied up in a ball of soft pink strands, unable to move. Or trying to assist some older woman in choosing a color for her latest crochet project."

Angel looked at me and shook her head. "Wow, you must be a saint to have taken those two on."

"Nope, just desperate for help." Just then, Winifred kicked my arm and let out a low growl.

Angel pointed to the cat. "I think someone is ready to go home."

"Yeah." I repositioned Winifred, so her claws were no longer in contact with my arm. "She's definitely ready. Hey, thanks again, you two, for Winifred's new duds. They're awesome!"

"You're more than welcome," said Connie, "and great to see you and your furry girl."

"Come on, kitty, let's get you home."

Winifred meowed.

I cuddled her closer. "Yes, you can try on your other new outfit again when we get there."

As I carried Winifred from the shop, I thought about Mike's strange wardrobe choices. There was something going on there. And I needed to find out what it was.

Chapter Sixteen

I stopped by the café an hour after it opened to see if Evie needed anything. The place was bustling, as usual, and my cousin was racing around like Winifred did when a strong wind ruffled her fur. When Evie spotted me, she came over and gave me a hug.

I took in her tired eyes and slumping shoulders. "Are you holding up okay, Evie?"

"Yeah, as well as anyone could." She waved her arm, encompassing the café. "As you know, I like to keep busy."

"Well, today should help you then." I smiled.

"No doubt about that."

Murray came out to stand behind the counter and waved us closer. "I've been keeping a close eye on what you found, but so far, no one has claimed it." He pointed to a sign he'd put up above the counter.

Lost something valuable?

Ask at the counter with a description of your lost item

to see if we have it here.

After I read it, I nodded. "Thanks, you've worded that perfectly."

He tapped his temple. "Smarter than I look, Seneca."

"Oh, I know you're a genius." I grinned.

He waved the comment away with his hand, mumbling something I couldn't quite hear.

"She's right," said Evie. "You really are. We couldn't do this, any of this, without you."

A pinkish hue rose up on Murray's cheeks. "You girls and your outrageous ideas." He was frowning, but right before he turned to leave, I noticed a smile forming beneath his mustache.

I turned to Evie. "Everything going okay here? No new…problems?"

"Thankfully, no one has yelled at me today, accused me of stealing from them, or…" She glanced at the place where Burlington took his final breath.

"Murray said there haven't been any inquiries into the br… Uh, the item?" There were lots of listeners nearby, and I had no intention of messing up Murray's clever way of advertising what was in our lost and found.

"No. Nothing. And let's just say, if I'd been the one to lose it, I'd be asking everywhere if somebody had seen it."

"Me too."

Evie sighed as she spotted something behind me.

"What's wrong?"

"Nothing, just…Mable is frantically waving at me from over there. Would you like me to ask her if the brooch is hers?" She raised her phone. "I took a photo of it earlier in case I had to show it to whoever said they'd lost it."

"That would be great, if you don't mind."

"I don't mind. I'll let you know."

"Thanks."

I glanced at the cup Murray had placed in my hand earlier, thankful he cared enough to take care of me in this small way. I took a sip. "Good as always."

From behind me came, "Hey, Seneca." I closed my eyes for a second. I knew that voice. And the ex-husband attached to it.

I turned. "Payne."

He got Murray's attention, ordered a black coffee, then planted himself right against the counter, his arms crossed over his chest. "Why didn't you tell me you had another murder on your property? Didn't you realize I'd hear about it sooner or later?"

"Honestly, Payne, it didn't occur to me to tell you. Why would I?"

"For one, I'm the only lawyer in town since your other one died over there." He pointed to the general direction of my greenhouse. "And for another reason, because you and I will be getting back together. You know it, and so do I."

I took a huge slurp of my drink, needing the caffeine fortification to have a civilized conversation with my least favorite person on the planet. "Look. I wish you'd stop saying we're going to get back together. It's not going to happen. Ever."

Payne shook his head. "From what I hear, you and Cody had a wild fling. But hey, I understand a person's needs. I'll still take you back. No questions asked."

My mouth hung open. It was a second before I snapped it closed. I took a breath and let it out, hoping my next words to him didn't come out as a shout. "Payne, honestly. When did you start listening to Maple Junction gossip? I'll tell you what I tell everyone else who's brought it up. Nothing happened."

"Come on. I know what I heard. And I…" He reached out to touch my hand. "I remember how it was. With us."

I jerked so hard I nearly spilled my drink on him. Although, that might have been a good thing if it had made him go away. "I don't want to have this conversation with you, especially here in my place of business."

"Whatever." His usual response to something he didn't like still made me livid.

"I have things to do, Payne, so…"

"If you won't see reason and talk about you and me, at least take into consideration that your cousin needs me."

"What?"

He crossed his arms over his chest. "She's under suspicion for murder, in case you forgot."

"No, she isn't. Cody doesn't suspect her. Because she's innocent."

"I see how it is. Because you and Cody are together, he's protecting your cousin."

A sound like a low growl had me whipping around to my left. Murray now stood there, eyes narrowed, muscular arms over equally muscular chest, and his glare was only for my ex.

"Payne," he said. "Here's your order." He edged the cup toward Payne as if not wanting to touch it because of who had ordered it.

"Yeah, thanks," said Payne. He tossed the money on the counter and picked up the glass.

"Now," said Murray, "it's time for you to go."

"I just got here."

Murray pointed at me. "The owner of this establishment obviously doesn't want to speak to you. So, now, you leave."

Looking first at me, then back at Murray, Payne shook his head. "You guys are all the same. I don't know why I bother."

I tapped my foot. "Neither do we."

With a huff, he turned and left.

"Thanks, Murray."

"No problem. Glad to take out the trash"—he tilted his head toward the retreating Payne—"that messes up Painted Wings."

Someone touched my hand. I whipped around, afraid Payne had come back, but it was Evie.

Her eyes were wide. "Seneca, I overheard some of what Payne said about me needing him as a lawyer. Do you really think that…"

"No. Not for one second. And neither does Cody, okay?"

She seemed to deflate as she let out a relieved breath. "Okay."

A customer called Evie's name. "Time for me to go too." She hurried to their table.

As I walked toward the door, I spotted Mable waving me over as she sat at her table. Maybe Evie had found the brooch's owner after all and hadn't had time to tell me.

"Hi, Mable."

She placed her hand behind her ear, indicating she couldn't hear me very well.

"Hi," I said louder.

"Hello, Seneca. Evie showed me a picture of the brooch. I'm sorry to say that beautiful piece of jewelry isn't mine. But I envy whoever it is. That brooch is worth a fortune."

"Thanks, anyway."

"What?"

I smiled. "Thank you."

She nodded, then picked up her cheeseburger, one of Murray's specialties.

I was nearly to the doorway when another person walked in. To my surprise, it was Penny. I tried to remember the last time I'd seen her in here, and couldn't. I tossed my empty cup in a nearby receptacle and headed toward her. "Hi, Penny. How are you?"

"Honestly? Quite frantic." She clasped and unclasped her hands, as if indeed at her wit's end.

"What can I do to help? Do you need to sit down? Drink something? How about—"

She stood, unblinking, as she stared at the front counter. More specifically, her gaze was above the counter. At Murray's sign. "I..." After a glance over her shoulder, she leaned closer. "Do you...I mean, that sign. Is it for real?"

"Yes, it's real." Why would she think it wasn't?

"I just..." She clasped her hands together again. "See, I've lost something and..."

"Then maybe what we have is yours."

"I hope so. How do we go about this? Do I tell you what I've lost first?"

I gently took her elbow and led her to the front counter. Then, I called for Murray.

He stuck his head around the corner. "Just a second. Let me finish this order."

"Sure," I said. "Penny, are you sure you wouldn't like to sit while we wait?"

She blinked. "I guess we could do that."

"There's a table right over there. By the wall."

As we walked past the counter, Penny's gaze dropped to the floor. To the same spot, everyone else looked at as they walked by. Penny's shoulders rippled. Had she shivered? That might not mean anything, though, aside from the normal reaction to someone having died.

But Penny hadn't been here that day. How would she know Burlington died right there? I shook my head. Just like we did here in the café, Penny heard all kinds of gossip from all the pet parents who came through their practice's door every day. It wouldn't take much to believe someone else had told her.

We sat at the table across from each other. "Penny, you're so pale. Can I get you something? Have you eaten today?" Now that I looked at her more closely, I could see subtle changes from just a few days ago when I saw her. Aside from her skin being paler, her cheekbones were sunken, and her eyes appeared dull. What in the world had been going on with her? Did it have to do with the phone call she'd gotten the day I had Winifred in their office?

"No, thanks. I'm not hungry."

"All right." I'd experienced that before, too, in times of severe stress. I felt bad for Penny, whatever was going on.

Murray approached us. "What's up, Seneca? I have lots of people waiting on their takeout orders."

"I know, Murray. Sorry. Um…Penny has lost something. She's wondering if it might match what we found."

He nodded, then glanced around the busy room. "But I only have a minute." He sat down next to me and leaned closer to Penny. "Can you describe what you lost?" His voice was low, something I wasn't used to from our gruff, burly chef. He was taking our mission to protect the brooch quite seriously, which I admired.

Her hand shook as she reached into her purse on her lap and pulled out an old, torn piece of paper. When she flipped it around, I could see it was actually a black-and-white picture of a woman.

"This is my grandmother," said Penny. "If you'll look closely, you'll see she has something pinned to her dress."

I squinted, then nodded. It was the brooch. Even though I couldn't see the color of the stones or the metal, it was obviously the same lovely piece.

Murray did the same. He stood. "I'll go get it."

Penny's eyes watered. "Oh, my goodness. You really have it?"

"Yes. I found it in the grocery store. In the cat food aisle. I tried to leave it with Tonda for their lost and found but she didn't want the responsibility of keeping it safe. Did you ask her if they had a lost and found? She could have directed you to me."

She let out a loud sigh. "I didn't want to draw attention to myself, or to what I'd lost. I even looked in the store, in that particular aisle, too. See, I buy some cat food there every now and then to keep on hand in case some of our furry clients need a quick meal to calm them down and I had been there recently. I think the latch on it had broken, because I got home that day and it was gone. I wear it every day."

My eyebrows lowered as I tried to remember seeing Penny wear it. It was so beautiful, I think I would have.

"I know what you must be thinking. Even though I wore it all the time, it was never visible. I kept it pinned beneath my cardigan sweater. No one knew it was there, but I did. I kept it close to my heart, making me feel close to my mom."

"I understand. Sometimes things are so special, we don't want to share them."

She wouldn't quite meet my eye. "That's part of it."

I wondered about her other reason for hiding her brooch, but Penny didn't elaborate.

I shifted in my seat so I was facing her directly. "The brooch had been moved, kicked by accident, I guess, under a bottom shelf. I barely noticed it."

"That might explain how I'd missed it."

Murray returned with a small sack. "Here, Penny," he said. "I'm glad you came in for your lost item. I was beginning to think we'd never know the identity of the owner. It's always good to reunite people with things that are important to them."

She accepted it with tears in her eyes. "Thank you, Murray. I'm so grateful."

With a quick nod, Murray turned and headed back to the kitchen. He really was a cream puff down deep, but normally kept that side of himself hidden, like a brooch in a sack.

Penny placed the sack inside her purse, then zipped the top, as if afraid she might lose her precious item again. I didn't blame her. It was obvious how upset and flustered being without it had made her.

I pointed to her purse. "I'm so relieved you thought to come in here. I was really wanting to reunite the person and lost item, too."

She brushed a lock of hair away from her cheek. "Actually, one of our pet parents had been in here recently and mentioned the sign above the counter. She said some people thought it was a joke. Others were curious about the wording, not telling the reader what the item is." She tapped her finger against her purse. "I was so hoping it was what I'd lost. My hopes weren't high, but…"

"I can see the relief on your face. The brooch is very beautiful and obviously old. My grandmother had a few pieces handed down in her family. Can you tell me a little about this one's history?"

At first, I thought she'd decline, her eyes widening as she stared at me. But then she relaxed and blinked, seeming to calm herself.

After taking a couple of deep breaths, she said, "It is beautiful, isn't it? It's my most prized possession."

"You were right about the latch. It is broken. I hope it can be fixed."

"So do I. You see, like I showed you in that picture, it was my grandmother's. Then my mother's, and then…"

"And she gave it to you?"

Penny nodded. "Right before she died."

"I can see why it's so special to you."

Suddenly, her eyes filled with tears.

"Is it about your mom? It must have been so hard to have lost her."

"Well, of course, that's always with me, but now there's someone who wants…" She inhaled sharply and watched me, as if fearing she'd said something she shouldn't have.

Penny stood abruptly. "I need to go. Th-thank you so much for finding this and keeping it safe." She rushed down the aisle, nearly colliding with a man who'd just entered, but veering out of the way at the last second.

Something terrible had happened to Penny. Did it have anything to do with Burlington's murder?

Chapter Seventeen

Wanting to find out more about Devan and his girlfriend, I headed back to the hardware store the next morning. Normally, Mr. O'Hurley would be the person I'd interact with, but there was one thing Devan did that his boss did not, and that was to carry merchandise to a customer's vehicle for them. I usually loaded things myself, with the exception of something very heavy, but I'd put my girl-pride aside and would ask for help this time.

I scouted around my greenhouse and barn for things I'd need some time in the near future. It wasn't an emergency to have them, but buying several items was one sure way to have a few minutes alone with Devan. Otherwise, Mr. O'Hurley might question my need for help. He knew how much I always tried to take care of myself.

When I entered the shop, Mr. O Hurley, as usual, stood behind the counter, beaming at me and waving. "Hello, Seneca. All right, let me guess…today you need…bailing wire."

It hadn't been on my list, but it should have been. I would need some in the coming months, so why not get it now? Plus, some of the bales were large enough it might seem plausible that I'd ask for assistance getting it into the bed of my truck. "Wow, Mr. O'Hurley. You're right."

His smile grew wider. "Ha, I knew it. How much do you need?"

I reached for a pen and list from my pocket, quickly wrote down bailing wire where he couldn't see me add it at the top of the list, then handed him the piece of paper.

His eyes widened. "Goodness. You seem to be out of everything today."

"Just stocking up. I like to be prepared."

He nodded. "You know what? So do I. Did I ever tell you about when my son was born? How I'd thought ahead to have everything packed for my wife's visit to the hospital, but went off and left it by our front door? Then, she had the baby in the car. And I had to deliver him. Oh, the icky sticky mess that was left on my car seat!"

I pressed my lips together as he finished his icky, sticky tale. It wasn't the first time I'd heard the story, but at least this was one of the briefer ones. "Yeah, that does sound… messy." I glanced at the list still in his hand. "Thanks so much for doing this. And… Is Devan around? I might need some help carrying all this to my truck."

He checked the list. "Yes, this does seem to be more than your usual order, doesn't it? Of course. Let me go get him."

When Mr. O'Hurley returned with his stockboy, Devan was stuffing his cell phone into his pants pocket. And he was frowning. Things on the girlfriend front must not have improved.

I chuckled when Mr. O'Hurley folded my list in half, tore the paper in two, and handed Devan part of the list.

"I'm not in that big of a hurry," I said. "I can wait."

"Nonsense." Mr. O'Hurley waved his hand. "You're one of my favorite customers. What kind of business owner would I be if I stood around, not using my time wisely when you have to get back to your own business?"

Maybe the retelling of his messy tale about his wife's delivery didn't count as poor time usage. But at least it would be that much sooner I'd be able to speak to Devan alone.

The two men rushed around the store, occasionally calling out to each other about certain items needing to be restocked. The inevitable trip into the storeroom followed, until Mr. O'Hurley gleefully pronounced with satisfaction that all items had been found and were ready to be loaded into boxes. As I looked at all the cardboard enclosures, I could already envision the gleeful party Winifred would have checking them all out. One of her favorite things was when I got home from a shopping spree, no matter where I'd gone. As long as it involved boxes, bags, or bubble wrap, she was in a great mood until she got tired of it and went to find a napping spot.

When Mr. O'Hurley handed me the total written down on a scrap of paper, I held in a groan. But I reminded myself that none of it would go to waste, and they were items I wouldn't have to buy later on. Besides, once I was done here, I'd better run to the grocery and spend even more money. Might as well get the misery over all in one day.

Why did I keep running out of Winifred's favorite food? This time it was her dry food. I hadn't checked it when I'd bought the other kind. Maybe I should stockpile it the way I was doing with items I was buying for taking care of the butterflies. But it seemed that even when I bought out the store of all of Winifred's food, it was never enough. Was it time to put my cat on a diet? A sudden vision of her attacking my ankles, claws out, because she insisted she was starving, caused me to forget that notion right away.

Then, a different picture made me laugh. One of me hauling in crate after crate as Winifred sat on a kitchen chair, nodding her approval, while wearing a queen's crown.

"Seneca?"

Devan's voice startled me. I gasped and turned. "Uh, yeah?

"You okay?" He watched me, seeming uncertain if I was in my right mind or not.

"Yes, sure." I forced a smile and glanced around. Oh no. While I'd been daydreaming, the men had taken the now-loaded boxes and placed them just inside the front door. How long had they been staring at me? My face heated. "Thanks, Mr. O'Hurley, this is great."

"You have a super terrific day, Seneca." He waved enthusiastically, probably due to the bump in his bottom line for his store that day.

I tilted my head toward the doorway and said to Devan. "My truck is just down the block a little. Ready to help me load?"

"Yeah. I guess." His expression wasn't anything like his boss'. Devan's face was downcast, and his shoulders drooped. Poor kid. It must be really bad with his girlfriend right now.

He picked up a large box filled with bailing wire. I held the door open for him, then grabbed a smaller box and followed him. After all this time, he knew which vehicle was mine.

Once we reached my truck, I set down my box, then opened the tailgate, watching as Devan hefted his box high and shoved it in.

"Thanks for helping me out," I said. "I ended up buying more than usual today."

"No problem."

Even though he said the words, I knew there was indeed a problem. I also knew I wouldn't have a whole lot of time to talk to Devan before his boss wondered what was taking so long. Might as well get right to the point. "Listen, Devan, I heard something."

His gaze snapped up to reach mine. "What's that?"

I glanced around, making sure we were alone and wanting him to know I cared about his privacy, as well. "It was about you. And your girlfriend."

He closed his eyes for a second. "I bet lots of people have heard by now."

"I'm really sorry you're going through this. I mean that." He was only a few years younger than I was, but somehow, the way he acted made the gap seem even wider.

He hung his head. "It's awful. I just love her so much. I… I don't know what I'll do without her. Who'll I'll be."

"I understand."

"You do?" His brow furrowed. "Did you ever get dumped by anybody when you were young?"

I tried not to bristle at the young comment. "What happened to me was mutual. My husband and I split, and yeah, that was awful too. We'd dated for years, then got married a couple years out of high school. We were very young." I added the last part, hoping he'd realize that even though true love can happen early, and often did last, there are situations when it didn't.

His eyes widened. "You were married. That's harsh. I mean, it seems like if you marry somebody it should be for life, right?"

"Yeah, it should; unfortunately, things don't always work out the way you want them to." I pointed toward the store. "Let's get another load of boxes while we talk."

"Good idea. Don't want Mr. O'Hurley breathing down my neck."

I nearly snorted out a laugh, trying to imagine the sweet, often clueless man being an ogre as a boss.

We picked up a large box each, then hefted them down the sidewalk, depositing them in the truck bed. I turned to Devan. "I'm a pretty good listener. If you want to talk more, that is."

He looked over his shoulder toward the store. "I should keep loading your boxes for you."

"Why don't we both carry boxes as we talk? Does that work?"

He rubbed the back of his neck. "Yeah, okay. Thanks."

I waited, hoping he'd say something else. And soon. I didn't want him to get in trouble with his boss because of me. Even though Mr. O'Hurley was a sweet cream puff, he was still the employer, and I didn't want to push things too far.

Finally, Devan stuck his hands in his front pockets and stared at the sidewalk. "See, my girlfriend, Kinley…well, her grandpa just died."

"I'm sorry to hear that."

"Yeah, it was awful." Then, his head snapped up. "But you already know about that since it happened in Painted Wings."

"I do."

"Yeah, it was her Grandpa Snare. Burlington Snare."

"Yep, I sure do know about Burlington. But that must have been awful for Kinley."

He nodded slowly. "It was. Still is."

"Did she give a reason why she wanted to break up? Was it because of her grandpa dying?"

"No, this happened…before."

"Really?"

"Yeah, see, right before he died, he said he was not going to allow his only granddaughter to marry a common stockboy and ruin her life, as well as Snare's family standing in the community that he'd worked so hard for."

"Oh, Devan, I'm so sorry."

I motioned back toward the store, and we each got another box. When I peeked inside the front window, I didn't see Mr. O'Hurley anywhere. That was good. It would give Devan and I more of a chance to talk.

"It's not like I don't work hard, I do," he said. "When her grandpa said that, I was so mad." His jawline formed a ridge as he clenched his teeth.

Before Devan's girlfriend had called it off, he'd been punctual and a good employee. But losing someone he loved might have put a crimp in that. Still, he was a good worker, and it pained me to have someone say he was unworthy simply because of what he did for a living. I'd had people scoff at my profession before. And yes, it stung.

"But since my girlfriend called and told me she wanted to break up with me, I can't seem to…" He shook his head.

"You can't concentrate on work and other things?"

"Right. And I'm so afraid I'll lose my job. Even though Mr. Snare hadn't thought it was worth anything, it means a lot to me. I like working here."

We reached the truck again, and I placed my box with the others in the back. "Devan, not to sound…insensitive, but since Mr. Snare has passed away, would your girlfriend reconsider taking you back? He wouldn't be here to stand in your way anymore."

"That's what I'd hoped for, deep in my heart." He turned his head, as if not wanting to make eye contact.

"But it didn't work out that way?"

"Nope. Now she's freaked out over having him die. I thought that once he…" His eyes opened wide. He hurriedly shoved the box he carried onto the gate of the truck. When he didn't seem to notice what he'd done, I reached up and shoved it further into the bed.

What had Devan been about to say? His expression almost looked guilty. Like he knew something. Or had done something?

My heartbeat sped up. Surely, sweet Devan wouldn't have committed a crime to get his girlfriend back. But love did crazy things to people. It wouldn't be unheard of for someone to want a direct path to the person they loved, no matter what they had to do to get there.

"What should I do, Seneca?"

I jerked, startled out of my thoughts. "What do you mean?"

"Well, that mean man is gone. But Kinley still won't take me back."

For now, I'd keep my thoughts about Devan's guilty expression to myself. In the meantime, it sounded as if he needed a little advice. "Sometimes things in life are so stressful, a person doesn't feel like they can handle anything else, except dealing with the huge thing that happened."

"Really?"

"Yeah. I'm not saying that's what happened with your girlfriend, but it's a possibility."

He crossed his arms over his chest. "Do you think she might want me back, after things…when she's feeling better about her life?"

"Again, I can't say. But it's possible. I know it's awful for you, and so painful. But maybe if you let her know that you're supportive, and there for her, with no strings attached, she might realize she still loves you. Losing a loved one is all-encompassing, especially at first."

He blinked rapidly, as if not wanting to cry, especially in front of me.

"Devan, have you ever lost someone?"

He started to speak.

"And I don't mean like Kinley breaking up with you, although that's bad enough."

"No, I've never had anyone I was close to die before."

"I'm glad about that." I patted his shoulder. "Someday, it may happen, but for now, try to imagine how Kinley must be feeling."

"You're right, Seneca. I've only been thinking of myself. And that's not right. It's not fair to her. I hadn't thought about it that way before."

"Please know I feel for you. What you're going through is very hard."

He slid a sideways glance in my direction. "But not as hard as what she is feeling."

"Exactly."

Devan gave a small smile. "Thanks, Seneca. This did help."

"I'm glad." And I was. My ulterior motives may have led me here, but I did want the best for Devan.

He glanced behind him. "I better get the rest of your boxes loaded."

"Great, let's get to work."

As we carried the rest of the boxes to my truck, I watched him closely, and my heart lurched. Was it possible he could have been the one to kill Burlington?

131

Chapter Eighteen

After having spent time with Devan, and trying to piece together what might have been going on with him and Burlington, I took my purchases home. When I pulled up into my driveway and parked in front of the greenhouse, I grumbled loudly. Sid and Norman were supposed to have been here at the greenhouse, cleaning out the larvae pens while I'd been gone. I'd even left the greenhouse unlocked for that very reason, not that I'd tell Cody that. He'd only lecture me on how I wasn't being safe with another murderer loose in Maple Junction.

But I was more ticked off at the two older men than afraid of Cody's ire. Since I'd expected Sid and Norman to have done the work for me, I'd taken off the time to see Devan at the hardware store. If I'd known the guys would have been no-shows, I would have stayed here and done it myself.

More grumbling followed, as I hefted the boxes out of the back of my truck and into the greenhouse. Why did I ever think it would work out, even temporarily, with those two men? But I'd give them another chance, because what choice did I have?

I got my phone from my pants pocket and tapped in Sid's home number. Neither he nor Norman used cell phones, so this was the only way to track them down, short of finding them myself, wherever they were.

Sid's number yielded no answer, so I left a message. The same thing happened when I called Norman. Where were those guys?

I went to my house and fed Winifred, then left her chomping on her food while I walked across the short distance to Painted Wings. With my current mood, the only thing that might help improve it was a diet cherry cola from

Murray.

As I stepped inside, I halted. Because there, sitting in the center of the café, each gorging himself on a huge hamburger, were none other than my wayward employees. I walked toward them, giving an occasional wave to other customers, then stood right beside their table.

Norman was the first to look up. Once he'd chewed and swallowed, he set down his burger. "Hey, Seneca. Nice to see you."

Sid bobbed his head. "Having a good day?"

I crossed my arms over my chest. "Nice to see me? Am I having a nice day?"

The men eyed each other and gave simultaneous shrugs. "Uh," said Sid, "No? I mean…yeah?"

Norman looked at Sid. "Maybe she's losing her hearing. You might have to repeat it."

"What I'm really wondering," I said, "is why you two might be sitting here enjoying a meal when you'd promised me you'd work in my greenhouse."

"Was that today?" Sid's eyebrows lowered, but he didn't relinquish his hold on his hamburger.

I tapped my shoe on the floor. "We just talked about it yesterday. Yes, it was today."

"Well," said Norman, "I guess we'll have to do it another time, then."

My mouth dropped open. Who were these guys? Lazy teenage boys? I studied them closely. Yeah, actually, they were. "The work doesn't go away just because you decide not to show up."

They glanced at each other again. Finally, Sid turned toward me in his chair. "Are we fired?"

"You haven't really even started yet."

"So, not fired?" He'd finally set down his lunch and lifted his hand in the I-don't-understand position.

I glanced behind me, realizing we now had other customers who were enjoying our conversation a little too much. "Why don't you fellows finish your food and meet me at the greenhouse, okay?"

"Sure, Seneca." Norman picked up his hamburger and took a huge bite. I turned to walk away, but could hear Norman, still with food in his mouth, say, "That girl sure does get wound up, doesn't she?"

"Yup," said Sid. "I think she needs another gooey kiss from the sheriff. Maybe that would put her in a better mood."

I shook my head and left the café. I hadn't spotted Murray while I'd been there, so assumed he'd been in the kitchen. And I'd only gone three steps outside the café entrance when Evie walked up.

"Hey there." She waved. "Are you stopping in to say hi? I just had to run to my car for something." She held up her cell phone.

"No, unfortunately, I went in for a drink."

She glanced down at my empty hands. "Murray wouldn't make you one?"

"I didn't even get that far. Sid and Norman were in there, stuffing their faces."

"Yeah, they each ordered a huge amount of food, like they hadn't eaten for a week. I don't know where they put it. It's like they're teenage boys or something."

I rolled my eyes at her description, only confirming my own observations. "How long have they been in there?"

She frowned. "Hmmm, a couple of hours."

"What?" My voice was so loud, I covered my mouth with my hand. "Uh, sorry."

Evie watched me for a few seconds. "Seneca, what's going on? Has something happened?" When her eyes widened and she grabbed my arm, I realized I might have given her the wrong impression.

"It's nothing bad. I mean, not dead-body-in-the-café bad."

She appeared to wilt from relief. "That's good, at least. So, what's going on?"

I pointed my thumb toward the café. "Those two guys were supposed to be working for me today."

"And there they were, a short distance away, eating hamburgers, fries, milkshakes, and cherry pie."

"That's two days' worth of food, at least. For you and me, it would be more."

"Yeah, I gained weight just serving it to them." She glanced at her watch. "Hey, I need to get back in there. Are you okay, though? I can hang out here for a minute or so longer."

"No, you go ahead. I'll be fine. Just need to get my wayward employees to show up."

The door opened, and the two men in question appeared.

My hands landed on my hips. "You're done eating those huge hamburgers already? It was like watching a couple of hyenas devouring their prey."

Sid gave a loud burp. "Those were our second burgers, so it was round two."

I glanced at Evie for confirmation. She nodded.

"Okay then," I said, "ready to go do some work?"

"Right now?" whined Norman. He patted his tummy. "But I'm so full. I'm not sure I can move, much less do actual physical labor."

"Ditto," said Sid.

"You're saying you can't do anything now?"

Evie gave me a quick wave and darted inside. The men looked at one another, rolled their eyes, then gave me head nods. "We can go," said Norman. "If we have to."

Kicking myself for hiring them in the first place, I pointed to the greenhouse. "Fine. Let's go get started. At this rate, we'll be working until bedtime."

"Bedtime?" said Sid, "but we have a poker game tonight and—"

"Look, maybe you could help me until it's time for your game. Does that work?"

"I guess," mumbled Norman. "If that's the best you can do."

They trudged behind me until we reached the greenhouse. But turned at the sound of tires on gravel coming up the long drive.

Sid pointed to the vehicle. "Isn't that the guy who gives out free money at the bank?"

Norman laughed. "You think it's free? He's giving you what's already yours in your own account."

"Oh, right. Sorry." He patted his tummy again. "Guess I'm not thinking straight now that all the sugar and whatnot has gone to my brain."

"I don't remember eating whatnot. How did it taste?" Norman guffawed at his own joke, causing Sid to join in.

I watched them for a few seconds and held in the thing I longed to say that wouldn't be very nice. This day wasn't going well at all. I squinted at the recent arrival until I could make out Lawrence in the driver's seat. He'd said he'd be here after work to help out. Was he early?

I dug my phone out again, and unlike when I'd gotten it out to leave messages for the men, I took a second to check the time. The afternoon was nearly over.

"Hey, is that the time?" said Norman, peering over my shoulder. I winced at the smell of onions on his breath.

"By golly," said Sid, "the game starts in an hour."

I held my tongue as I put my phone back in my pocket. "Perhaps you guys could work for that hour? It would really help me out."

"Yeah," said Sid, "I guess we could do that much, right, Norman?"

"Yep. Always glad to help out a damsel in distress."

Not acknowledging them, I instead waited for Lawrence to get out of his vehicle and join us.

He walked over, giving a nod to the other men. "Hi, Seneca, ready for duty." He smiled.

"Thanks, Lawrence. I appreciate you coming."

I glanced at the other two to see if they were feeling any remorse about not showing up when they were supposed to. There didn't seem to be any. They were bent over, watching a ladybug make her slow progress up a stalk of grass poking up between some pieces of gravel on the drive. When they stood back up, they appeared bored. Or maybe just sleepy from carb overload.

I thought about the lateness of the hour, calculated how much daylight was left, and decided to tackle the most important duty for right now. "Change of plans. We're going to the milkweed fields and rake out the weeds from the milkweed plants."

"Sure," said Lawrence.

Norman leaned over to Sid and must have thought he was whispering when he said, "That sounds like real work."

"Yeah, but guess Sergeant Seneca isn't going to let us off the hook."

Acting as if I hadn't heard them, I motioned the three guys to follow me. We walked past the café, past my house, and down a path until we came to an open dirt walkway across a grassy expanse. When we reached my barn, I handed them each a rake, then grabbed one for myself.

"Good golly," said Norman, "the last time I picked up an actual yard tool was in 1973. Not sure I even remember how to do it."

I held in a laugh. "Just watch and do what I do, and do the same, okay?"

Norman shrugged. "Sure, I guess." But he rolled his eyes at his cohort as they carried their rakes and complained the whole rest of the walk about how heavy their tools were, that there was a danger of them tripping on them and ending up in the hospital with injuries, and that the sun was too hot.

Lawrence walked next to me. "Seneca, your farm is spectacular."

"Thank you. I think so, too." How nice to have someone who appreciated the things that I did. Unlike Sid and Norman, who were now complaining about blisters on their feet from the long, treacherous walk.

Lawrence glanced up at the blue sky. "I'm usually stuck inside the bank, standing behind a counter. This is wonderful. You get to spend time out of doors."

"Well, it is nice on days like today. Not so much in February. Snow. Ice. Wind that goes right through you." I shivered.

"No, I suppose not."

When we reached the nearest milkweed field, Norman spied the bench that was nearby. "Thank goodness. A place to rest my weary bones."

Sid rushed behind him, taking a seat. "Ah…." He leaned back, folded his arms behind his head as a makeshift pillow, then closed his eyes.

Were they going to take a nap?

I walked to the bench and stood in front of them.

"Hey," said Norman, squinting. "Do you mind? You're blocking my sun."

Norman elbowed him. "Give her a break, Sid. Seneca is a youngster. Maybe she's concerned about your risk of skin cancer with too much exposure to the sun."

Sid waved away the comment. "Nothing to worry about there. If all my years riding on a boat in the Navy didn't hurt me, this won't either."

I let out a sigh. Would it be easier to just tell these two to forget the whole thing? I glanced back at Lawrence, who was frowning at his rake as if he'd never seen one before. Maybe he'd always worked in an office environment like he did now at the bank. Did he not have any experience with any kind of manual labor either?

Perfect.

These three were all I had, and I was determined to make it work. Or, make them work, which would be a better way of putting it. At least I knew Lawrence was a hard worker at the bank and was punctual when showing up here, so I had high hopes for him.

"Guys," I said to Sid and Norman. "Ready to get some work done?"

Norman groaned. "If we have to."

Sid nodded. "And only if we have to."

I placed my hands on my hips. "You have to." I tried not to laugh at their petulant expressions. But if they actually wanted this job, then they had to do some work.

Lawrence stepped up beside me. "I'm ready, Seneca. Where do you need me?"

Norman leaned over to Sid and placed his hand around his mouth as if to whisper. "That guy is a kiss-up," he said, rather loudly.

When I dared a glance at Lawrence, his expression was a cross between annoyance and amusement. At least he didn't seem terribly upset.

Norman stood, reached down, and assisted Sid to his feet. "Come on, Sid. Time to pay the piper."

"I thought we were the ones getting paid."

"Just an expression." Norman picked up one of the rakes they'd tossed to the ground when they'd claimed their seat. "Here. Take this." When Sid had his rake in hand, Norman grabbed the other one. "Let's get this gravy train rolling."

Lawrence leaned over to me. "What does that even mean?"

"It's better not to ask."

I motioned for them to follow me and then demonstrated how to carefully rake out dead leaves and weeds from between the milkweed stalks. When the three of them seemed like they mostly understood my instructions, I walked a few feet away and began to do the same on the other end of the row. A commotion came from the older men. When I turned to see what was going on, I snorted out a laugh. A monarch butterfly had landed on Sid's head, and Norman stood in front of him, trying to wave it away.

"Hey guys, they won't hurt you. If you just wait, the butterfly will leave on its own. Don't try to touch its wings, or you might injure it."

Norman elbowed Sid, who still hadn't moved and wore a terrified look on his face. " Sid, do you suppose when that Betty Rollings chained herself to a tree, she was attacked by these frightening woodland creatures?"

Chapter Nineteen

When I drove past the parking lot of Precious Posies, I was surprised to see Betty standing beside a community bulletin board near the front of her building.

After hearing the scuttlebutt from Sid and Norman about Betty chaining herself to a tree way back when, I decided to see what she was up to now. I drove around the block and pulled into the lot. Betty was no longer there, but after I parked, I hurried over to the bulletin board. There was only one paper on the board that appeared to be new, not tattered, faded, or torn. It must have been what she'd been posting. When I leaned closer, I could read it.

SAVE THE TREES in MAPLE JUNCTION!!

That seemed innocuous enough by itself, but if Betty had indeed attached herself to a tree, was there something else going on with her?

A light tinkling sound came from a tiny bell on the door when I opened it. I was there to hopefully glean information. But I also knew I'd need to purchase something to keep in Betty's good graces and also just to be polite. Small-town people did sometimes have certain expectations. I was happy to do it, especially since Betty was so diligent about bringing beautiful flowers into Painted Wings, unasked, and she would never take any payment for them.

Betty, who'd been flipping through a pile of papers on her glass counter, straightened when she saw me. "Seneca, hi."

"Hi."

"What can I do for you today?" She placed the papers off to one side.

"I thought my house needed a new houseplant. Something that won't upset a kitty's tummy. And I knew this was the right place to find one."

"Winifred is a little too nosy around plants?" She laughed. "Gee, sounds like most cats I know."

"She's nosy like you wouldn't believe. And takes it as a personal challenge to check out every square green inch."

Betty tapped her chin. "Let me see…" She glanced behind her at a gorgeous display of green plants in colorful ceramic hanging pots. "What size were you thinking?"

"I don't want anything huge. Maybe a small one to hang above my kitchen sink. There's great light there if that helps."

She pointed to an adorable red and yellow painted pot filled with cascading green spikes. It was small enough I wouldn't bonk my head on it every time I stood at the sink. And the hanger looked adjustable. Maybe I could keep Winifred out of it. I could try, anyway. She was a tough one to control.

"Yes," I said. "That one would be perfect."

She grinned. "Great! Let's get you and your newest family member properly introduced."

Some people might have made fun of her attitude toward plants, but I totally got it. Not only did I continually talk to Winifred, but I also kept up running conversations with my adult monarch butterflies, as well as the caterpillars.

As Betty reached up to remove the hanger from the wall hook, I took a moment to study the stack of papers on her counter. It was the same as the flier I'd read on the bulletin board.

She turned and placed my new green friend on the counter, then raised one eyebrow when she noticed me checking out the pages.

"Sorry. Didn't mean to be nosy." Of course, I had, but she didn't need to know that.

She waved her hand. "Please go ahead and check it out. I just got those back from the printer this morning."

Since I had permission, I picked one up. When I took the time to read the smaller print beneath the Save the Trees sentiment, I noticed another line beneath it:

Join other Tree Custodians, as we discuss how to save the trees of Maple Junction, and in effect, the whole world!

It listed a time and place, with a picture of a smiling maple tree waving one of its leaves at the reader.

"I admire your devotion to plants and trees, Betty." I replaced the paper on the stack, attempting to keep the pile straight, as she'd done.

Her eyes crinkled as she smiled. "Thank you. That means a lot. Not everyone gets that, you know."

"Everyone's different, I guess."

"Yeah, they are. But the people who don't like them, or even harm them"—she shuddered—"I just don't understand."

"I totally agree with you. Have you always loved trees?"

Her gaze took on a faraway, dreamy expression. She pressed her hands to her chest. "Oh yes. As long as I can remember. My dad had a tree farm."

"That's amazing. You don't hear about those much anymore. At least not around here."

"No, you're right. His tree farm was a few miles from here, out in the country. He'd take me there every day after school and on weekends to see it. It was beautiful. I used to follow him around, and he'd tell me all about the trees, if they had blooms, or sap, or leaves or…" She gave me a sideways glance. "I'm boring you, aren't I?"

"Not at all." And I meant it. People might have thought my devotion to butterflies was over the top, but like Betty, a family member—my grandma— was the one who showed me a whole new world of how butterflies lived and how amazing they were. "Is the tree farm still in your family?"

Her face fell. "Unfortunately, no. It…you see, there was a forest fire and—"

I gasped. "Oh no."

"I'm afraid so. It was awful, and besides that, my mom wasn't really into horticulture or arboriculture. Actually, I think she was secretly pleased when he didn't have the farm anymore."

I frowned, sad for Betty and her father at their loss.

Her frown matched mine. "Mama had thought after the farm was gone and I grew up, that I would lose my love of trees."

"But you didn't, obviously." I pointed to the fliers.

"No, if anything if fueled the fire—oh, shouldn't use that word I guess—my passion for them grew even more. It's my life's calling."

"Yes, I understand that."

"I'm sure you do, with your butterfly farm." She smiled. "We have that in common, don't we?"

"We sure do."

"I have to say, though, that after Dad's farm burned down and he didn't have the heart to start over again, something took hold of me. Something inside." Her eyes brightened, her face took on an almost feverish appearance, and she gazed up at the ceiling. What was going on with her?

"What do you mean, Betty?"

She jerked as if my question had startled her. Then she crossed her arms tightly over her chest, as if needing to hold herself together. "What I mean is, I have an almost…how do I put this… fierce need to protect trees."

I thought of what Norman and Sid had told me about Betty chaining herself to a tree. Wanting to hear more of her thoughts, I said, "You know, when I was a kid, I had a lemonade stand to raise funds to help my grandma pay for costs on her farm because she was struggling to keep things afloat. You mean doing something like that?"

She dropped her arms, and her face hardened. "Nothing like that. Mine was more…well, let's just say the police got involved with what I did."

When it was clear she wouldn't elaborate anymore about it, I tapped the pamphlet. "Um, this looks very interesting. Will you be leading the meeting?"

"No, I'll be just one of many people who will stand up to encourage others in our quest for a safe, green environment. I'm going to put these up all over town. Hopefully, we'll have a good turnout." She glanced at the pages and back at me. "I don't suppose…"

I tilted my head and waited.

"Would you mind terribly if I put one up at Painted Wings? If you'd rather not, I understand. It is your business, after all."

I had no problem with someone who wanted to improve our community.

"I don't mind at all. Would you like me to put it up for you?"

Her eyes lit up. "Would you? That would be great. I have a new shipment of roses coming in today and will be very busy here."

"Then let me take one with me, along with my new little roommate." I ran my fingers across the top of the plant.

"Your spider plant will be a wonderful addition to your home. As well as something Winifred can bat at and not be in danger of ingesting anything harmful. Plus, every time a person spreads the plant love and adopts a new one for themselves, the world becomes a better place."

"Thank you, Betty. I'm sure Ingrid will love her new home."

Her eyebrows rose. "Ingrid?"

"Yep." I laughed. "My grandmother used to name all of her houseplants. She had a rubber tree named Hortense."

Betty clapped her hands. "I love it! Your grandmother used to come in here and check out what new additions I had. She was such a jewel. And yes, I think Ingrid will love looking out of your kitchen window, too."

After paying Betty, I took Ingrid and one of the fliers out to my truck. Once I had Ingrid safely seated—yes, I belted her in—I drove slowly and carefully back to my farm. I couldn't stop thinking about Betty and the meeting she was going to have. I hadn't learned anything specific from her today, but maybe more would come out at a meeting where others who were passionate about trees attended as well.

The moment I entered my house, Winifred was there to greet me. Actually, it was more like yelling, but she did that every time she ended up stuck inside the house when I was presumably racing off to adventures unknown, leaving her to wither away in feline solitude.

I placed the plant on the table, knowing she'd immediately jump to a nearby chair to check it out, which she did. Her paw reached out toward the potted newcomer, tapping lightly at the ceramic base.

"Winifred, I got this plant for the kitchen. Her name is Ingrid, and I want you to be nice to her. What do you say?"

Winifred sniffed every possible inch from every conceivable angle, contorting her furry body into positions that would cause a human to groan in pain. But once she seemed satisfied that Ingrid wasn't going to harm, attack, or maim her—I'd need to keep an eye on the situation to make sure Winifred didn't do those things to the plant—my cat sat back on her haunches, opened her mouth wide, and let out a screech."

I rolled my eyes. "I know that sound. Hold on." I opened a nearby cabinet and removed a can of salmon. Winifred's tail wagged as her paws danced up and down in a rhythmic display of kitty ecstasy.

Once I grabbed a clean cat bowl from the dishwasher, I spooned some of the vile-smelling concoction into the base, barely getting the bowl positioned on the floor before Winifred shoved her head into the bowl and snarfed away.

When a knock sounded on the door, Winifred hissed and hid beneath the kitchen table.

I hurried toward the door. When I opened it, I grinned. "Hey there, Cody. What's up?"

He stepped inside. "Just checking on my two favorite girls."

I turned, laughing, when Winifred emerged from her hiding spot and trotted over to rub against Cody's legs. "She'd just dived under the table when you knocked. But when she saw it was you—"

"What about me?"

"My cat obviously loves you."

He picked up Winifred, cuddling her in his arms. "The feeling is mutual."

My skin prickled. What was that about? I normally only got that reaction when I was envious of what someone else was doing or who they were with. I shook my head. Nope. Not going there.

"What's wrong? Why are you shaking your head?"

"Um, sorry. It's nothing."

"Wait. Are you sure? Is everything okay?"

Definitely not wanting to discuss the weird vibe I had around Cody lately, ever since our near kiss at the auction, I forced a smile. "I'm fine."

His eyebrows lowered. "Okay..." His glance snagged on the table. "Hey, new plant?"

"Yep, I got it from Betty at Precious Posies. Don't you love her?"

"Love…Betty? She's all right, I guess."

"No, Ingrid."

He glanced at the plant, then back at me. "Wait. You used to always name your stuffed animals as a kid. Don't tell me you name your plants, too."

"Of course I do. Don't you remember Hortense?"

"Not ringing a bell."

"Gram had that big rubber tree plant. She used to keep it on the screened-in porch."

"That's right. The one I plowed into accidentally as a kid when you and I were playing catch in the house."

"That's the one. Poor Hortense."

"Wait. Did she…I mean, was that the end of her plantness?"

I smirked. "No, she recovered nicely. Gram even allowed me to place a couple of bandages on leaves that had gotten bent. But, if you'll remember, that's the last time, ever, you and I were ever allowed to play catch in the house."

"Sure, I remember that very well. Your grandma was a sweet woman, but don't mess with her plants."

"Or her butterflies."

"Speaking of which. Are your monarchs doing okay?" he asked.

I nodded. "Better than okay. They're thriving."

"That's something I hoped to hear after you nearly lost them from your wicked former neighbor."

"Yeah, I agree. Speaking of how he tried to wreck things for me, I'm really concerned about Evie. She's having a hard time with what people are saying about her."

He rubbed the back of his neck. "So am I. She puts on a good front, but I can tell she's scared to death she might be found guilty of Burlington's murder."

"But she's not?"

His eyebrows lowered. "Of course, she's not. And I keep telling her that. Just like I told you the same thing when you were worried I'd arrest you for your attorney's murder. Not going to happen. You weren't guilty and neither is your cousin. Believe me, I'm looking in other places for whoever the guilty person might be."

I gave his arm a light squeeze. "Thanks, Cody."

He repositioned Winifred in his arms, causing her to let out a kitty harrumph. "For what?"

"For always looking after us."

"I can't imagine doing anything else." He placed Winifred next to her food dish. It took her all of three seconds to reposition herself with her face so far in her bowl, I could barely see her eyes above the rim.

I clasped my hands together in front of my waist. "Now that we're talking about Burlington's death, I thought I'd fill you in on what I've found out."

"Seneca."

"Yes?"

"Didn't we have this discussion the last time you were involved in a murder investigation? I reminded you that I'm sheriff and you don't need to worry about any of that. Besides, with Bud helping me, I don't see any problems in figuring out what happened to Burlington."

"I know I'm in the minority when I say this"—I didn't really think I was, but would stay on team Cody for Bud's benefit—"but I don't always have the highest confidence in Bud."

"He's okay. Just a little…"

"Weird." And that was putting it kindly. Bud was a good guy, but Cody seemed to wear blinders when it came to his deputy.

"I was going to say unique."

"Cody, the other day, Bud was standing on the sidewalk with a fishing pole, trying to hook his mail out of the mailbox."

He waved his hand. "But that has nothing to do with how he does his job as my deputy, does it?"

"I suppose not. I still think it's weird, though."

The left side of his mouth rose in a half grin. "Enough about Bud. I know that no matter what I say to dissuade you, you'll keep searching for clues to help Evie."

"You've got that right." I placed my hand on my hip.

"All right. Why don't you fill me in on what you've found out so far."

"Sure."

I filled him in on Sid and Norman telling me that Betty had chained herself to a tree, and the upcoming meeting, finding the brooch, and last but yes, definitely least, about Payne's visit to the café, which made Cody frown, as always. Payne and Cody had never gotten along, which used to put me in the middle when I was married, but thankfully, not anymore.

Chapter Twenty

I'd been concerned about Karen ever since her meltdown in the bank. Knowing her love for Murray's cheesy fries from the café, I did what I'd done before when I needed to speak to her privately and took her a batch of fries to cheer her up.

Murray, as he'd done the previous time, narrowed his eyes at me when I helped myself to a large portion of fries. He crossed his arms and tried to look gruff, but I only shrugged and smiled as I placed the food inside a take-out bag.

Evie waved at me with her free hand, her other arm clamped tightly by Mable's fingers. My cousin was so much more patient with her, and others, than I would be. But that was why I worked with butterflies, and Evie ran the café. Win-win.

I hoped her spending time with Mable might take her mind off of Burlington's demise, and the way some people were still blaming her for his murder. Busyness at work would help her day go faster, but I knew from experience, no matter how she tried to distract herself, she'd still have that vision of the man lying face down in a pool of his own blood, stuck in her mind.

A quick movement from the corner of my eye caught my attention. From a table nearby, the twin sisters sat across from each other. Nora held a crumpled napkin. Had she just grabbed it from her sister's hand as she'd done when I'd been sitting with them? When I peered closer, I could see a small pile of napkin bits sitting in front of Flora. Why was she so agitated?

Then, Nora pointed down to the floor. Right where Burlington had been found dead. Flora's face paled and she slunk down further in her seat. I shook my head. Were Flora's apparent nervous reactions tied somehow to his murder? I'd have to keep my ears open around those two.

Johnny Overmyer was in his usual seat as I walked toward his table. His bright blue eyes sparkled beneath his bushy white eyebrows. He winked. I grinned and winked back, glad to have him as a friend and faithful customer nearly every day in Painted Wings. I was almost past him when I heard a sound like a tire releasing air.

I angled back around to see Johnny waving his arm in a come here motion while he made the pst-pst sound again.

Holding in a sigh, because I wanted to get to see Karen on her scheduled meal break, I nevertheless went back to Johnny and waited.

"Seneca," he said as he dabbed his napkin on his mustache. "I wanted to tell you something."

"Sure," I said, folding the bag securely closed so the fries would hopefully stay warm.

"I was in the hardware store again." He held up his hand. "Never fear, it wasn't about a hammer this time."

I nodded, hoping his story wouldn't take too long. He had a tendency to ramble.

"See, this visit, I went in to get a vice," he said.

My eyebrows lowered. "Um, do you mean a vise?"

"What's the difference?"

I started to tell him, then decided it would only prolong things. But the thought of Johnny going shopping for a 'vice' something that would make most people blush made me nearly laugh out loud. Hopefully, he wasn't going around telling people about his newest purchase. Had Mr. O'Hurley noticed the faux pas when he'd sold him the vise?

"When I was in the store, Mr. O'Hurley was once again absent. This time, he had a dentist appointment. Boy, you'd think he could find a better time to have a rotten tooth removed than when I need to buy something."

I felt more sorry for the guy with the sore tooth than the one who was slightly inconvenienced, but I knew it wouldn't do any good to say that to

Johnny. "So when you were in there, what happened?"

"It's about Devan. You know, the stock guy?"

I nodded again.

"Anyway, he waited on me again."

"Was there more crying, like with the hammer?"

"Nope." Johnny leaned closer. "This time, he seemed happy. Triumphant, even."

"I'm glad to hear he's happy. But what was that about?"

"He said he's thrilled that his girlfriend decided to take him back. Then he said, 'It was worth it, everything I went through, everything I had to do. It all turned out okay. Things will be much better for everyone now that he's gone.'"

"He said that? Do you think he meant Burlington?"

"That's the only explanation I can come up with. When I asked him about it, he just bagged up my vice."

Once again, I bit my lip, thinking of whatever malicious vice he would have in his bag that he'd purchased from Devan. "That's very interesting, Johnny."

"I thought you'd want to know."

"Yes, I do. Thanks. And if you come across anything else interesting, feel free to send it my way." I patted his shoulder, then worked my way toward the door. I said hello to Angel and Connie, then waved goodbye to Evie.

I walked out into the bright sunlight, smiling when a butterfly landed on my arm. "All right," I said, "I'll give you a lift as far as the truck, then you'll need to stay here with your friends. Besides, with those gorgeous wings, you don't need me to take you anywhere. You can get there yourself."

I walked slowly, so I wouldn't startle her, then, as gently as possible, brushed her from my sleeve, watching as she fluttered away toward the milkweed fields on the other side of my barn. I never tired of monarchs' beauty and grace. I had my grandmother to thank for that. Her love of them became mine, and I'd be forever grateful.

A strident meow came from the area of my shoes. I glanced down. "Winifred, I have to go on an errand right now."

She gazed up at me, her eyes wide and pleading, mouth slightly open, as if wanting to tell me all her troubles. I'd heard them all before, of course, and it always sounded the same. My guess was she either wanted me to pick her up or feed her. I took another step toward the truck, but she darted in front of my feet.

"No, I'm sorry, kitty. Mama can't take you along this time."

She stood on her hind legs and batted at the French fry sack. Then she mewed, which sounded an awful lot like begging.

"Ah, I see. It isn't that you want to be with me. You just want to eat."

At the word eat, her ears perked up, and she rubbed her face against my pant leg, her paws bobbing up and down in a dance.

With a glance toward the house, I figured I could toss out some food, then hightail it out of there, hopefully still making it on time to catch Karen on her break. "Okay, but it needs to be quick. Come on."

I speed-walked to the house, opened the door, and followed Winifred after she darted into the kitchen. I gave her a handful of kitty treats, then hurried back outside. She'd be mad when she realized I'd left her shut inside the house, but for now, it was probably best. There was no doubt, though, that I'd get a long list of her complaints when I returned.

Finally in my truck, I placed the French fry sack on my passenger seat. Hopefully, between talking to Johnny, giving the butterfly a lift, and keeping my cat marginally happy, the food would still be warm for Karen by the time I got there.

Thankfully, just as I arrived inside the bank lobby, Karen was putting her closed sign on the counter of her teller station. I glanced to my left, but Lawrence wasn't at his.

Karen saw me and waved. "Hi, Seneca. Good to see you." Her gaze dropped to the sack in my hand, and her eyes widened. The last time I brought her some, I'd put it in a pretty basket, but I hadn't taken the time for that on this trip. But the pleasing scent of the fries was drifting out, and Karen's grin told me the plain old sack would do just fine.

I held it up, moving the sack so the fries rustled inside the paper enclosure. "Got time for a snack?"

Her eyes lit up. "You bet I do. Wow, thanks. And right on time for my break. How did you know?"

"Just a guess." Karen had been going to lunch at the same exact time every day for years. It really hadn't taken much guessing on my part. "It's gorgeous out. Want to sit at the picnic table?"

"Yes, sounds great." She stepped out from behind her counter, then went to the entrance. She turned a sign on the door to CLOSED and locked the door with a loud snap. "Don't worry, we can go out the back entrance to the picnic tables. And with the door locked, nobody can just walk in here while I'm outside."

As I followed her toward a hallway behind the tellers' area, I glanced at Lawrence's empty workstation. Many times, they covered for each other so they could each take a lunch break, unless one of them was ill or out on vacation. "Is your coworker off today?"

"Yes, he is. They've bumped him down to part-time."

"That's too bad."

"It was because of Mr. Snare's death."

I hated to hear that, but glad that at least he'd get some additional income from working at Majestic Monarchs. "I'm sorry. That must mean more work for you, then, too."

"They're doing some restructuring at the bank now that... well, things have changed. I feel bad for Lawrence." She frowned. "Hey, didn't I hear he was going to speak to you about working some for you?"

"That's right. He's actually started already. But I didn't realize he was only part-time here." Maybe I could use him for more hours and the gossipy older guys a little less. From what I'd noticed, they didn't want to work anyway.

We passed by a small bathroom and what I assumed to be a closet. Karen shook her head. "I didn't actually hear it from him, though. It was from a customer who seemed to know about it."

It did surprise me somewhat that Lawrence hadn't confided about his new job with Karen. I looked at her. But truthfully, even though I liked her, if I had to work that closely with her every day with her sudden mood changes and tendency to gossip, I might not want to tell her anything personal either.

"I bet he's glad to have the extra work," said Karen.

"Yes, I think so." He did seem appreciative of the work and the fact that it was a change of pace from the bank. I couldn't imagine Karen, however, wanting to change jobs. She loved working at the bank. It almost seemed like she'd been born to do it. And good for her. I was glad she enjoyed what she did.

We were all different. There might not be many people out there like me who loved working with butterflies and their larvae. I was so grateful I had the opportunity to do it.

When we walked outside from the back door, the sound of our footsteps startled a pair of doves, who cooed at us and flew away. I placed the sack on the table, then reached into my purse for the smaller sack with disposable napkins, forks, and, of course, packets of ketchup. Karen had grabbed a couple of sodas from a fridge that we passed by on our way out.

Once seated, we spread out napkins to use as impromptu place mats and ate in companionable silence for a while. Two doves, maybe the same ones as before, landed close by on the recently clipped grass. One cooed and looked straight at me, ruffling his feathers, which reminded me of the way Winifred had begged, with her costume wings fluttering as she pawed at me. It seemed Mr. Dove requested some fries, but I wasn't sure if birds were supposed to eat them, so I did my best to ignore him.

Besides, I knew for a fact Lawrence put out food for them, since I'd seen him carrying a filled bird feeder more than once when I'd pulled into the parking area.

Karen wiped her hands with a napkin, then took a swig of her drink. "Thanks again for bringing these by. It really cheered me up."

"I'm glad." Even though I adored Murray's fries, I'd only taken a small amount, leaving the rest for Karen. If she needed cheering up, the extra food could only help. "You're down because Mr. Snare died, right? I mean, that's understandable."

"Well, that and..." She glanced around, though there was no need. I doubted anyone besides wildlife was within blocks of us. "See, I've been upset. You may have noticed the last time you were here?"

I nodded but kept my expression neutral. Her sobbing explosion had been kind of hard to miss.

"While I'm sad at how my boss, um, former boss, died, I mean, no one should be killed that way, right?"

"Uh, right."

Karen's eyebrows lowered. "Mr. Snare had accused me of talking openly about customers' private business. Me!" She placed her hand over her chest. "Can you imagine?"

I twisted my fingers together on the tabletop, trying not to fidget. "Gee, so very hard to imagine." Lying wasn't right, but if I didn't agree with her, she'd start bawling again, and no one wanted that. Besides, I needed information, and this was my best opportunity to have time alone with her.

"I know, right? I'm the poster girl for discretion and professionalism." She watched me, waiting for me to reply.

All I could do was give a quick nod. It was getting harder to control my expressions.

Karen's sigh was so loud, it caused a squirrel sitting beneath a nearby tree to chatter at us. But my tablemate didn't seem to notice. She placed her elbows on the table, and her chin rested in her hand. "Anyway, right before Mr. Snare had been, you know, murdered, he'd taken me aside and threatened to fire me."

I jerked at the unexpected news. "That's terrible. But you must have convinced him otherwise." I pointed toward the building. "I mean, you're still working here."

Her cheeks reddened. "Not really. Um, actually, before he could back up his threat, he, well, died." She broke eye contact with me and gazed down, suddenly very interested in her red-painted fingernails. Why did she suddenly look so guilty?

"I'm sorry about Mr. Snare, too. But glad you didn't lose your job here. I know you like it, and I'm sure it's important to you." She'd worked in the bank for years. I couldn't remember her ever working anyplace else.

"You're so right, Seneca. I need this job desperately. You see, I give money every month to help out my two sisters. We're paying for our grandmother's care as she gets older."

"That's very commendable." And I meant it. Not everyone would or could do the same.

"We love her and want her to be comfortable. Our parents aren't around anymore, and we feel it's our duty to take care of her. So, if I'd lost my position here…let's just say I did what I had to and don't regret a second of it. Sometimes, a person has to stand up for herself and take what she rightfully deserves." Karen's mouth curved up in a slow, satisfied smile, reminding me of Winifred when she was quick enough to snatch a piece of food from my plate.

I blinked. What did she not regret? Taking care of her grandmother, standing up for herself to protect her job, or something worse, like taking matters with her boss into her own hands?

Chapter Twenty-One

Even though it was a few weeks early for Winifred's next vet appointment, I called to schedule for today, then went ahead and took her in for her exam. Something was going on with Penny, and the more opportunities I had to be around her, the more I might be able to find out. Winifred always knew it was vet day. Even before I'd gone to the garage to get the cat carrier, I must have given off some sort of vibe, because as soon as she inhaled her breakfast, she raced up the stairs and hid.

Knowing this might happen, I'd left extra time before her appointment for any possible kitty searches I might need to perform.

I set the carrier on the kitchen floor—no use antagonizing her until the last possible minute at the sight of the enclosure of doom—grabbed the container of kitty treats, then climbed the stairs. My house wasn't large, it was an old farmhouse, so there weren't as many hiding places as Winifred might have preferred. And, since we'd been through this before, many times, I knew her favorite places to hide.

When I was nearly to the top step, I shook the container. Sometimes, she couldn't help herself and raced out to see me in hopes of satisfying her tummy. That always made my job easier and quicker. But not this time. I looked up and down the hall, peeked into a closet door that was partway open, and checked beneath my desk in the guest room.

Nothing but dust bunnies. Probably should take care of that soon.

I shook the container again and stood still, listening closely for any tale tell scratching noises and tiny plaintive mews.

Still silence.

"All right, fine." She was going to make me get on my hands and knees to find her this time. I could picture Winifred crouched down beneath or behind a piece of furniture, giggling into her paw because she'd outfoxed Mama. "Well, not today, little sister. We're going to that place." I glanced at my watch. And we needed to leave soon.

With not very high hopes, I rattled the container one last time. Winifred was still playing her little game.

Gritting my teeth, I headed to my bedroom, set the container on the floor behind me, then got on my knees and peered beneath my bed.

A slight movement caught my eye, but it was dark under there. The intelligent thing would have been me bringing along a flashlight, but apparently, I wasn't that smart.

I scooted closer to the bed, my head now beneath the box springs. Was Winifred back there, maybe in the far-right corner where the bed was pushed against the wall?

I jumped when I heard a sound behind me. Like that of a plastic container being pushed across the floor.

With effort, I backed out slowly from beneath the bed, sneezing as a local dust bunny crossed right in front of my nose. Whipping around, I spotted my cat, who whapped the container with her paw, no doubt hoping her claws would pop the lid off.

I dove across the floor, scraped my elbows, then grasped her beneath her tummy with one hand and grabbed the container with the other. Finally, I awkwardly transitioned from my knees to my feet, letting out a yelp when a muscle spasm attacked the back of my calf.

Winifred struggled against me, kicking my side with her hind feet, but I held firm.

"Listen, I know you don't like going there, but we need to. It will help you stay healthy and strong. I'm doing this because I'm your mom, and I love you." I kissed the top of her head, right between her ears.

Her answer was a growl, then a pout as her whiskers drooped in defeat. She hung over the side of my arm like an orange dish towel with wings, but at least she stopped growling.

As soon as we were downstairs, I gently pushed her inside the carrier, then poured out several treats beside her as a consolation prize.

The look she gave me would have melted iron. "Sorry. But we have to go now."

Once I had her inside the truck, she turned in her carrier so her back was facing me.

"Yeah, I know. You're making a statement. I get it. I don't like having doctor's appointments either."

She stayed silent, but her tail smacked against the wire of the tiny carrier door. When we pulled into the small parking area, she gave out a hiss. Oh great, usually the hiss waited until we were actually in the exam room. This wasn't going well.

I lugged her carrier to the door, grateful when a pet parent on their way out with a beagle held the door open for us. Another hiss came from the carrier when the dog got too close to the cat. When we stepped inside, I let out a breath. The appointment probably wouldn't be long, then I could get my kitty back home where she could grumble to her heart's content. And I knew she would.

Penny sat at her desk and was on the phone. She had her head turned away and hadn't noticed us yet, so I sat down by the picture window that faced the street and set Winifred's carrier on my lap. My cat was still grumbling. It might be in my best interest that I couldn't decipher what she was saying.

From behind the glass partition, Penny said, "Hey, I don't appreciate you calling me on this work number. Or calling me at all, for that matter."

Was this the same caller who had upset her when we'd both been in the bookstore?

As upset as Penny was and as loud as she spoke, maybe it was good the waiting room was empty except for Winifred and me. Wanting to calm my cat down, one, because of Penny's loud voice, and two, because of where we were at the moment, I took a chance that Winifred wouldn't take a nip at me as I put my fingers through the metal gate of the carrier.

At first, nothing happened. Then, a whisker brushed against me, tickling my skin. I wiggled my fingers, glad when a wet nose bumped against me.

Maybe she wouldn't make me wait the normal two and a half days following the appointment to forgive me.

Penny pounded her free hand on her desk. I jumped, causing the carrier to tilt slightly. Winifred hissed again.

With another bump on her desk, Penny said, "You can't blame him for that. It was unavoidable. I understand that your family's dog is…"

From the back area, a door opened, then closed. Was Dr. Cummings walking out to see what all the fuss was about with his daughter? I waited, watching the doorway that led to the side hallway, but he didn't appear.

A sob came from Penny. "Please don't do this. I…I'm begging you…wait, don't hang up. I—"

She pulled the phone away and stared at it, then placed the receiver back on the base. She reached for a nearby tissue and wiped her eyes.

Footsteps came from the back, and Drew appeared. Where was Dr. Cummings? Maybe in one of the exam rooms?

When Penny spotted Drew, she jerked, as if startled. Drew gave me a friendly wave, causing Penny to look my way.

Her mouth dropped open, and she stood. "Oh…hi Seneca. How long have you…"

"We just got here." I tapped the top of the container, wincing when Winifred let out a long, low growl.

Drew came toward us. "Hello again, Seneca. Good to see you."

"Thanks, good to see you too." I leaned a little to the side, hoping for a glimpse of Winifred's doctor.

Drew's face turned pink. "Dr. Cummings had an appointment of his own outside the office, so you and Winifred will be seeing me today."

"Great!" I sat up straighter, not wanting to cause anyone to be more embarrassed than they were, or in Winifred's case, grumpier.

"If you'd like to follow me to the back?" Drew waved his hand toward the doorway beside Penny's desk.

"Yes, of course." I stood, adjusting the carrier so it was held more firmly in my arms. It had a handle, but when I used it, sometimes Winifred had a bumpy ride. And that didn't end well for either of us. But then, I might not like it either if a giant carried me around in a plastic enclosure and I bounced around inside like a ping pong ball.

I followed Drew. When I passed by Penny, she was still snuffling and dabbing her nose and eyes with more tissues. I hated to see her so upset. With Drew here and Penny's dad away for who knew what, I desperately hoped Dr. Cummings was all right.

"Seneca?"

I stopped just past her desk and turned.

"Sorry about…" She waved her hand toward her phone.

"It's no problem. We really didn't wait that long."

She blinked. "But you might have heard something that…well…"

Drew had gone on ahead but stopped in front of an open doorway. He motioned to me that he was going to go on inside, and I nodded.

"Penny, I don't want to pry, but if there's anything I can help you with, I'm glad to. Even if it's just to listen."

"Thanks, I appreciate that." She grabbed another tissue and wiped moisture from her cheeks.

The entrance door swung open, and a woman with a Great Dane on a leash walked in. Winifred thrashed around in her carrier. She shook so violently at the dog's barks that it took all of my arm strength not to drop the carrier.

Penny gave me an apologetic smile. "Sorry, I'd better get back to work."

"It's all right. We can talk later. If you like."

She nodded, then waved the woman and her barking horse closer to the desk. Not wanting to upset my cat any further, although being here was upsetting enough for her, I hurried down the hallway, hoping I wasn't jostling Winifred worse than usual. I had no doubt she'd have more than a few choice words for me when we got home.

The door was open to the exam room. It was odd, stepping into the familiar area, but having a new veterinarian standing on the opposite side of the counter where I set the pet carrier. But Drew seemed like a nice guy, so I was willing to give him a chance.

"Thanks for coming in today, Seneca." He bent down until he was at eye level with Winifred, through the grate on the door. "And you too, Winifred. Nice to meet you."

A sound like air leaking from a tire came from inside the cage. Drew straightened and grabbed a paper towel to wipe the kitty spit from his cheek. "Really can't blame her. I'm sure she knows what goes on here, right?"

"Yep, she sure does. Not her favorite place, I'm afraid." But I winced at the thought of my cat actually hissing on his face.

Drew shrugged. "That's perfectly normal. They don't understand why their parent would bring them to some terrible place where only scary things happen."

"That's the way I see it too. She always knows when It's vet day."

The left side of his mouth rose in a half smile. "Did she run and hide from you?"

"How did you know?"

"Cats are like that. When they sense danger, they want to get as far away as possible, the more hidden the better. Let me guess. Did you find her in your closet?"

"Under the bed."

He chuckled. "Another good spot. Would you like to get her out of her carrier? It's more reassuring for the cat if their parent is the one to bring them out into the bright light and different smells of the room."

"Sure, give me a second."

"I'm not in a hurry."

And he didn't appear to be. Drew seemed relaxed and confident, which was reassuring to me, even though Winifred wouldn't find those qualities all that wonderful in the guy who was soon going to invade her personal space.

I opened the door and reached in. Winifred backed up until her whole body was crammed against the far wall. I'd taken off her costume before we left the house. It would have been difficult to have a thorough exam while wearing clothing.

"I know, Winifred, But Dr. Drew"—I glanced at him to make sure the moniker was okay, and he nodded—"is a nice man and just wants to make sure you're all right. Come see Mama."

When she wouldn't budge and even tried to nip my hand, I plunged in deeper and caught her under her armpits. With her front legs now unable to help her scoot back, I gently slid her on her back paws out onto the counter.

At least Drew could actually see her now.

When she tried to dart back into the carrier, I picked her up. Drew quickly closed the carrier door so she wouldn't have a convenient place to hide.

"Thank you, Winifred," said Drew, "for coming out to join us."

She pressed her face into my neck, her back claws scrambling to find a good place to latch onto. Her sharp toenails poked into my arm, but I held firm. She needed to have the exam done, and the sooner she allowed it, the better.

Drew performed the usual things that Dr. Cummings always did. He did them quickly and gently, for which I was grateful. Once Winifred had been checked, poked, petted, and finally kissed on the top of her head by Drew, she dove back into the carrier as soon as I opened the door.

"Thank you, Drew," I said. "I appreciate you seeing Winifred and me today."

"It was my pleasure. She's a beautiful cat."

"I think so, too." When Winifred meowed, I laughed. "She says thanks."

He raised one of his eyebrows. "Are you sure that's what she said to me? I have my doubts."

"Well..." I grinned. "You may be right."

Drew typed a few notes about Winifred's visit at his computer on a nearby desk. I moved the carrier closer, ready to pick it up and go out to pay at Penny's desk. But when he turned to me, his eyebrows lowered, I feared he'd found something about Winifred that wasn't good.

"Is something wrong with her?" I asked.

"No, she's perfect. It's just...I noticed you stayed behind to speak to Penny. And I'd have to have been deaf not to hear that she was upset on the phone a bit ago. I'm not going to pry into her business. It's not my place. But you seem to know her well, and...I just want to make sure Penny is okay. Do you think she might confide in you about whatever it is?" He held up his hand. "I don't need to know any details. Just that she has a friend who cares that she can trust the information with."

"Yes, of course. I was hoping to speak to her after Winifred's appointment anyway."

"I'm really worried about her. That's not the first call she's gotten here that has upset her."

"Thanks for checking on her. She's so sweet."

He nodded. "Yes, she is."

I readjusted Winifred's carrier in my arms. "I'll do my best to be there for her."

"I appreciate you doing that. If there does turn out to be anything I can do to help her, please let me know."

"I will."

As we left the exam room, I leaned down so I could see Winifred through the opening. "Don't worry, as soon as we get home, we'll get you dressed again."

I hefted Winifred's carrier back to the front desk. Why did it seem heavier than when I'd carried it in? After placing it on the counter, I smiled at Penny.

"Did she do all right?" Penny pointed to Winifred.

"She did great. Just the usual, uh…"

"Right. Cat stuff."

"Exactly." Penny had worked here so long I had no doubt she knew more about animals than most people ever could.

She printed out something, then handed me the paper. "That's the total for today."

"Great." I handed her my credit card, wondering how to bring up again the phone conversation I'd heard.

As soon as Penny handed me back my card and receipt, her phone rang. "Sorry."

I nodded, knowing it wouldn't be right to hang around here and wait for her to get off the phone. She was working, after all. And I was behind on work, too.

As I was stepping out the front door, I heard Penny say, "You have to stop calling me. You have to…. Please."

Chapter Twenty-Two

I'd done as Betty had asked and had placed her flier about the meeting on the bulletin board just inside Painted Wings' front door. When I entered to check on Evie, I glanced at it again to be sure of the time for tonight. Six-thirty. Not long now. I hoped I'd learn something else about Betty if I attended her meeting.

I walked to Evie, who had just stepped away from Mable Kane.

My cousin leaned in close and whispered, "Bless her heart. She just wants someone to talk to."

I remembered my conversation with Mable in the library and the scolding I'd received for reading kids' stories to Winifred. But I had to admit, Mable did like to be around people and Evie was the nicest person there was. "Good thing you're so patient with her. She seems to really have latched onto you."

"Yes, sometimes literally." She rubbed her wrist as if Mable were still attached. "But it's a small thing to do for her."

"You're always doing things for other people, Evie. But how are you?"

"About as okay as possible. Working helps. Staying busy."

"Yeah, it does."

She pointed in the direction of the bulletin board. "Still going to the tree thingy?"

"Tree thingy?"

"You know...the meeting? I'm not sure what to call it, since I don't know what's going to happen there." She looked around the room. "Of course, I'd go with you. If I could. You know, to see if you find out anything about..."

When her voice drifted off, I knew she meant about Burlington's murder, but didn't want to say it out loud. Smart girl. There were too many flapping ears in this place, and gossip was already at its peak. "Yeah, I know you would. Just like I'd stop in here at closing time to help you out."

"No, you need to go. And thank you for doing it, since I know it's mainly for my benefit."

"You're welcome. Anything for you."

She grinned. "Back at ya."

"Okay, I need to get over to the meeting."

"Does Winifred need anything while you're gone? Supper?"

I rolled my eyes. "She might think she does, but I just fed her. She's stuck in the house and not at all happy about it."

"Want me to check on her before I go home tonight?"

"No, but thanks. I'm hoping the tree thingy"—Evie laughed —"won't last too long."

I checked my purse to make sure I had my keys and phone, then headed out to my truck in the parking area.

As I pulled away from the greenhouse, I took the long gravel driveway, which led me directly past my living room window. And there, sitting on the back of my couch, staring forlornly out of the picture window, was Winifred. And she was pouting.

I'd have to make it up to her when I got home, that was for sure.

Even though this meeting wasn't something I'd ordinarily spend an evening attending, I wanted to learn more about Betty. We were friends, but not close. If we had been, wouldn't I have known about her tree-hugging days? It had taken Norman and Sid to clue me in. And they'd seemed mighty pleased to do it.

When I reached the community center, there were already lots of vehicles in the lot, mostly trucks, as nearly everyone in town had one. Or two.

I climbed out of mine, started to walk away, then imagined Cody's scowl if he discovered I hadn't locked it. After hitting the remote lock button, I headed inside the building.

Metal folding chairs, the uncomfortable kind that no one ever wants to sit on, were lined up in rows across the small room. I hoped Betty wasn't expecting a huge mass of people, because I didn't particularly want to sit on anybody's lap.

Except maybe Cody's.

No. Stop thinking about that almost kiss. It won't get you anywhere but in trouble. Was I thinking about it more because some of the townspeople liked to bring it up when talking to me? Sure, that must be it. Otherwise, why would I spend time dwelling on something that didn't actually happen and probably never would? The fact that I might, deep down, want it to was beside the point.

A scraping sound startled me. Two men were pushing a wooden podium a whole six inches to the left of where it had been, across a small wooden stage. I glanced around. Had anyone noticed me just standing here like a dolt, thinking about Cody? That wasn't my reason for showing up tonight. Time to find out what this meeting was all about.

At least a dozen people, none I knew, were now buzzing around like insects at a smelly picnic, arranging and rearranging the rows of chairs, the podium—again—and a few chairs on the stage. Three fiftyish-age women were busy placing what looked to be stacks of various fliers and pamphlets, for what I assumed to be information about trees. Because, at a tree meeting, what else would they be about? Did they ever stop to think that the paper from those fliers came from trees?

Others wandered in and chose seats. Maybe I should grab one, too, in case it did become crowded. I nabbed one in the very back row, near the door. That would make it easier if I became claustrophobic in the small, warm area, got an emergency call from Evie, Murray, or Cody, or if a person attending the meeting went crazy and upended the whole affair. My money was on the last choice.

I sat on the chair—yes, quite uncomfortable—and placed my purse on my lap. The squeaky metal contraptions posing as seats were so close together that if I left my purse on the floor, someone might trip over it. Voices rose from right outside the doorway. I recognized a couple of them. Betty and her part-time assistant, Marla Tiegs. At first, I thought they were laughing, then I realized they were upset about something.

We had drama, and the tree thingy hadn't even started? I checked my watch, and forced myself to remain calm and wait it out. I'd come here for information, and if I left now, it would have been a wasted trip.

After a few deep breaths to relax, I glanced around to notice that most of the seats were indeed filled. The two right next to me were still empty. Maybe I could put my purse on the nearest one, acting like I was saving it for someone so nobody else would sit right beside me, and…

Bad idea. With the drama already circling around me in conversations, my causing more turbulence by denying someone a seat would only fuel the flame for the reason people had come here tonight.

A shadow loomed from my left. I looked up. It was Norman. And Sid.

"Hey, Seneca, mind if we sit next to you?" asked Sid.

I hoped my smile would come off as sincere. "I don't mind. Have a seat." They were both husky men, to put it kindly, and would flow over their allotted seating space. I moved my chair a few inches the other way, hoping I wasn't now blocking the aisle, but finding it the only way not to be knocked off my chair. If Cody showed up, would he site the place for an overcrowding violation?

I checked out the room, not recognizing anyone but Betty, Marla, and of course, my two seatmates. Who were all these people, and where did they come from? Maybe the tree people society was more spread out than I'd realized.

Sid, right next to me, elbowed me in the ribs. Hopefully, that wouldn't be a common occurrence the whole time. I turned my head, assuming he wanted to tell me something.

He waved his hand at the room. "What do you think they'll talk about?"

Was he kidding?

Norman leaned toward us, crowding Sid, who edged even closer to me. I slid a little toward the other end of my seat but didn't have far to go.

I clutched my purse tighter against me as I braced one foot firmly against the floor. "Um, the meeting is about trees, so…"

Norman elbowed Sid, who bumped into me again. "Sid, tell her what we heard outside, before we came in."

"Oh, right. See, we were waiting to get in the door—there was a crowd out there."

"Now it's in here," pointed out Norman.

"Yes, right, so we stood there, wondering when we'd get in and—"

I held up my hand. "You guys heard something you wanted to tell me about?"

"Yep, surely did." Sid bobbed his head.

"And it was…"

He frowned.

"Go on, tell her," said Norman.

His eyes lit up. "Oh, right. It was Betty Rollings. She was out there joking around with… oh, what's her name?"

"Marla," said Norman.

He snapped his fingers. "That's the one."

"What were they joking about?" I asked.

Norman crossed his arms over his chest. "Marla teased Betty about being chained to a tree."

"Did Betty laugh about it?" I asked.

"At first, then she got real quiet and gave a sort of, I don't know, growl."

Sid shook his head. "It was more of a snarl."

I'd never known Betty to be anything but kind. "Okay, anyway…"

"And," Norman went on, "then Betty pointed her finger right at Marla and said, 'Actually, if I had to do it over, I'd gladly do it again. Even today, right now, if the situation warranted it.'"

"Wow," said Sid, "you remembered it word for word. Especially the use of warranted. Good job."

"Thanks. Took my vitamins right before we came." He gave us the thumbs-up sign. "After Betty's tirade, Marla started to cry."

Poor Marla. I didn't really blame her. If Betty had done that to me, I might have done the same. It would have come as such a shock.

I tried to balance on the edge of my chair without falling off completely. "Betty seemed pretty adamant about her cause? That she was still very serious about saving trees?"

"Oh, yes," said Sid. "I'd say the word to use about her tone is 'mean.'"

Norman nodded. "Yes, definitely mean."

Surprised that Betty might have seemed that way to the guys, I waited for more information. Maybe they'd misunderstood or weren't paying attention. It's possible Betty and Marla were having a disagreement about something entirely different. Or, more likely, Sid and Norman were trying to make it into something more dramatic than it had been.

But they'd already lost focus on our conversation and were huddled together, pointing at someone across the room, whispering loudly, about the large, feathered hat the older woman wore.

From the podium, a man clapped loudly, several times, to get people's attention. "All right, time to get started."

While Norman and Sid were focused on the front of the room, I moved my chair a few more inches away from protruding elbows. Who knew how sharp that part of a person's anatomy might seem when it made contact with another person's ribs?

Even though the guys still crowded me, at least no one sat on my other side, behind me, or in front of—

And just my luck, the feather-hatted lady took the seat directly in my eyeline. Even with me positioned into the aisle now, I couldn't see past the blue, green, pink, and was that a deep purple?—voluminous feathers that danced about every time the woman turned, tilted her head, or apparently, breathed.

A glance behind me showed that the back wall was standing room only. To leave my seat now would only serve to draw attention to me. It was either run away right now and not look back or sit here and act like I enjoyed it.

So, sit here, I would.

Mr. Clappy Hands was still behind the podium, giving the attendees a death glare until we settled down to his satisfaction. If the guy wasn't an elementary school teacher, I'd be shocked.

"Now," he said, "on with the show."

I blinked. The show?

Since I couldn't see over the feathers, and leaning to the side wasn't promising me anything but a quick trip to the floor, I finally stood, placed my large purse on my seat, and sat on it.

I gave my favorite purse a silent apology, and could now see at least partially through the forest of bird paraphernalia.

Although the man had announced things would get moving, nothing changed. The room had gone deathly silent. Was there going to be anything happening, or—

Stomping feet came from behind me. I turned awkwardly to see the source. It turned out not to be stomping, but marching. A group of a dozen people, mostly women, and a few men, stood in a single-file line and came in through the back entrance. Had they been hiding outside when we'd all entered earlier?

Not only were they marching, but each sported a T-shirt that had a cartoon man with a megaphone announcing, "Save our leafy friends!" Plus, they each carried a sign with pictures of various sorts of trees with happy smiles.

And leading the pack was Betty.

When she passed by me, she grinned, then winked.

Sid elbowed me in the very same tender spot as before. "Did you see that? She was flirting with me."

"No, she wasn't," said Norman, "she looked right at me."

Didn't I get enough of this when the guys actually remembered to show up for work at Majestic Monarchs?

The marching squad made their way past the rows of unreliable chairs and stomped up onto the small podium. I held my breath until the final sign holder was safely on board, wondering how they all fit at the same time, especially with their large placards. But their expressions were that of glee and determination, a united front.

Squeezing past the rest, Betty set her sign to the side of the podium and leaned toward the microphone. "Citizens of Maple Junction, and those from surrounding areas, thank you for coming!"

A cheer rose from those seated. Sid and Norman looked at each other, then tried to do a two-man wave by standing and raising their arms. The lady on the other side of Norman glared at the men and shook her head when they tried to get her to stand.

Not wanting any more attention directed our way, I poked Sid in the arm, tilted my head toward his chair, and let out a sigh of relief when they finally sat back down.

Betty, normally so mild and even-tempered, now resembled a fireball, in her orange tee-shirt, waving her arm in the air, yelling, "Protect our friends, the trees!"

Her marchers soon joined in the mantra, accidentally smacking each other in the heads with their signs. After tonight's episode, there'd be lots of black-eyed tree-huggers running around.

Three of the ladies in the group stepped one at a time to the podium, giving their heartfelt stories of how they loved trees and what a tragedy it was that so many were cut down, literally, in the prime of their lives. Just as a man from the end of the line moved closer to the podium, Betty waved him away. He frowned, and his face reddened, but didn't say anything. If I were him, I would have been mortified.

Betty then motioned to the group standing beside her to step down and form a line in front of the podium, facing the audience. By the uncertain looks the members gave each other, Betty's request must have been unplanned. They did as asked but appeared confused.

What was she doing? She'd told me she wouldn't be leading the meeting, but from all appearances, that was exactly what was happening.

Betty planted herself behind the podium, grasped the sides firmly, and leaned into the microphone. "Friends and townspeople."

She sounded as if she was starting a political rally speech.

"We're here this evening to pay tribute to our friends, the trees." She held her arms up in the air and wiggled her fingers. Was she trying to look like a tree with leaves? A few people in the audience responded with wiggling fingers as well.

Sid elbowed me in the side. "Sounds like she's revving up for something exciting. Maybe this won't be as boring as I'd thought."

Betty pointed toward the crowd. "But aside from that, we need to protect our bark-covered friends. Right?"

Applause came from those around me. Norman and Sid looked around, eyed each other, then clapped enthusiastically. Sid even let out a wolf whistle so loud that my ears rang.

Betty gave people a minute to show their appreciation for her comments. Then she held up her hand for them to settle down again. "But the real reason we are here. The main purpose of this meeting is to let you know that I have a personal vendetta."

Personal vendetta? Betty hadn't mentioned anything like that to me when she'd asked me to put up her meeting flier in Painted Wings.

The room became so quiet that I could hear Norman's stomach growl. Or maybe it was mine. The way the two men now stared at me gave me my answer. I slid down in my seat a little and wrapped my arms around my middle, hoping to contain any further outbursts from my internal organs.

"You see," Betty went on, "Burlington Snare was in the process of hiring a company to raze an entire small forest of beautiful pine trees to build himself a lavish home. Can you imagine the waste, the devastation, the poor trees who would lose their lives because of one man's greed?"

I looked around me to see if others were as shocked as I was by Betty's outburst. And indeed, many of them were. A few of those standing in front of the podium even turned to stare at Betty.

"He got what he deserved and more. I, for one, am thrilled the man is dead! How about you all? Are you with me? Are you glad Burlington Snare's blood was spilled on Seneca James' café floor?"

My mouth dropped open. Why had Betty just dragged me with her into her terrible tirade about a murdered man?

Every head in the room turned to gawk at me.

Sid turned toward me. "Gosh, I thought this would be boring, but it turned out to be a real kick in the pants."

Norman shrugged. "I just came for the snacks."

Chapter Twenty-Three

On a rare day when Evie and I could enjoy lunch at the same time, we decided to meet at the park. Murray had told her to scram—yes, his exact word—because business was slow today, and I had woken up early, so was ahead of schedule in my farm duties. It was thanks to Winifred's whiskers poking me in the ear this morning that had gotten me up early in the first place.

I'd suggested visiting the park because Mike told me once he often went there on his own lunch hour from working at the convenience store. Maybe I could talk to him again.

"So," I said, as we ducked beneath a low-hanging branch on the park trail, "are you holding up okay in the aftermath of Burlington's murder?"

"As you know from experience, it's scary and frustrating all at the same time."

"Yeah, I sure do know."

"It's like…everyone is staring at me, watching me when I'm in Painted Wings."

"Oh, I'm sure that's not…" I sighed. "Yes, you're right."

"So, you felt that way after your lawyer died in the greenhouse?"

"Definitely. All the time. I even had people say things like; the bodies are sure piling up out at your place lately."

Evie's horrified expression probably matched the one I'd worn during that time. She shook her head. "People sure do love to gossip, don't they?"

"Yep, we're all guilty of that, of course. But when someone is murdered? It's a free-for-all of words, accusations, and pointing fingers."

"You're right about that."

We strolled on for a while, stopping to admire some ducks in a nearby pond. When one of them quacked loudly, startling another into scuffling in place, its wings thrashing in the water, Evie giggled.

"That laugh is good to hear."

She grinned. "It feels good too."

A person yelling made us both gasp.

"What in the world?" Evie squinted to better see the group of people standing beneath a shady grove of trees. "Hey, isn't that Mike Larsh?"

I did the same narrow-eyed squinty thing and agreed. "Yeah. He comes here for lunch sometimes. That must be his historical club. See? They're all wearing those Civil War uniforms."

"Huh." She frowned.

"What?"

She pointed toward them. "All of them have white shirts. Except the color sticking out of Mike's looks yellow."

I thought back to the one Mike had been wearing at Angel and Connie's shop. It had looked odd with his coat then, but seeing it now, when his friends all had matching ones of a different color, made me notice it even more. "You're right," I said. I watched Mike, who seemed to be holding court, as he paced back and forth in front of the group of men of various ages.

"Gosh," said Evie. "I've never seen Mike look so frantic before. Usually, when he comes into the café, he orders his drink, then sits and reads a book."

"Yeah, I agree. Something must have really upset him for him to act that way." I glanced behind us, then to the left and right. Other than Mike and his friends, we seemed to have this area of the park to ourselves. "Do you still have a little time left for your break?"

Evie checked her watch. "Yep. A little. And Murray hasn't sent me an SOS text yet, so he must be okay."

"Want to get closer and see what Mike is up to?"

Her eyes widened. "Are you thinking we might learn something valuable about what's been going on around here?"

"You never know."

"Let's do it. I'm up for anything that might tell us who killed Burlington. Since we both know it wasn't me."

We backtracked up the trail a bit, then stepped onto the grass, which disguised the sound of our footsteps better. When we came to the back of the tree grove, we stopped, standing still as we waited for Mike to say something else.

Just when it seemed we'd missed our opportunity, that maybe Mike was finished talking, he shouted, "We cannot allow this to happen!"

The group of men mumbled their agreement, some bobbing their heads.

I stepped a little closer to see between a few pine tree branches. Evie followed and did the same. When Mike waved his arms, something sloshed onto his sleeve, but he didn't appear to notice. What was he holding? It had a shape like a liquor bottle. Maybe whiskey?

"Evie," I whispered, "check out what's in his hand."

She peered through the branches, then nodded.

Now that we were closer and I could see the glazed expression in Mike's eyes, I was fairly sure the guy was drunk. I'd never seen him consume anything alcoholic at the café, or anyplace else, for that matter, when I'd run into him in restaurants.

Evie held her hand as if it was cupped around something, then mimed drinking.

I nodded.

"As you men know," said Mike, his words a bit slurred, "my whole family loved history and were all members of the local historical society. Changing anything about the production we put on every year for the town would put a black mark against my family's legacy."

The other members of his group mumbled their agreement.

"Listen, my great-great-great..." He scratched his head with his free hand. "Well, I've forgotten how many greats, grandfather...was part of the original Civil War battle. No way I will allow anything in our reenactment to be altered."

Evie's phone pinged. She gasped and grabbed it from her pocket. I checked on the excitable group, but they were all talking loudly and obviously didn't hear her phone. "What is it?" I mouthed to her.

She held up her phone. It was from Murray, SOS. "Sorry," she whispered. "I can't stay much longer."

I nodded. I should get back to the farm, too. Without Annie around, there was even more work to be done, even though Winifred had woken me up early today, and I'd gotten a head start. Sid and Norman were turning out to be more work for me than if they weren't around. I'd give it a little bit longer, but I couldn't go on this way for long.

Just as I was ready to sneak back out of the grove to the trail, Mike spoke again.

"Men, there is something I must tell you. It's important. But for your ears only, is that understood?"

Everyone nodded.

"Although I'd shared with you what's been going on with someone putting a roadblock in front of our group for the reenactment to be historically correct, I have not yet told you who the culprit was."

Each man either took a step closer to Mike or leaned in.

"That person, the one who tried to throw a wrench into our plans, was none other than Burlington Snare."

They gasped.

Evie gasped.

I gasped.

Mike held up his hand. "Although I'd desperately hoped that once Burlington Snare was dead, we'd be in the clear to perform our production as we wanted, it seems some members of his family want to honor his wishes and keep us from doing it."

A man closer to Mike's age stuck his hand in the air, as if asking for permission to speak. "Mike, what do you have in mind?"

When Mike hesitated, an older man with a long white beard said, "We're with you. Just say the word, and we'll storm the castle gates!"

What castle? We lived in Indiana, for Pete's sake. Unless he meant one of our many barns or sheds, I had no clue what the guy meant. Had the rest of them been drinking this early in the day, too?

The other men agreed. But Mike gave a confused look. After a few seconds, he blinked his bloodshot eyes, raised the bottle in the air, and shouted, "Yes! Storm the castle!"

The men cheered.

Evie stared at me, her eyes wide.

I shook my head, not knowing what to make of these guys either. Of course, there was no castle, but could the older man have meant someplace else? Another building they were planning to invade?

After taking out my phone from my pocket, I sent Cody a quick text to keep an eye out for unruly Civil War reenactors. I knew he'd have more questions, but for now, that would have to do. I didn't want to miss anything else Mike or one of the others might say.

"Onward, men!" Mike turned and led his volunteer brigade away from the trees and back to the trail. As Evie and I watched them awkwardly march-stumble-amble, their voices warbled out some song I couldn't understand.

I stared at the backs of the swaying men as I took in what I'd heard. Could Mike have been so angry he'd actually killed Burlington?

Evie looked at her phone. "Sorry, Seneca, but I really need to go."

I wavered on what to do. I had so much work waiting for me back at the greenhouse, but was seriously concerned about what Mike and his inebriated friends might be up to. "I understand. You go ahead."

"What will you do?"

"I think I need to follow Mike and see what happens next."

Evie stared at the rag-tag crew. "I think you should too."

We rushed back toward the trail, not worried about if the men would notice us. They were too sauced to notice anything at all. And they had driven here! I gasped as I watched them get into trucks that were lined up along the side of the road.

This time, wanting Cody to have more information, I bypassed texting and was ready to call him when he beat me to it. When his name popped up on my phone screen, I quickly answered.

"Seneca? What does this text mean?"

"Listen, there's something weird going on with Mike Larsh and a bunch of other men. They're all drunk and—"

"Wait, this early in the day?"

"Right, and I'm getting ready to follow them."

"To where? Where are you now?"

I rushed to my truck and slung open the door, glad I'd left it unlocked this time. As I climbed into the seat, one-handed, I held onto my phone. "I'm at the park. I'll explain later."

"Where are you going?"

"I don't know."

"Then how—"

"I'm following them."

"Seneca, what's going on?"

"I'll talk to you while I drive."

"Wait. You're driving? You can't do that. It's illegal and dangerous and—"

"Fine." I punched the speaker button. "You're on speaker and the phone is on the passenger seat. I'll talk to you as I drive so you'll know where to meet me, okay?"

A loud sigh came from the other end. "Just please be careful."

As I peered through the windshield. I could barely make out Mike's vehicle in the line of other trucks. Never had I seen such awful, zig-zaggy driving in my life. Cody would have a cow when he reached us. Wherever that turned out to be.

My main concern was that they all stayed safe. And didn't harm any other drivers on the road, including me. At least Evie had left before the Civil War guys had taken off, so she'd be okay.

As I followed the line of trucks, I felt like I was in some sort of demented parade that no one in their right mind would come to watch. I didn't want to be here either, but something was going on with Mike, and I wanted to make sure he, and his friends, didn't do anything stupid or get themselves in trouble with the law, or worse, end up in the hospital.

"What's going on, Seneca?"

I jumped at Cody's voice from my phone. "Right now, I'm following the truck train down Pear Street."

"Okay, since you mentioned the park, I'm headed in that direction."

"Um, wait, are you holding your phone? That's illegal, you know."

There was silence, then shuffling. "Uh, it's on speakerphone."

"You dork! You only did that because I said something." I could picture him rolling his eyes.

"Just keep your eyes on the road, Seneca."

"Hey, how did you know I wasn't…?" I bit my lip.

"Because I know you. Where are you headed now?"

"We're driving pretty slow. Now it looks like the truck in front is turning left onto Mason Street."

"All right. Any idea where they're headed?"

I shook my head.

"Seneca?"

"Sorry. Um, no. They were yelling about storming a castle after Mike had said that Burlington had been the one to cause all the trouble."

"What trouble?"

"You know how much Mike loves the Civil War reenactment?"

"Sure."

"Burlington had been instrumental in trying to change things about how Mike and his crew did it."

"That's weird."

"I thought so, too."

A noise came from Cody's end of the conversation. Like the squeak of a hinge. Was he opening his glove compartment? "So, what's this castle business?"

"Not sure. One man said they should storm the castle."

"There aren't any castles in Maple Junction."

"That's what I told Evie."

"Wait, she's with you?" His next words were muttered, and I couldn't make them out. Probably something not meant for me to hear anyway.

"No, she had to go back to Painted Wings," I said.

"Don't you have a ton to do at the farm, with being so behind?"

"Yes, of course. But when I heard what the men said, and that they were drunk and…"

"Yeah, Okay. Good move on your part."

"Thank you."

"Where are you now?" he asked.

I leaned down over my steering wheel to try to make out where the first truck was turning. "Oh, now we're turning onto Embassy Drive."

Silence.

"Cody? Are you still there?"

"Isn't Embassy Drive where Burlington's son lives?"

"Yeah, you're right. They're going to storm that house."

"What does that even mean, storm it?"

"I'm not sure I want to know." I kept my eyes on the line of trucks in front of me, keeping my foot near the brake as I noticed brake lights coming from the first couple of trucks in line ahead of me.

"Neither do I," said Cody, "but now that I know where you're headed, I'll meet you there."

A long, loud, screaming blast of Cody's siren filled the inside of my truck. I cringed. "Uh, okay, Cody! Bye!" I yelled. But I doubted he could even hear me.

I focused on the line ahead of me, which had slowed down even more. Any slower and we'd all be parked in the middle of the road.

Sure enough, every truck ahead of me turned onto the street where Burlington's son lived. I kept right behind the vehicle in front of me, not super worried they'd wonder who I was or what I was doing. Actually, whoever I was directly behind was drinking from a bottle. Only a little ways to go, and they'd all stop at the house. Then, at least, Cody could show up, and they wouldn't be allowed to drive again until they'd sobered up.

Chapter Twenty-Four

I heard the wail of Cody's siren getting louder. Suddenly, he zoomed past me, past the whole line, and raced to the front of the parade, forcing the trucks to finally stop. I let out a relieved breath, glad that Cody had made it in time due to our town being so small and that he'd take care of whatever mayhem Mike and his buddies had planned.

The slow line of vehicles parked haphazardly in front of the house, with a couple ending up in the grass. That wouldn't make for very happy residents of the houses near there. I parked at the end of the line, putting me quite a distance down the sidewalk. But that was okay. Maybe a quick walk to the house would help get rid of some of my nervous tension from the slowest-ever car chase.

When I reached the group, who had formed a haphazard bunch in the driveway, Cody was already there, speaking to Mike. I crept toward the back of the group, trying to be unobtrusive, hoping none of them would wonder why I was there since I wasn't part of the historical club.

But looking around, I shouldn't have worried. They were all still inebriated. I doubt they'd give it much thought. Thank goodness they'd all made it safely here.

Cody, standing taller by several inches than any of the other men, crossed his arms as he faced them. He made eye contact with me, but mainly focused on the men. "All right. It's painfully obvious to me that you've all been drinking and—"

"What?" shouted Morty Burns. "No. Why would you think that? We were having a meeting in the park. A perfectly mornal—I mean normal—thing to be, uh, do."

Cody frowned. "Don't try to con me, Morty. I know drunk when I see it. And smell it." He wrinkled his nose. "Now, the first thing you're all going to do is hand over your truck keys."

They all moaned and protested, and one man even started to cry.

"Listen," said Cody. "It's my job to keep you safe. If I'd known about the drunken park soiree, I would have put a stop to you driving before you had a chance to show up here."

I wondered how Cody was going to hold onto all the sets of keys, since there were several, but I should have known he had a plan. He reached into his pocket and got an evidence bag. As he held it open to allow each man to drop his keys into it, he said, "I'll hold onto these until you all are deemed sober enough to drive back home."

A communal groan rose, growing louder. It took Cody several seconds to quiet them down.

He glanced around for a place to set the bag, but shook his head. Looking at me again, he lifted his eyebrows. He wanted me to hold the bag?

I stepped forward and took the plastic bag he held out, wondering if the guys would start asking why I was there.

It didn't take long.

"Hey," said Cliff Smiff—yes, his mother actually named him Cliff with that last name. "What's she doing here?"

Barry Golden piped in, "There've never been women in our group. Did someone invite her and not tell us?"

But the most annoying one was another one from Morty. "Hey, Sheriff, do you normally bring your kissing buddy to work with you?"

My face heated, and Cody's turned red. The whole lot of them hooted and laughed, smacking each other's shoulders as if they were the one to come up with such a clever comment.

Cody shook his head. "It's none of your business why Seneca is here. Just listen to what I have to say."

They sobered quickly, but not in the I'm-not-drunk-anymore way. Still, they did mostly pay attention with the exception of Morty and Cliff giggling in the back row. Barry swayed slightly and let out a loud hiccup. I widened my eyes at Cody, then pointed to the sidewalk.

He glanced that way, then nodded. "I'm sure the Snare family doesn't want all of us standing on their lawn. So, all of you follow me. You're going to have a seat on the sidewalk and—"

"What? You're going to make us sit down like a bunch of school kids at a picnic?"

Mass grumbling came from the men.

Cody ran his hand through his hair. "Just follow me." He walked a few feet to the sidewalk and pointed down. "Please sit in a row."

Lots of grumbling and eye-rolls followed, but they finally did as asked, even though a couple of them misjudged the distance to sit down and landed on other guys' laps before being brusquely shoved to the side.

Cody paced back and forth in front of the motley crew like a general in front of his troops. With the way the men loved historical battles, would any of them notice?

"Now," he said, "normal protocol would be to haul you all into jail for drunken driving."

When they started to protest, he held up his hand, getting them to quiet down. "But since there are so many of you and only two in my department, this is what we're going to do instead. I've called ahead to have Bud join us and—"

One older man in the group laughed out loud. "Bud? He's so daft he might get lost on the way here."

Another round of chuckling came from the group until Cody stared them into silence.

He pointed his finger at the guys, one by one. "When Bud gets here, he's going to write each one of you a fine for driving drunk. And before you start moaning again, consider it a favor from me that you're not all sitting in a cell right this minute."

I held in my own laugh, picturing this many people in Cody's two tiny cells. He had no choice with his limited resources but to handle this awkward situation the way he was. I grinned at him, feeling proud of my friend for his quick thinking.

A loud siren sounded from down the street, and soon Bud zoomed up the block, jerked to a stop, and hopped out of his vehicle. He halted, spun on his heel, and ran back to his car. When he turned back around, he held a handful of forms and a couple of pens, then joined Cody on the sidewalk.

After Cody had given Bud some brief instructions, he started at one end of the line and began to fill out forms, had each man sign, and collected the appropriate fee. When a couple of the men complained that they didn't have their wallets, meaning they'd also driven without a license, they begged others to lend them some cash.

Cody stopped pacing and stood in front of them. "Now, from what I've heard, you men were talking about issues with this year's historical reenactment. And also mentioned storming a castle, as well as talking about Burlington Snare."

Several sets of eyes widened. One man elbowed Mike and said, "Either the whole park was bugged, or the sheriff has supersonic hearing." The way he'd leaned close to Mike and cupped his hand around his lips told me he thought he was whispering. But the volume level was actually like a Circus Ringmaster with a megaphone.

Mike jumped at the loud voice and frowned at the other guy. "I don't know, man. Just be quiet and listen to Sheriff Bales, okay?"

Chagrined, the man nodded and edged a few inches away from Mike, though he couldn't go far without bumping into the man on his other side.

I stepped off to one side, giving Cody space as he started to pace again. He watched Bud for a few seconds, then said to him, "Thanks, Bud, for having those statements signed and collecting the money. Now, I'll need you to assist me in questioning these men individually about what was said at the meeting and any pertinent information about Burlington Snare and their possible involvement in his death."

Several from the crowd gasped at the word death. I was sure Cody had done that on purpose, to make sure they knew the severity of why they were here sitting on the sidewalk like a bunch of wayward kids.

Bud, having completed his money and form collection, stuffed those papers and pens into his pocket. He headed back down the line on the sidewalk and helped the first man to shakily stand, then move a few feet away on the sidewalk to question him privately.

Cody, starting at the other end, did the same. Once he had his first guy off to the side, he made a quick call to Dana at the sheriff's station, gave her an update of what was happening, then questioned the first man.

I stood, wondering if I should leave, stay, or wait in my truck. I was still the keeper of all the keys so I should probably hang around until Cody took the bag from me. I glanced up at the house. Was anyone home? If so, what were their thoughts on the loud, obnoxious people sitting in front of their house?

The place was big, so not a stretch that someone in Mike's club had called it a castle, at least by Maple Junction standards. Most of the town was farm ground, but this suburb on the edge of town was ritzier and definitely more upscale than where I lived. Not that I would ever trade, not for a minute.

My mind wandered as the sheriff's department personnel went about their duties, but when I caught Mike's name, I listened more closely.

Mike and Cody were now several feet away from me, but when I stood quietly, okay, when I leaned closed and strained to hear, I got most of their conversation.

Mike attempted to stand up straight, but ended up wilting a little, like an un-watered tulip. "Cody, I don't understand…what, I mean why…" He rubbed his hand over his face as if trying to force some coherence into his thoughts.

"For one thing, you and your group broke the law by driving under the influence."

"Yeah, kinda figured that part out," Mike mumbled.

"Maybe you should have done that before driving around with a snootful of alcohol."

He hung his head. "Yeah, I know. Sorry about that."

"Don't do it again."

"Nope, I sure won't. Can trust me on that. But what about…" Mike frowned. "Uh, that other thing you mentioned."

Cody crossed his arms over his chest. "That other thing was about Burlington Snare. And his murder."

"Um…"

"The way I see it, and from things I've heard you say from others, you've been talking about Burlington Snare and his involvement in changing the way your club does its reenactments."

Mike looked upward, as if trying to remember. "Not sure…maybe?"

"And I heard from the two ladies at the quilt shop something about trimming bushes in your good shirt that's your favorite? They thought it sounded odd, and told me. So now, I'm asking you. Does that have anything at all to do with Burlington?"

Mike's face reddened. "I might have been, uh, spying on him from outside his window. In the bushes. And, um, my shirt got torn."

"Why were you spying on him?"

"He was going to ruin everything. I couldn't let him."

"What do you mean, he'd ruin everything?"

"I…" He rubbed the back of his neck. "See, that reenactment means the world to me. The whole world. If I can't use the experience to get into the college course I want, I'll never fulfill my dreams."

I focused on Mike, not wanting to miss a word he said.

"That reenactment might seem like something silly to others. But Cody, this goes way, way back in my family's history. My dad, and his dad….well, it's a long line of dads who have been involved, either in the actual battles themselves or in the retelling of them. When I was little, my dad took me to see my grandpa, who was in poor health. Even though I was young, I knew he didn't have much longer to live. And he'd always been so good to me. Made me feel important and cared about. I wanted to do whatever I could to make him happy."

"And did that have to do with the reenactments?"

He nodded. "That's right. Dad had always been a part of them, and I'd go along and watch him and his friends when they acted it out. But it wasn't until my grandpa said how important it was to preserve history, especially our family history, that I got it. It made sense. If people who are still living don't tell the stories of what went on in the past, how will the kids of the future ever learn what happened? And ever see how to hopefully avoid the same mistakes?"

The more Mike talked, the more he seemed to have sobered up.

"While I was with my grandpa, he also said he'd always wished he could have gone to college, to study history. Really study it. But he never had the chance."

"What about your dad? Did he go?"

"No. He wasn't able to go either. Finances were tight, so it didn't happen. But see, if I could use this reenactment to get into college, there's a scholarship attached. It would pay for most of my expenses. I could go do what I love and make my family proud of me at the same time." He pressed his hand over his chest. "It's my life's most deep desire."

There was silence between the two men. I knew Cody well enough to know that he wanted to believe Mike. But he'd also need to stay tough until he'd proven who had killed Burlington, and who he could disregard as being not guilty.

Cody watched Mike for a few seconds. "And what about him wanting to change your reenactments? What did you do about that?" Cody didn't blink as he stared down Mike.

"Yeah, okay, I may have been… All right, I was definitely mad about him wanting to change it. But there were other people who wanted to also."

"Burlington is the only one in the morgue as we speak."

Mike's face went pale. "Morgue—"

"That's right. Why would you be surprised? You know he's dead."

"Sure, but…." He cleared his throat and coughed.

I desperately hoped he wasn't about to spew stomach contents all over the very nice, manicured lawn to his left. For my own benefit, I took three steps in the other direction, just in case.

Cody glanced at me, then back to Mike. "What I need to know is, can you verify your whereabouts on the night Burlington died?"

"But what about the other people who wanted him out of the picture, too? Aren't there more than just me?"

"Just getting all my information together. You have been saying things around town that made you sound guilty." Cody's hands landed on his hips, the effect making him appear even taller.

"I didn't do it, Cody. You have to believe me."

"I want to, honest, I do. But I need more than your word, Mike."

When he blew out a breath, Cody's head jerked back. Alcohol breath on someone's face was never fun, and Cody would get that more than most, in his line of work. "All right, it's like this," said Mike. "On the night it happened, I was at work."

"Can you prove that?"

"Uh…." His eyebrows lowered. "Oh, right! There were several customers who came in. I can show you who they were by their receipts."

"That's a good start. Anything else?"

"Our store cameras. One is posted right by the cash register. I was standing there the whole time. Well, I think I did leave once to, you know, use the restroom. But I was only gone for a minute. Not long enough to kill anybody. You have to believe me!"

"Let's go over your receipts and camera footage and go from there, okay?"

Mike seemed to wilt with relief. "Yes, sure."

"Here," said Cody, "let's have you sit down again for a while until I have everything sorted out."

"Sure, Cody. Thanks. Anything you say."

Bud had finished over half of the guys. He'd gotten through them quickly. Maybe they'd all had consistent alibis. Anyway, Cody and Bud would follow up on everything they were told. But I was guessing that would have to wait until all the guys were okay to drive again. The open sidewalk made for an interesting impromptu jail. But Cody hadn't had much choice. It wasn't as if he had a huge paddy wagon to cart them off in or enough jail space to hold them overnight. And it would have been irresponsible of him to have allowed them to drive on their own yet.

I had to give him credit; it was a creative idea made on the fly.

Before Cody could get to another of the men, his phone buzzed. He answered.

"Hello? Oh hey, Dana."

Maybe Dana had questions after Cody had called her earlier about what was happening in front of the "castle."

Cody frowned. "Wait, what?" He blinked. "Uh, yeah. Let me check into that now. Thanks."

He hung up, then looked at me and rolled his eyes.

When I lifted my hands in the 'what's up" pose, Cody walked over to me. "That call I got was from Dana. Apparently, she just got a 911 call from here."

"You mean one of these guys called the station?"

"No. From this house." He pointed his thumb over his shoulder.

I leaned around him to better view the large residence. An angry face was staring out of an upstairs window. I couldn't tell from this distance if it was a man or woman, but I thought it was an adult. "When no one came out with all the commotion, I figured they weren't home."

"My thoughts exactly, although I was planning to make sure of that before leaving today. I should have checked right when I got here but was distracted by all the drunkenness."

"Yeah, I was too. Not your fault."

"Thanks. Someday, it might be nice to have a bigger sheriff staff," he said.

I touched his arm. "But that might mean we'd live in a larger town, and would you really want that?"

"No. I guess I wouldn't."

"You're going to talk to someone who lives here? Right now?" I glanced at the window again, but the angry face had disappeared.

His left eyebrow rose. "The way you asked that, it sounded like you want to tag along."

"Well…"

"You're not part of my department, Seneca."

"No, but I clued you in to what was happening here today after what I heard at the park. That must count for something, right? And you wanted me to hold the evidence bag full of keys. So, I was assisting you in your duties."

He sighed. "Yeah, I guess. But again, you're not a deputy."

I grimaced. "I would hope not. I mean…" I tilted my head toward Bud, who was doing a weird sort of dance, trying to escape a ladybug as he floundered across the sidewalk to the amusement of the tipsy men.

Cody smirked. "Just come on. Let's go see what's up at the house."

We walked up the driveway, but I stayed behind Cody. Even though he said it was all right, I didn't want to appear like I was getting special treatment, which I was. Once we reached the wide front porch, Cody rang the doorbell. I listened to the sound from inside, some sort of opera tune I couldn't place. Fancy indeed. If I had that as my doorbell sound, Winifred would hiss every time anyone came over.

When no one opened the door, Cody tried again. I still couldn't place the tune, but then, Classic Rock was more my music style anyway.

The door opened with a squeak, and a man in a long black coat, black pants, and equally black hair, stood before us, wearing a frown. "How may I help you?"

Cody had already reached into his pocket and now held open his badge so the man, who I assumed to be a butler, leaned over to see better.

"Sheriff Bales. Now that I know your identity, how may I be of assistance?"

"I just received a call from the sheriff's office that they'd received a 911 call from inside this house."

Mr. Black Coat blinked slowly, peered over Cody's shoulder to the group, then back. "I can only imagine it had to do with those vermin who've taken up residence on the front lawn."

"They're not actually on the lawn," I said. "At least, not now. They're on the sidewalk, which isn't your, um, your master's, uh, it doesn't belong to whoever owns this house."

Cody had turned and was staring at me, eyes wide.

"Sorry," I mouthed to him.

"She's right," he said to the butler. "Legally, they aren't on the homeowners' property."

"How long might the cockroaches be staying?"

Even though I hated that the guys out there were inebriated, the way this man talked about them was downright rude.

"The *men*," emphasized Cody, "will sit there until I deem them sober and responsible enough to drive safely back to their residences. Allowing them to drive yet would be negligence on my part, putting them and other citizens of Maple Junction at risk."

The butler sighed. "As you wish."

Cody leaned a little to the side, trying to see in the house. "Any chance I could speak to whoever called the sheriff's station about this?" He pointed over the other man's shoulder.

"I'm afraid not."

"Why is that?" I blurted out, once again earning a look from Cody.

"Because," said the butler, "I've been instructed not to allow anyone into the residence with the exception of family members for the time being."

I narrowed my eyes at him. "Until when?"

"Until they instruct me otherwise." He switched his gaze back to Cody. "So, if there's nothing else, Sheriff?"

Cody mumbled something under his breath that my grandmother would have scolded him for.

The man in black raised one eyebrow. "Perhaps, if you feel that strongly about it, you might procure a court order next time you'd like to make a visit? Good day, Sheriff. And Miss…" He glanced at me, shrugged, and slammed the door.

I followed Cody back down the driveway to the sidewalk. Were the club members finally sobered up? A couple still looked bleary-eyed, but several were more alert. So much so, two men sitting closest to me pointed at me, then Cody, and elbowed each other as they laughed. When I thought of the guys' comments earlier about Cody bringing his kissing buddy along, my face heated. When would people stop bringing up something that nearly, but not quite, happened?

Chapter Twenty-Five

I dropped into the café shortly after it opened the next day. Evie was rushing around, but I knew she preferred it that way. If she had to sit very long without something to do, she'd go crazy.

I was the same, but I didn't go at warp speed like my cousin did. Mine was more slow and steady. We both got our work done, so I never thought the end result was much different.

When I glanced toward the counter area, Flora was standing exactly on top of the spot where Burlington had been found. She was crying. Nora grabbed her arm and told her to be quiet.

I hurried toward them. "Is everything all right?"

Flora opened her mouth to speak, but Nora shushed her.

"No, everything is not fine," said Nora. "That man" —she pointed toward the floor— "tried to ruin our lives."

I glanced down. "Do you mean Burlington Snare?"

Flora let out a gasp at the mention of Burlington's name and slumped down halfway to the ground, but Nora grabbed her and tugged her back up.

I stepped closer. "Is there something I can do to help?"

Again, Flora opened her mouth, but a glare from her sister made her snap her lips shut.

Nora didn't let go of her sister as she looked right at me. "I'll have you know that Flora and I are so very glad, giddy, in fact, that Burlington met his most deserving demise."

I jerked. That was a bold statement. Did either of them have something to do with that?

Flora's eyes widened. "No, don't say—"

"I must," said Nora. "The good news that he's dead should be shouted from the rooftops."

I held up my hand. "But why—"

"Because he tried to have my sister committed to a mental institution."

My eyes bugged out. "What?"

Flora whimpered. "I didn't want to go. He was going to make me. We had to do something!"

Nora released her sister's arm and gave her a single pat on the shoulder, a kindness I hadn't witnessed before from her. "Calm down, Flora. You're safe now. I didn't let that happen, did I?"

Flora shook her head.

"Didn't I promise Dad that I'd always take care of you?"

"Yes," she nodded sheepishly. "Thank you, Nora."

"You're quite welcome." She continued to keep an eye on Flora.

"Listen. Why don't we all sit down over there?" I pointed to a far corner. "There's no one else over there right now, so it might be a little more private." Anything would be more private than where they now stood, right in front of the counter, where a line of people was forming to place their food orders.

Murray came out and watched us, then raised his eyebrows. I pointed again toward the corner. "We're going to go sit down. Would you mind having Evie stop by in a minute?"

"I can do that." He disappeared behind the wall that separated the counter from the food prep area. Since I didn't spot Evie, that must be where she was.

"No." Nora's voice came out gruff and loud. "We don't need to sit down."

When Flora started to wilt again, I clutched her right arm as she sagged against me. "I don't mean to be rude, Nora, but I think your sister needs to get off her feet."

"Please." Flora's eyes were wide and pleading.

"Fine." Nora huffed out a loud breath. "Let's get you on over there, then." She took her sister's other arm, and we assisted her to the table. Several people turned to watch us, but thankfully, I didn't hear any whispers or see anyone pointing at us.

Once we were seated, Flora leaned forward, placing her arms on the table and her head on her arms.

When Nora didn't do anything to comfort her, I reached over and rubbed her upper back lightly, before I realized it was exactly what I did for Winifred when she was upset. But it must have worked, because Flora let out a sigh and her body relaxed.

Nora tapped the table. "Now, what's all this business of us having to sit over here? Aren't we allowed to leave when we want to?"

"Of course you are. But Flora seemed like she needed a rest. And maybe some food?"

When Nora started to object, I touched Flora's shoulder. "What would you think of some of Murray's cheesy fries? On the house."

She sat up straighter and nodded. "That sounds delightful. Thank you, Seneca."

Evie came by, took the order, then left.

I fully expected Nora to put up a fuss, but thankfully, she remained silent on the subject of the food.

I clasped my hands together on the table. "All right, after what you two just said over by the counter just now, I'm really concerned."

"About what?" Nora's eyebrows rose. "The fact that a madman wanted to commit my twin sister to an asylum?"

A whimper came from Flora, but I patted her arm again.

"Yes, about that." I looked at Flora. "Of course, that's no longer a threat, since he's dead."

Flora blinked rapidly as if trying not to cry. I grabbed some napkins from the dispenser, then handed them to her. She gave me a grateful look and wiped her eyes with one of them.

Nora let out a noise like a low growl, but I ignored her. Flora was obviously in terrible distress, and I intended to help her if I could. "Since I already know what Burlington had threatened to do to Flora, why don't you tell me a little more."

"Why should I?" Nora's voice came out sounding belligerent.

Flora sighed, then tore one of the napkins to little bits.

"Don't." Nora tried to grab it from her.

I shook my head. "It's okay. Really. I can see it helps calm Flora when she's upset. Am I right?"

"Yes." Flora scooped the bits of napkin into a compact pile in front of her. "It does help."

"Fine." Nora glared at me. "I'll tell you more." But when she glanced at her sister, her eyes softened. "Maybe it will help a little."

Evie came over with our food. Once we were all settled and ready to eat and drink, I sat back against my seat. "Please." I pointed to their plates. "Eat the fries while they're hot." When neither woman moved, I took a bite of one from my plate and made a yummy sound. The noise didn't need to be faked. Murray was an amazing chef.

Flora took a hesitant bite, and a slow, satisfied smile appeared on her lips. "So tasty."

With a scowl, Nora grabbed a fry and took a tiny bite. She blinked. "My, this is… very good." She grabbed another, then they both dug in. I did the same, suddenly realizing I hadn't eaten much today.

It didn't take long for us to finish. I picked up a napkin, wiped my hands, then waited for one or both of them to tell me more.

With a resigned sigh, Nora set aside her empty plate and turned toward me. "When my sister and I were little, she was teased relentlessly by the other kids."

"Yes, it's true." Nora's fingers infiltrated the neat pile of napkin bits, spreading them out into a circle in front of her. "I didn't like school very much. Kids were cruel."

My heart broke for the little girl who was mocked and teased.

"I took it upon myself to make sure Flora was okay. You see, our mom died when we were little, and our dad had to spend all his time being both father and mother to us. So it was up to me to protect my little sister."

"You're only older by two minutes," Flora pointed out.

"Be that as it may, I became the protector. I forced myself to harden against others, in order to be that person."

Now it made sense why Nora came across as gruff. She wasn't so much rude, as putting up a tough front for both of them.

I looked right at Nora. "I think you've done a good job for your family."

"Thank you."

"And Flora is lucky to have you."

"I am," she said. She glanced at Nora. "Quite lucky indeed."

I spread my hands. "I guess the big question is, what happened between you and Burlington?"

Flora stiffened and tore up another napkin.

"I'll tell you what happened," Nora knocked her fist against the table. "We were minding our own business, working our shift at the pharmacy. And that man, Burlington Snare, came into the building."

Flora didn't speak but watched her sister closely as if to ensure she quoted the story correctly.

I focused on Nora. "What did he do?"

"We were restocking some items on shelves. He walked by, then whipped around and came back. He stared at Flora. Then, he starting yelling."

Flora's destruction of the napkin increased in speed.

"What was he yelling about?"

Nora glanced around the table. Was she making sure no one might hear her for the next part? "He was waving his arms and getting too close to Flora. He said she was just like his aunt from when he was little. That she'd been crazy. A witch."

I gasped. "A witch?"

Flora snuffled. I handed her an unshredded napkin so she could dry her eyes.

"That's right. He accused my twin sister of being that terrible thing."

I shook my head. "But why would he do that?"

"It was my fault," Flora finally said.

"What was?" I watched her closely.

"He saw me doing things. And he…he said his aunt did the same things. That they locked her up." She focused teary eyes on me. "Seneca, he wanted to do the same to me. Lock me up in an asylum! I…I do things sometimes that are…strange."

"Sometimes?" Nora let out a snort. But when Flora gave her a sharp look, something I hadn't witnessed before, Nora said, "Sorry."

"Anyway," continued Flora, "I've always done things to make others laugh at me. Like, I count my steps when I walk, and I tear things up." She poked her finger into the smashed pile of white pieces.

"Don't forget the washing," said Nora.

"Uh, yes."

Did she mean clothes? Floors? Taking showers?

She glanced at her red, dry hands, then pulled them into her lap. "I wash my hands. A lot."

How much was a lot? I didn't want to embarrass her, so I didn't ask.

But that didn't stop Nora. "Thirty times a day. At least."

My mouth opened, but I quickly closed it. Maybe Nora was exaggerating. But Flora's reddened face and lowered head told me it was true.

I leaned closer to Flora. "That's nothing to be ashamed of, you know."

"Thank you, Seneca. I've been told that before by our doctor. I do take medication, but when I'm stressed, I still…" She shrugged.

"Everyone has something they do that might be different from others."

Nora's eyebrows rose. "Really? Then what's yours?"

Flora's head turned in my direction, her face full of questions.

I looked from one to the other. "You know that I raise butterflies?"

"That's fairly obvious," said Nora.

Why was she so antagonistic? Was it because of looking after her twin her whole life? "Yes, anyway, I talk to them. All the time. I even name some of the ones who like to land on me when I'm in the milkweed stalks." I pointed behind me in the direction of the fields.

"That doesn't sound so strange," said Flora.

I smiled. "Then there's my cat, Winifred."

Flora grinned back. "I like cats."

Nora's huffed out a breath, but I chose to ignore her.

"Me too." I focused on Flora. "And I talk to Winifred all day long. Just like she's a person."

"That's sweet." said Flora. "But I don't find it strange."

I held up one finger. "Also, my cat wears little outfits."

Both sisters blinked.

A rustling sound came from behind me. When I turned and looked down, there sat the kitty in question. "Look who's here right on time. Come up and meet my friends, Winifred." When I picked her up and placed her on my lap, the wings of her costume moved, giving the illusion that my cat was ready for takeoff.

I ran my fingers across the fur on Winifred's neck, much like I'd done for Flora. Winifred purred loudly, as if she knew I needed her to act like a little lady today instead of a wildcat.

"But…"Flora continued to stare at the cat. "She's….you…."

I laughed. "That's right. I dress my cat in clothes. And not just this outfit. She has a tiny dresser where we keep all of them. And each morning, I open the drawer and Winifred places her paw on which one she wants. She even wears pajamas to bed. So then I—"

Nora sat up straight in her seat. "You really are crazy, Seneca."

Flora's mouth dropped open. "That's not nice."

I tugged Winifred closer in case Nora's rough voice might upset her. "I'm sure there are people who make fun of me and talk about me, but I don't care. Now, Flora, I realize what I do is a choice and not like what you experience. You didn't ask to have these thoughts or reactions to things. And I'm sorry you have to deal with it. I just wanted you to know that I understand, a tiny bit, what you might go through at times. The way other people might react."

"May I touch her?" Flora's hand slowly crept toward Winifred.

"Of course."

Thankfully, my cat remained still and quiet as Flora petted her between her ears.

Winifred put up with being petted, but a minute later, let out a huff, her way of telling me she was ready to leave. I placed her gently on the floor, and we all watched as she ambled toward the open doorway and outside.

I turned back around.

Nora laid her hand on Flora's arm. Then, she stood so suddenly, her chair scraped loudly on the floor. Several people looked in our direction, the very thing Nora had wanted to avoid before.

With her arm around her twin, Nora led them out of the café. I sat there, stunned. Now I understood what had happened between the women and Burlington. But it still didn't answer the question as to whether or not they'd killed him.

Chapter Twenty-Six

I was ready to leave the café when Penny approached from the parking area. I was surprised. She so rarely came to Painted Wings. Had something else happened to her brooch? She glanced around the café until she spotted me, then made her way across the room.

"Hi, Penny. Is everything okay?" Since it was twice in a short period of time for a person who rarely stepped foot in here, I assumed there was a problem.

"It's not an emergency or anything." Her brow furrowed.

"Were you able to get your brooch repaired?" I said it softly since Penny seemed sensitive about the subject and might not want others to overhear.

"Yes. I took it to the jeweler, and he was able to fix it right then and there." She tapped her upper chest in the spot that I assumed held her brooch beneath her sweater.

"That's great." A few seconds elapsed, and when Penny hadn't said anything else, I went ahead. "How can I help you today? Would you like to order lunch?"

She waved her hand. "Um, no thanks. I…" She seemed very interested in the café floor.

"Have you, by any chance, lost something…else?"

With a roll of her eyes, she nodded. "I'm afraid so. This seems the logical place to have lost my compact. I think it might have been dislodged from my purse when I was getting other things out to show you and Murray."

"Purses can be that way. One day they eat something and you can't find it, the next, items are leaping from the purse trying to make their way to freedom."

Penny laughed. It was the first time I'd heard her do that in quite a while, and it was a wonderful sound. "You're right."

"So, do you have an idea where you might have dropped it?"

She narrowed her eyes. "I can't be sure, but the most likely might be around where we were sitting."

"All right, we can look. Evie does a nightly check, but sometimes things are hard to see." I glanced over to the table where we'd been sitting, and it was empty. Evie hadn't had a chance to clean it yet after the previous customer. I'd take care of that so that when Penny and I were finished looking for her lost compact, another customer could use the table.

I motioned for Penny to follow me, and we veered around the tables situated in the center of the café. When I checked over my shoulder to make sure Penny was still behind me, she had stopped and was staring at the place where Burlington had died, just like she'd done when she came for her brooch.

Why was she so mesmerized by that spot? Or was it only the normal curiosity I'd seen by several other café patrons?

When I reached the table, Evie had just walked by. Then she stopped. "Do you need this table? Let me clean it for you."

"No, I can do it. We just need to see if Penny lost her compact here the other day."

Evie frowned. "I don't remember seeing anything like that, but beneath some of those corner tables are dark by the time I close up the shop. I'll go get the cleaning supplies if you want to take a look underneath."

"Thanks, Evie." I smiled.

Penny watched her make her way toward the counter. "Evie seems so nice."

"She is. She's my cousin, but we're more like sisters."

"You're fortunate. It's just me and Dad now." She blinked rapidly. Was she going to cry?

"I'm so sorry about you losing your mom, Penny."

"Well, it's more than that. I…" She waved her hand as if shooing something out of the way. "Something terrible may happen if I don't do a certain thing for a certain person."

What did that mean? "I'm sorry you're going through so much. Is there anything I can do to help?"

She let out a long breath. "This is all on my shoulders, I'm afraid."

Even though Penny's expression was troubled, she didn't elaborate. When it seemed she was staying silent on her situation, I crouched down to check beneath the table. I crawled forward on my hands and knees. Glamorous, it wasn't. But then, I was used to that when working with the butterflies and larvae.

I shoved a chair out of my way so I could reach the wall. A ray of sunlight streaming through the front window caught onto something shiny. Could that be her compact? Edging closer, I saw that it was. No wonder Evie hadn't spotted it while doing her nightly check, because the compact was nearly the exact same shade as the wall.

"Hey," said Penny from above me. "Any luck?"

"Yeah. Still trying to grab it." I had to get my fingernails between the compact and the wall. It was really wedged in there. I tried once more and heard a light popping sound. I grabbed the compact and backed out from under the table. Several onlookers who'd been watching me clapped, my gyrations having apparently been entertaining.

When I stood, Evie handed me a wet wipe. Gratefully, I took it and cleaned off my hands. Evie wiped off the table and chairs, getting it ready for the next occupants.

Penny smiled when I handed her the compact and another wet wipe from what Evie had brought with her. "Thank you, Seneca."

"No problem. It's a little dusty back in that corner under there. Might want to give it a quick cleaning off."

She did as suggested, then tossed the wet wipe into the trash. "I feel silly, losing two things in such a short time and having to come here and bother you."

"You're not bothering me at all. Honest."

Penny glanced toward the door.

Maybe she'd take me up on my offer from when I'd last been in the vet's office, to listen if she needed to talk. "I'm heading out. If you're ready to leave now, would you like to walk out with me?"

After hesitating a few seconds, she nodded. "Yes, I think I would."

We stepped outside into the bright sunlight. Northern Cardinals trilled their sweet tunes, and Blue Jays squawked their peculiar melodies as we walked across the graveled parking area toward Penny's car. I'd seen it so many times at the vet's office, I knew it on sight, even though she rarely drove it here.

I pointed in the direction of my milkweed fields. "Have you ever been around back to see the monarchs?"

"No, I haven't."

"Would you like to? It's not far from here. And it might cheer you up." I smiled. "I know it always has that effect on me. "

She glanced at her watch. "All right. Just for a bit."

It surprised me a little that she'd agreed, but maybe this was just what she'd need to unburden herself from whatever had been on her mind.

I led her past my house, waving at Winifred who sat in the window, frowning because of her plight of being stuck in the house. Once Penny left, I would let my cat out. But even though Penny liked Winifred, Penny might focus better on talking to me without my cute kitty performing her usual antics.

As we walked along the path, her shoulders relaxed. She inhaled deeply. Was taking a walk outside helping her? I hoped so. I wasn't kidding when I told her going to see the monarchs always lifted my spirits.

"Penny, you'd said there was something you had to do for someone. It sounded a little, I don't know, ominous."

"That's how it feels, I'm afraid."

"Can you talk about it?" I held up my hand. "It doesn't have to be with me. But you should talk to somebody. Keeping things pent up is hard on a person."

Her sigh was long and deep. "I know. You're right. It's… What's going on involves me. And my dad. And…a couple of other people."

I nodded. I so wanted to ask more questions, but forced my lips closed. It seemed like she was open to sharing what was going on. I needed to be patient and let her tell it when she was ready.

When we reached the milkweed field, Penny's eyes opened wide. Monarch butterflies were everywhere. Orange and black works of art, flying and twirling in the air and throughout the milkweed stalks. I did let out a contented sigh. How blessed was I that I got to work with these incredible creatures every day?

She touched my arm. "Oh, Seneca. They're breathtaking."

"Yes. They are."

"I see why you would feel better just being out here with them. I envy you that. I love my job working for Dad and the animals, but this is…"

"You're welcome to come here any time. Just to hang out." I pointed to a bench a few feet away to the left of the path. "There's even a place to sit. We could do that now if you'd like."

"Yes. I really would."

We made our way to the bench. When Penny sat down on the smooth, weathered wood, her shoulders sagged, as if all the fight had gone out of her. Whatever was going on was big, and it was taking its toll.

A female monarch meandered through the air, in the graceful way of butterflies, and landed on the seat between us.

Penny's eyes widened. "Wow. Is it all right to touch it?"

"Better not to touch the wings; they're very fragile. But if you place your hand next to it, she might decide to climb on board."

Slowly, Penny laid her hand, palm flat, on the bench seat. As we watched, the butterfly stuck out her antennae and checked out the new landscape in front of her. I glanced at Penny, who was holding her breath. I didn't blame her. It was an amazing experience to have a monarch butterfly decide to make you their new friend.

Sure enough, the butterfly walked up and onto the back of Penny's hand, causing her to giggle. "Its feet are tickling me."

I laughed. "Yeah, I know. Great, isn't it?"

"It really is." She tilted her head as she watched her new acquaintance.

"You'd called it a she. You can tell a difference between them?"

"Yes." I pointed very close to one wing without actually touching it. "The easiest way to tell is that males have two distinct black spots on the lower, hind wings, that females don't have."

"Oh, I see. I mean I don't see, because they aren't there."

"Right. The two sexes are very much alike, though. If they're flying, it's harder to spot the difference than when they're resting."

"Especially on your hand."

"Yes, especially then."

Mrs. Butterfly hung around for a couple more minutes, then lifted into the air in a graceful arc, finally landing on a stalk of milkweed on the other side of the path."

"Thanks for suggesting this," said Penny. "Even with all that's going on, I do feel a little better."

"Good. I'm glad."

She crossed her arms across her middle, as if for protection. "All right, so here's what…" She cleared her throat. "Here's what's been going on."

I turned a little on the bench so I was facing her, wanting her to know that she had my full attention.

"It all goes back to my brooch." She touched her sweater again, like she had earlier in the café. "As I'd told you, it's a family heirloom."

"Yes, it sounds like a very valuable piece, for sentimental reasons, if nothing else."

"It is. But it's also valuable in the monetary sense. Believe me, if it hadn't been my mother's wish that I always wear it, I'd be scared to even take it out of the small safe I have at my house."

I didn't blame her. I had a ring that was my grandmother's. It was beautiful, but with the way I worked with my hands in soil and butterfly larvae, the thought of something happening to the ring if I wore it would make me feel ill.

"There's a second wrinkle to all of this. It has to do with my dad."

I sat up straighter. "Is he all right? I have to admit I was worried about his health when Drew told me he was working there now."

She shook her head. "Dad's okay, physically. And… well, he doesn't even know part of this. What he does know is that when he treated Burlington Snare's dog, there was a complication."

"Burlington?"

"Yes. He'd brought his dog to us for years. Unfortunately, the dog got hit by a car."

I gasped, hating to ever hear that about any animal, especially a pet.

"The dog survived the accident, but even though Dad treated him, his leg was too badly damaged and had to be removed."

"That must have been awful for everyone involved. I can't imagine how hard it was for your dad to have to do that."

"Dad was devastated. I tried to reassure him since he'd saved the dog's life, but he wouldn't be consoled."

"But the dog lived, so everything turned out okay."

She shook her head. "Unfortunately, not."

"What happened?"

"Burlington was livid. Blamed Dad for causing his dog to lose his leg."

"That's not fair. Your dad did his best."

"Yes, he did. Just like he always does. But Burlington was trying to get back at my dad."

I lowered my eyebrows. "I don't remember hearing anything about them having a fight about it. Or Burlington doing anything to your dad."

Her eyes narrowed as her gaze held mine. "That's because he didn't say anything else to Dad directly. But he sure did to me."

Everything in me wanted to ask, but again, I forced myself to stay silent as I clutched my hands together in my lap. She was going to tell me something big. I could feel it.

"What I'm going to tell you…I haven't breathed a word of it to anyone. But I can't hold it in any longer. It's making me physically ill, trying to keep it inside. And, Seneca, I trust you. Just the fact that you wanted to show me this part of who you are"—she waved her hand to indicate the field of butterflies—"tells me you're someone who really cares."

"Thank you, Penny. I appreciate your kind words."

"I've known you so long. Your reputation as a good friend and listener is stellar. Please, if I tell you, can you not tell the sheriff? I know that you and he are close. I'm…he can't know about this, please."

A small shiver ran through me. If Penny was in trouble, Cody might need to know. But how could I tell her I wouldn't say anything and then go back on my word? "I won't tell Cody. Not without your permission." Somehow, I'd make it work. If need be, I'd try to convince Penny she might need help from the authorities. But not yet. For now, I'd simply listen and be her friend.

"Thank you." She closed her eyes for a few seconds, then blew out a long breath, as if any fight she'd had left inside was now gone, floating away on the wind along with the monarchs as they twisted and looped through the air.

I took her hand, wanting her to know I was there for her. She gave me a sad smile, squeezed my hand, then placed hers in her lap. "Burlington, being so upset, told me he was going to do a smear campaign against my dad. Tell the whole town that Dad was incompetent and too old to practice. And that he purposefully ruined the dog for the rest of its life."

I shook my head. "That's horrible."

"It would have led to my father's early death if that happened. I have no doubt about that. His veterinary practice has been his world for nearly his entire life. I begged Burlington not to do it. To leave Dad alone and let him finish out his career in peace, leaving his caring legacy intact."

"But Burlington wouldn't?"

"No. He…" She reached into her purse and removed a couple of tissues to dab her eyes. "He said there was only one way to make him not carry out his plan."

I blinked. "What was that?"

She pressed her fingertips near the top of her sweater. "He wanted my grandmother's brooch."

"Why on earth would he want that? How did he even know about it?" My gaze dropped to where her fingers were. "It isn't as if you wear it on the outside of your clothing for all the world to see."

She lowered her hand and placed it in her lap. "This story goes back many years. You see, when my grandmother was young, way before she had my mom, or even met my grandfather, she worked as a housekeeper for Burlington's grandmother."

"Wow. I had no idea those connections even existed for your two families."

"Unfortunately, yes. My grandmother, much like me, used to wear it beneath her maid's uniform jacket. It was so precious to her, something her own mother had handed down as well."

"What happened?"

"She was cleaning in the kitchen, and the maid in charge of cooking accidentally spilled some hot grease on her."

"How terrible. Was she injured?"

"Thankfully, no. But she ripped off the jacket, which took the brunt of the grease. Burlington's family member happened to walk in at that moment and spotted the brooch on her blouse. He said there was one from his family that had come up missing. He accused her of stealing it."

My mouth dropped open. "She must have been so scared to have been accused like that."

"She was. She was innocent, of course, but he wouldn't leave it alone. He tried to get her to give it to him, but she refused, and they fired her."

"I'm so sorry. And her being so young. It must have been heartbreaking."

"I'm sure it was. That's how I would have felt."

"Me too."

Penny waved her hand. "So fast forward to now. I started getting calls from Burlington."

"Calls about your dad?"

"That's right. He said unless I gave him the brooch, he was going to shout from the rooftops about how Dad had ruined his dog. I'm not sure Dad would have survived that. Besides, it was in my family. And my mother's last wish is that I keep it always. How could I give it to that scoundrel when it never belonged to his family in the first place?"

"Obviously, you said no. I mean, you still have the brooch."

She touched her sweater. "Yes, but for how much longer?"

"What do you mean? Burlington is gone. Didn't the calls stop?"

"I wish. Shortly after he died, I started getting similar calls."

"From who?"

"His son."

My heart lurched. Just when she'd thought the nightmare was over, Burlington's son took up the awful cause. "Oh, Penny. I'm so sorry. What will you do?"

"I don't know. I really thought...hoped...that once Burlington was dead, my life would go back to normal, and Dad's reputation would be safe." She shuddered. "Why couldn't his death have solved the problem, like I'd thought it would? I was so certain my life would return to normal once he was dead and buried."

I swallowed hard. Penny had just plainly stated a very compelling motive to have killed Burlington. Cody needed to know. But I'd promised her I wouldn't do it without her consent.

"Penny," I grabbed her hand. "Please, you need to tell Cody. He can help you with the blackmailing."

She shook her head so hard, her dangly earrings swung back and forth. "No. I can't. If Cody were to investigate and bring this out into the open, it would be devastating. Don't you see? Then everyone would know what happened, and Dad would be dragged into the middle of this mess, the very thing I've been trying to avoid. My dad is not a young man. He couldn't take it. I don't want his career, his life, to end on such a terrible note."

She stood suddenly. "Thank you so much for bringing me here and for listening. I do so appreciate it. But I need to leave now. And I'll trust that you'll keep your word and not tell Cody what I've said."

Penny walked back down the path and around the house, until I could no longer see her.

I slumped against the back of the bench. What was I going to do?

Chapter Twenty-Seven

The next day, I was still concerned about Penny. The blackmailing needed to stop. I'd told her I wouldn't tell Cody. And I wouldn't. At least not until I felt Penny was in physical danger. Then, all bets were off. I'd feel terrible knowing what I know and allowing her to be injured. Or worse. I'd try again, and soon, to convince her to talk to Cody. For her own safety and to have Burlington's son arrested for blackmail.

However, there was one person I could confide in who wouldn't say a word. I had to talk to someone, and Evie was the one I could trust. She'd be on her break right now. I knew because she always took it at the same time every day, and Murray watched over things until she returned.

I stepped into the privacy of my greenhouse, called her, and told her about Penny. I was so glad I did. She was as shocked as I'd been, but had, of course, promised to keep it between us. At least I didn't feel the entire burden of knowing about Penny myself. I slipped my phone into my pocket.

But for now, I had work to do, and taking care of the butterflies had taken a back seat to another murder in town, plus the fact that two of the workers I had weren't even close to being reliable. Lawrence seemed like a good worker, but would he stick around for a temporary job when he needed full-time with benefits? Unfortunately, that was something I couldn't offer him.

I headed out to check on my milkweed fields. The weather had been dry, and I wanted to make sure the crops were okay. A rustling in the grass at my feet caught my attention. It was Winifred, of course.

"Hi, kitty. Want to help me out this afternoon?"

My cat glanced up at me, meowed loudly in what seemed the affirmative, and trotted along beside me, her tail in the air like a flag and the wings of her butterfly costume flapping in the gentle breeze.

We made our way down the path of flattened grass, made from years of me making this daily trek and my grandmother before me. Every few feet, Winifred stopped to sniff something: grass, a dandelion, a tiny moth, which ended up settling down on the cat's nose, causing Winifred to sneeze. We didn't see the moth much after that, not that I blamed him.

When we reached my barn, Winifred darted in as soon as I opened the tall doors. I came for a rake, while she'd probably find lots of interesting things to stick her paws, nose, and whiskers in. My guess was she'd need a thorough fur brushing later, which, of course, she'd hate.

I returned to the milkweed fields and raked out leaves and weeds for about an hour with no sight of my cat. But the barn would be warm and toasty now in the afternoon sun, which was an ideal place for cat naps. On occasion, I'd been known to take a nap with her, but not today. Too much to do.

A noise came from behind me. Soft rustling in the grass. There were footsteps, quiet ones. I turned, thinking it might be Evie, who occasionally ventured out here and might want to know more than I'd told her on the phone about Penny. But it wasn't my cousin.

It was Lawrence.

I smiled. "Hey, how are you? I wasn't expecting you until later this afternoon."

His normally pleasant expression had been replaced with a downturned mouth and sad eyes.

"Lawrence? Is something wrong?" I placed my rake down on the grass beside the edge of the milkweed where I'd been working.

He shook his head. "It's not good, I'm afraid."

Maybe something happened to Karen. Or Lawrence had lost his job altogether. "What's going on?"

I laid my rake in the grass, then stepped toward him, ready to listen. In our time working together at Majestic Monarchs, I'd come to appreciate his calm demeanor and good work ethic. As I got closer, I realized he was wearing clothes he normally wore at the bank. Not older jeans and a shirt to work out here with me. "Did something else happen? I mean, is it something to do with the bank?"

He shook his head.

"Karen? Is she all right?"

He waved his hand. "She's fine. As whiny as ever."

I blinked. It wasn't like Lawrence to sound so unkind. But if he was having a bad day, which seemed apparent, maybe he wasn't feeling like himself.

Lawrence spread his hands. "I thought, was hoping, maybe you and I could just talk. I need to get some things off my chest, and you seem like you're a good listener."

I'd actually been told that many times, and I was thankful people had found that to be true and helpful for them. I counted it a privilege to listen and hopefully lend support to others, just like people had done for me. "I'm happy to listen." I glanced toward the bench my grandma had placed a few feet away near the path. She'd done that for me when I was little, and I would always get worn out before she was ready to head back to the house. "Would you like to sit down?" I pointed toward it.

He looked at the bench, sighed, then shook his head. "I think I'd better stand. There's a lot of pent-up things on my mind, and I might need to pace."

"Sure."

"You sit if you need to."

"Thanks, I'm okay for now."

"All right." He flexed his shoulders. "Well, my story goes way back. To my dad, and when I was little."

I crossed my arms over my chest, hoping whatever Lawrence had to say wouldn't be as bad as he was making it seem.

"See, my dad was a deadbeat. Never amounted to anything."

That wasn't something I'd expected him to say. "I'm sorry to hear that."

"Yeah, not much fun for me. Not only did he not provide for me after my mom left us, but I was also teased at school mercilessly when he was carted off to jail for theft, and I had to go live with a foster family."

"That sounds terrible. Was your foster family kind to you?"

He shook his head. "No. Never. They were hateful and rude, and the only reason they took me and two other kids in was for the money. They told us that."

"How awful for you, especially as a little boy."

He began to pace back and forth in front of me again, reminding me of how Cody had done in front of the drunken sidewalk crew.

"Are you sure you wouldn't like to sit down?" I asked.

"I said no."

I held up my hand. "All right. Um, please go on." He really was wound up. Poor guy.

Lawrence took ten paces to the right, then back to the left. Had he been doing that the whole time, and I hadn't noticed? Sure enough, he kept up the pattern, as if trapped in some sort of box he couldn't escape. Was he thinking of what his father had endured, living in a jail cell?

"You see," he said, not missing a step, "as a foster kid who was treated unfairly, I was also poor. Not that it was a new concept for me since my own dad hadn't bothered to work much, but I'd hoped living with someone else would have made things better. It didn't."

"I'm sorry, Lawrence." I wanted to say more, but he seemed so agitated, I didn't try.

Without acknowledging I'd spoken, he kept moving. "I guess I should clarify about my dad working. He did, some, but it was never on the up and up. He was a thief, stole anything he could get his hands on, and sold it for cash to buy booze, but never for house payments and rarely for food for us."

The longer I observed Lawrence, the more alarmed I became. I could understand him being upset about his dad and childhood, but why was it coming up now? What had happened to cause him to need to vent about it as an adult to someone he really didn't know all that well?

Lawrence glanced down, then bent to retie his shoe. He stood and continued pacing. "Because of what I went through, being poor, my dream was to grow up and work at a job where I'd make lots and lots of money. So, when I got the job at the bank, I was thrilled. Being a teller doesn't pay a huge salary, but it was a start. And I was sure there would be opportunities for me to move up, if I worked hard and was a good employee."

"You work hard when you're here, Lawrence, which I appreciate."

"Thank you. See? You can see the value of a person who tries their best." He waved his arms as if agitated.

"Do they not appreciate you at the bank?" I thought about Karen's words that Lawrence had been cut to part-time.

He jerked to a stop and stared at me, his eyes huge. Then, he let out a loud, long laugh.

It was such a foreign sound coming from him that I shivered.

"Seneca, if you only knew. But how could you if you've never been told." He stood still and placed his hands on his hips. "Why don't I tell you right now? Then maybe you'll understand why things have turned out like they have."

I frowned. What was he talking about? When something brushed my ankle, I jumped. My heart slowed down a little when I realized that Winifred had been hiding in the milkweed and had stuck out her paw to tap my leg.

I bent down and picked up my cat from between some milkweed stalks. She had a few bits of stalk caught in her fur, all the more reason to brush her later and all the more reason for her not to like it.

"Hey!" yelled Lawrence. "Are you listening to me?"

My mouth dropped open at his sudden eruption. "Um, yes, sorry. I..." I glanced down at Winifred, who was now pressed against my chest. I could feel her little heart beating fast—or was that mine?—at Lawrence's loud exclamation. "See, I didn't realize Winifred had been down there and..."

"I don't give a crap about your stupid cat."

Winifred's growl was long, but low. Had Lawrence heard her?

"Hey," I said, "please don't talk that way about her. She's my family."

"Why are people so stupid when it comes to their animals?"

"Listen, Lawrence, I like you. I really do. And I'm very sorry for what you've gone through. It sounds like there's a lot going on with you, so maybe it would be best if you talked to someone else who could—"

"That's not going to happen, Seneca."

What was going on? How had this conversation gone south so quickly? I, for one, had had enough. It was time to end this strange encounter with my employee, who, after saying that about Winifred, might no longer even be that.

Just as I was ready to insist that he leave my property, Lawrence reached into his pocket. What he had clutched in his hand stopped me cold. A small, but very dangerous, handgun.

I gulped. "What are you doing? Put that away!" I clutched Winifred tighter, causing her to let out a hiss. But no way was I going to put her down in case the crazy man in front of me decided to use my baby for target practice.

Instead of doing as I'd asked, Lawrence stepped closer. "I'm not done talking. Letting it out is actually quite cathartic, so thanks for that."

He narrowed his eyes. "Let's see, where was I?"

As Lawrence tapped his chin in thought with the revolver, I realized my phone was in my pants pocket. Sometimes, I forgot to bring it when I was going to be out here, getting dirty and messy, but today, I'd brought it with me. Would I have a chance to reach for it and dial Cody?

When Winifred squirmed, I pressed my lips close to her ear. "Sweetie, I need you to hold still for Mama, okay? Let's try to get Cody out here to help us."

At the mention of Cody's name, she instantly relaxed. If anyone could calm her down, it was him.

I kissed the top of her head, then glanced up. Lawrence had stopped his agitated movements and was now openly glaring at me.

"What are you doing, Seneca?"

"I was… um, talking to Winifred."

The snort of laughter he let out was anything but amusing, or amused. "Leave it to someone like you to do something so asinine."

My teeth clenched together, tight. I couldn't have replied even if I'd wanted to.

He watched me for a second. "Anyway, I remembered where I'd left off. So once I was firmly entrenched in the world of banking, I wanted to move up, to be in charge of other people, and to get control of my own destiny. Also, I wanted tons of money. A bank is full of it, right?" He tilted his head.

"Aren't you going to ask me what happened next?"

Even though I didn't want to, I decided it might be best to appease him, for now. "Fine. What happened next?"

"I'm so glad you asked." He smiled, looking every bit like a menacing crocodile. "During my time working with Mr. Snare, he bullied me and called me worthless, much like my dad had. Much like my foster father had. What was the deal with the men in my life being like that?"

If I could only get him to change his mind about holding that gun. If he set it down, or put it back in his pocket, could we possibly resolve this without anyone getting hurt?

I glanced down at my pants pocket. If only I could call Cody. He'd know what to do.

Lawrence was pacing again. "One day, while at work, I let it slip to Karen that I had that dream for the future, wanting to excel and move up in the bank. You know what happened? Mr. Snare overheard us and laughed at me. Laughed! I was humiliated. His very words to me were this—'The only way you'll ever get a better job at this bank is after I'm dead!'"

He gave a slow smile. "Seneca, aren't you going to ask me again what happened next?"

I swallowed hard, having a good idea what the answer would be. "What happened?"

"I gave him his wish. I killed him."

Chapter Twenty-Eight

My heart thudded wildly. Winifred pressed so close to me, stiffening in my arms. She knew something was wrong, that we were in danger. Her claws flexed against my arm, but not to harm me, only to let me know she was here and she was ready. For whatever happened.

I pointed toward the bench, unable to control my shaking hand. "Why don't we sit down over there? We could talk some more, or maybe…I don't know, have you speak to someone else?"

"Oh right, like who? The sheriff? No thanks. He'd only try to talk me out of my future plans. And I doubt he'd be too happy about me killing Mr. Snare." His eyes narrowed. "I bet he'd really be unhappy if I killed his girlfriend."

My normal comeback for his comment—that I wasn't Cody's girlfriend—died on my lips. What did it matter at this point if I corrected a murderer of his false ideas?

Lawrence tapped the gun against his palm. "Say, I have an idea. Why don't you shut up and let me finish my story?"

I nodded quickly, not wanting to antagonize him any further. When I ran my fingertips through Winifred's fur, she nuzzled my neck, something she rarely did. Poor kitty was just as scared as I was.

He began pacing again. My hope that he'd wear himself out walking back and forth wasn't going to happen. The guy was too keyed up, too delusional to think clearly or even realize that having killing Burlington was wrong. Never mind that he now might kill me. And the possibility of something happening to Winifred nearly did me in. I shoved the thought from my mind. If there was any way out of this, I needed to focus on Lawrence and what he was saying.

"Anyway," he went on, "earlier today, when you were in your greenhouse, I overheard you tell someone that you knew who the killer was and that you were ready to confront them about it."

Taking a chance that he wouldn't pull the trigger just for spite, I said, "But you weren't there. I made sure I was alone in there when I said it."

"That's the amusing thing. I was there all right. Those windows at the back of your greenhouse were just the right height for me to crouch below and hear what you were saying. Nice touch that you left them open today. I was ready to head into the café, but I saw you walk into the greenhouse with your phone in your hand. When I saw you start to dial, I thought maybe I could get some useful information if I hung around. And I'm so glad I did. I'd love to know who you were talking to, but I'm guessing you won't tell me?"

I shook my head. "Never."

He shrugged. "I thought as much. Well, anyway, that day when I decided to meet Mr. Snare in your café to make sure it was his last evening on earth, I hadn't realized that you consider yourself some kind of amateur detective. Imagine my chagrin when I heard about you asking questions all over town. When I realized what you were up to, I knew I had to act, and fast."

Anger sparked hot in my chest. "So you thought you'd get to me first, huh?"

"That's right. You should know after listening to my story that I'm resourceful."

I had to give him that. "But wait. If it was really you, then how did you get into the café to meet Burlington? That door was locked. Evie is positive of that."

He waved my comment aside with his gun. "No sweat. Remember when I told you my dad was a thief? Some of my early years were filled with him teaching me how to pick locks. It only took me a few seconds, and I was in."

I hunched forward, feeling deflated. Lawrence was smart and knew what he wanted. What were my chances of escaping this situation unharmed? I could take off running, but he was in better shape and could easily catch me. Besides, I couldn't outrun a bullet. I glanced at my pocket again, thinking about my phone.

"What are you looking at?" he asked. "Pay attention to me."

My head snapped up, and I looked at him. I needed to be careful and not give him an excuse to pull the trigger. But I also needed to keep him talking if I had any chance at all of getting out of this mess. There was always a possibility that somebody might come looking for me. A friend, a neighbor, or even someone who was lost needing directions. I'd take any of that now, if it would stop Lawrence from doing what he planned to do.

"All right," I said. "I get that you knew how to unlock the café. But how did you get Burlington there in the first place? It was after hours. What would make him meet you there?"

"That's the beautiful part, Seneca. See, I knew a secret about Burlington. He was blackmailing the vet's daughter, Penny. He said he'd tell everyone he knew that her dad had maimed his dog, and then no one would ever go to Dr. Cummings again. It's amazing the kind of stuff you can overhear when you skulk around in corners and follow people on the street when they're on their cell phones and don't pay attention to who else might be listening."

I kept quiet, not wanting to let it slip that I knew about the blackmail. I didn't want to infuriate him further. He seemed proud of himself that he had something on Burlington, and me already knowing that information might set him off again.

His mouth formed into a smirk. "To get Burlington to meet me, I sent him a note using some of Penny's personal stationery."

"How in the world did you get a hold of that?" I gasped at my own outburst. Would he turn more of his anger on me? But he didn't even look in my direction as he kept pacing. By the time he was done, I'd have nothing on that path but a bare patch of dirt. The reality hit me. When he was done…. Would I even be here to see the path, or anything else, anymore?

He shrugged. "I can pick locks, remember? I saw some stationery in her purse once when she was looking for deposit slips one day while at the bank.

I asked her about it, telling her how nice it looked. She loved the compliment and said she had a whole case of it at her house, that before her mom died, she had insisted Penny have it to use for all of her correspondence."

"So you broke into her house and stole some?"

"Of course. I typed a note to Mr. Snare, asking him to meet "Penny" at the café after it was closed. I said we needed privacy for what I had to say. In the note, I implied that I'd bring the brooch for him so he'd stop the blackmailing."

It was an ingenious plan, not that I'd say that out loud. Instead, I asked, "What about using the frying pan to kill Burlington? Why did you choose that?"

He grinned. "Didn't you love that? I wanted something I wouldn't have to carry into the café with me, like this" —he waved the gun. "I'd been in the café enough times to see that huge frying pan Murray used for cooking. It seemed a great weapon to use and would help implicate your cousin in the process."

Suddenly, my phone buzzed with an incoming text, and I jumped. Winifred hissed when I jostled her. And Lawrence's eyes widened.

He rushed toward me, his ever-present gun way too close to me. "Hand it over, Seneca."

"But—"

"Now!"

The barrel of the gun edged closer until it brushed against my cheek. I swallowed hard. "I...um, I can get it for you, but you'll need to back up. Just a little. It's in my pants pocket."

Suspicion was clearly written on his face, but he finally nodded. "Get it, now. And maybe I won't shoot you. Or your furry orange vermin."

Winifred's hiss went on so long, tiny flecks of her saliva hit his arm. Thankfully, he seemed too focused on me to notice.

He did as asked and backed up, but not very much. I wrapped one arm tightly around Winifred. She squirmed, making it difficult to get my phone, but I held on to her. I slid my other hand into my pants pocket and drew out the phone.

"Toss it over there." He pointed to his left with the gun barrel. I didn't waste any time throwing it a few feet away. But my heart ached to know who had texted me. Was it Cody? Evie? Murray? I'd even love one of Murray's SOS calls right about now to do a ketchup run. Not that Lawrence would allow it.

He kept the gun pointed at me, causing me to squirm and sweat. Winifred must have had enough, because she clawed my arm, this time using force, and leaped to the ground. She disappeared into the milkweed until I could no longer see orange fur or butterfly wings. I let out a relieved breath. Maybe she'd be safe if she stayed hidden.

"Now, I guess I'll only need one bullet," said Lawrence.

I whipped around, hoping he'd now forget about Winifred. However, my own future didn't look all that bright.

My phone buzzed again, hopping in the grass. Whoever it was really wanted to talk to me. If it was urgent would the person drive over here to find me?

I wrung my hands together, wishing I still had Winifred to hold on to, but glad she was hiding somewhere behind me. If I knew her, she was crouched down, still listening, and watching. If only there was some way she could help me out of this mess. But it seemed I was on my own.

"You know," said Lawrence, "I'm tired of this game. And I have things to do, so why don't we get this over with."

Was I the "this" in his equation? I didn't like that scenario at all.

"Hey, Lawrence, right now, I'm the only person who knows what you've just told me. If you let me go, I promise I won't rat you out." I would, of course, rat him out, but under the circumstances, it didn't seem wise to say it.

"Not on your life." He smiled. "Actually, it is on your life. Ha! See what I did there?"

A scratching sound came from the tall grass a few feet away. Was that where I'd tossed my phone? It would be my luck that some hawk or owl had flown down and taken off with it, then there'd be no chance for anyone to know what was going on.

"The time has come, Seneca. If you don't want to see the bullet coming, you better close your eyes. Right now."

It was up to me to stop this lunatic. He had a gun. But what did I have? As my gaze took in the grass around me, I spotted it. My rake. I took a step to the right, trying to get closer.

"What are you doing?" He moved his gun, so it followed me.

I took another step. That rake might be my only way to get him to drop his gun. But I needed a distraction. How could I—

An orange blur ran past me and zipped in between Lawrence's feet. When Lawrence glanced down at Winifred, I dove for the rake and snatched it up. By the time he'd regained his balance, I was only a few inches away. With one sharp motion, I struck the gun with the rake, hitting the weapon a few feet away to my left.

Lawrence's eyes narrowed. "Oh, no, you don't!" He tried to grab the rake handle from me, but I took a swipe at his cheek. Then, I hit him right above his eyebrow.

Lawrence screamed, putting his hand to his face. Drops of blood ran down between his fingers, landing in the grass.

Taking advantage of Lawrence being temporarily blinded by the blood, I hurried to toss the rake away and trade it for his gun. I had no desire to kill him, but pointed the barrel at his knee. If I had to, I could at least stop him from coming at me again, or getting away.

"Winifred? You've been a very good girl. Come to Mama, and there will be salmon in your near future."

Winifred turned her head toward me and gave a tired mew. She ran toward me, then climbed up my leg and torso, gluing her body to my chest. I patted her back a few times, then quickly took hold of the gun again with both hands. Now that I had the weapon, I could retrieve my phone and call Cody.

Then a noise I normally hated, but at this moment loved, came from the base of my gravel drive on the other side of my barn. A siren!

Lawrence wiped away blood from his eyes, then gasped as he craned his neck to see who was coming. But he had to know it was either Cody or Bud, since our department was tiny. He took a step back, then another. He was trying to get away.

"Stop!" I yelled.

"You won't use that gun, Seneca. We both know you won't." His voice sounded confident, but his hands shook.

"Really? Want to try me?" Even though it was hard, I held my hands firm and straight. No use letting him know that I was scared as a fidgety cat.

The blessed sound of tires on gravel got louder, and then Cody's car came into view.

Winifred disengaged herself from my front and jumped to the ground with a thump. What was she doing?

Cody's car jerked to a stop, and he leaped out, leaving his door open. "Seneca? Are you all right?"

"I am now." I released a pent-up breath and tossed the gun on the ground, because Cody had one of his own, and it was aimed right at Lawrence, but not at his knee. Winifred tore across the grass ran around behind Cody, vaulted into the air, and landed on his back. Cody's pained expression told the rest of the story until my cat appeared on his left shoulder. And the whole time, Cody's gaze never left Lawrence, nor did the gun lower even a fraction.

Admiration for Cody's skill as a sheriff, along with relief that he was here, caused me to wilt into a lump on the ground.

"Seneca?" Cody's voice reached me even though I didn't look up.

"I'm okay," I said.

Cody walked toward Lawrence, who had drooped, arms hanging listlessly at his sides, knees ready to buckle. Once Cody had handcuffs on him and made him sit on the ground, he put his gun in its holster. Keeping his focus on Lawrence, Cody grabbed his phone from his pocket and called Dana.

"She'll tell Bud to get right out here," said Cody. He came toward me, arms out, and engulfed me in a hug. "Seneca, I was so scared when I heard what happened."

I enjoyed the hug for a minute, then frowned. "Wait, how did you hear about it?"

"Well…" He tilted his head toward Winifred, who was sitting on his shoulder.

"What are you saying?"

"Did you at some point lose control of your phone?" he asked.

"Yes, but how…" I glanced over to where I'd tossed my cell in the grass and remembered hearing something scratching earlier, having assumed it was a bird. But what if it was….

I reached up and gathered all the furriness and wings that was Winifred into my arms. "Kitty, how did you do that?"

Cody petted Winifred between her ears, causing her to let out a rumbling purr. "I think I might know what happened. See, I'd sent you a couple of texts."

"So that was you. Lawrence had already forced me to throw my phone over there. But I heard it go off."

"And where was Winifred?"

"She'd been hiding in the milkweed."

Cody's eyebrows rose. "So you never saw her come out?"

"No, I heard a noise in the grass, but I couldn't see what it was.

He rubbed my shoulder, then petted Winifred again. "Since I had already texted you, my number would have been the last one on there. If she put her paw on the phone—"

"Or sat on it," I added.

He smiled. "—right. Then that would explain how I heard you talking to Lawrence."

"You did?"

"Yep. Then I heard a quiet meow. It was like she was whispering. Winifred called me, and I heard what was going on."

Tears ran down my cheeks as I kissed Winifred, then hugged Cody with Winifred between us. "Thank you. Both of you, for helping me."

Cody glanced at Lawrence. "You're welcome, but it looks like you were doing great on your own."

Lawrence groaned.

Cody smiled.

Winifred purred.

Chapter Twenty-Nine

The following evening, after closing time, Murray went all out and prepared a victory dinner at Painted Wings. His food was always amazing, but for some reason, tonight's looked spectacular. Everything appeared the same, but there seemed to be an added ingredient. Maybe it was that he cared so much about us, and providing us with nourishment was his way of showing it.

Evie, of course, was already at Painted Wings when I arrived, having worked her shift. She looked tired, but somehow energized, and her hug nearly squished the life out of me. Winifred, who'd trotted in behind me, rubbed against Evie's ankles until she picked her up.

Those two had gotten closer since Evie had been accused of Burlington's death. It was as though Winifred knew that Evie needed extra attention. I truly believed cats knew when people had something going on and needed love. But with felines' stubbornness and independence, sometimes they didn't bother. I was glad that this time Winifred had gone the extra mile, or in her case, extra yard.

When Cody walked in, I laughed, pointing at the top of his head.

His eyes rolled up as if trying to see it for himself. "What? I remembered to brush my hair today." He raised his hand to touch his hair, but I shook my head.

"Don't move, Cody."

"Come on, Seneca. What is it? Is it a spider? You know I hate spiders. Is it one of those big ones? Remember the one when we were little and at your grandmother's barn?"

"No, it's not that." I walked to him. "Now, slowly, bend down a little toward me, but don't touch your hair."

"I don't know what's going on, but I don't think I like it."

"It'll be fine. Don't you trust me?"

His eyes met mine. "You know I do." He bent down, as instructed.

With care, I reached up and coaxed two monarch butterflies onto my fingers. They sniffed my fingers with their antennae for a few seconds, then settled into one spot on the back of my hand. "Okay, you can stand up now."

His grin was wide when he saw who he'd given a ride to. "Aww, look at that. I didn't feel them land. I wonder how long they'd been there."

I held my hand in the air, and the two beauties fluttered together in a spiral of orange and black as they rose to find places on the rafters to perch. When they landed, I could just barely make them out, as they slowly moved their wings up and down in a rhythmic dance all their own.

Murray came up beside us and glanced at the butterflies. "They got the best seats in the house. Can see what's going on, but are out of harm's way. Pretty smart little creatures."

"You're right about that," said Cody.

Evie let out a contented sigh. "Such a great sight. And the butterflies should be here with us, right? To celebrate the good outcome of Burlington's investigation"—she smiled at Cody—"and for you"—she grabbed my hand with her free one—"that you're okay!"

Murray, who'd stepped out of the room after admiring the butterflies, came out from the back area and placed an additional bowl on the counter. "All right, you people, dinner is served." He waved his hand at the counter, which was laden with his culinary delights.

We all filled our plates and approached one of the café's larger tables, which had been set with silverware, napkins, and drinks at each seat. Very fancy compared to how we sent customers home with their food in Styrofoam containers. It made this evening feel festive.

I sat down, with Cody to my left and Evie to my right, while Murray sat across from me. "Thank you, Murray, so much for all of this. It looks and smells wonderful."

A slight blush rose to his cheeks, peeking out above his white mustache. "Well, somebody has to feed you guys. Take care of you." He wiped his eyes, but didn't say anything else. When Evie squeezed my hand beneath the table, I knew exactly what she meant: that Murray cared so deeply for us, and this was his way to show us.

Cody reached for his glass and took a drink. "I wholeheartedly agree. Thanks, Murray, for including me in this celebration."

Evie tilted her head. "But, Cody, it was your investigation that led to my great personal outcome."

"Personal outcome?" I looked at her. "Are you talking about more than being found innocent of the murder?"

"You bet I am. Well, also, I'm guessing you might have heard that Karen Blain is now the new bank manager?"

"I didn't know that. It's wonderful. I know for a fact she can use the extra funds to help her family. She must be thrilled."

"She is. I saw her this morning before the café opened, and..." She looked at each of us in turn, wearing a grin. It was obvious she was bursting to tell us something but wanted to increase the suspense of the moment.

"And..." Cody moved his hand in a circle. "Don't keep us hanging. What else happened?"

"Karen approved my loan. I'm getting a house!"

I screeched, startling Winifred, who'd been sitting beneath my chair. She scrambled in place and hid beneath a small table in the corner usually reserved for singles who wanted some time alone.

"Uh oh. I've done it now. She might not come out of there until Christmas."

Murray waved his hand in the cat's direction. "She'll be okay. I'll give her a treat when we're finished. I'll bet my mustache that she'd come out for that."

And that was quite the bet. It had taken Murray years to grow his long, thick facial hair, to get it just how he liked it, like that of an old western gunslinger ready for a high noon brawl.

Winifred must have heard the word treat, because her ears perked up, and she looked right at Murray.

Cody leaned forward to look directly at Evie. "That's great news. Do you have a house in mind?"

"Maybe. I have my eye on a couple. I'm so excited I can't stand it." Her eyes widened, as if she couldn't take the amazing news in herself.

I clapped. "I'm so happy for you. And you know that I'll help you move, or whatever."

"We all will," said Cody.

Murray gave a nod. "Count me in, Evie."

I took a few bites of food, made an appreciative yummy noise, then faced Evie. "Did Karen happen to say anything more about her new job?"

"She's thrilled, of course. But she's also heartbroken that her coworker turned out to be a killer. She had no idea that all this time he'd been up to 'nefarious actions'—her words."

"Yeah," said Cody, "that's a good way to describe it. That guy was up to no good. I was fooled at first, that's for sure."

"And to think," I added, "I had Lawrence working here too. Believe me, I had no idea either, since I thought it was Penny who'd done the deed."

Evie nudged me with her elbow. "But you still have your other two, um, employees."

I groaned. "Well, I guess so. When they ever decide to show up. Things can't go on much longer like this. I really have to get someone permanent."

"Annie's shoes will be hard to fill," said Murray. "As odd as she is, she does love those butterflies, and taking care of them."

"That's for sure." When Annie had helped me care for the monarchs, even the larvae, her habit was to ask them every morning if they slept well.

Evie nodded. "I've even seen her in the café when a monarch or two floated in. She watched them, a smile on her face, as if she'd never seen one before. I know we all miss her, especially you, Seneca. But I'm glad she's finally getting to pursue her dream of being a doctor."

"So am I. Even though things are difficult without her, I wouldn't take that away from her for the world."

Murray held out his hand to Winifred and wiggled his fingers. Although she was often frightened of him, his offer of treats must have convinced her otherwise. Because she raced across the floor and rubbed her whiskers against his hand. "All right, Winifred, how about a nice piece of chicken?" He glanced at me, his eyebrows raised in question.

"Okay." Winifred didn't normally get people food, but this was a celebration, after all. "Small piece." I held up two fingers a half inch apart.

"Of course." He cut off a piece, not small, but I didn't say anything, and he placed it on the floor. Winifred had it gone in three seconds flat. She looked up at him hopefully.

"No, Winifred," I said.

She frowned at me, then sat next to Murray's chair, licking her paws.

When we'd finished the meal and complimented Murray once again, we all relaxed in our seats. I for one, was relishing the time with friends and family. Although, in my heart, they truly were all my family, not just Evie. When my grandmother died, it had been so difficult, so heartbreaking. But these three people had stepped in and given me even more love and support than they normally did, which was a lot.

Cody leaned forward, placing his forearms on the table. "Now that the scary stuff is over—"

Murray's eyebrows rose.

With a laugh, Cody said, "Not the meal, of course, but the murder and investigation. I'm still trying to absorb all that happened. Who was actually involved. And who wasn't."

This was pure Cody. Wanting to know the answers to everything. Wanting every small piece to fit, to make sense. It was what made him an excellent sheriff. Maple Junction was lucky to have him.

"Well," said Evie, "I was shocked when I learned that Lawrence had been the one to kill Burlington, as we all were. He seemed so gentle, so unassuming. But I guess he's also a great actor, good at fooling people."

"I agree." I frowned. "Once he started working for me, I got to know him. Actually, I guess I didn't, since what I believed about him was a lie."

Cody shook his head. "Hey, don't feel too bad. It's my job to know these things, and I didn't get it at first either."

Murray gave one of his customary grunts. "You all are too hard on yourselves. I saw him in here frequently, and I didn't see it either. And you know I'm often the first one of us to think the worst of people." His lips quirked.

We all laughed. Even though Murray was making a joke, it had some truth to it. He was never one to immediately trust a person. It took him time to warm up to people. But once he liked a person he was all in.

I drummed my fingers on the table. "I believed in my heart it was Penny. I'm relieved to be wrong, because I like her so much."

Evie nodded. "I wondered about her too, but I also didn't trust Mike after you and I overheard him talking to his troops."

"Troops?" asked Murray. "I knew he dressed up in military garb but didn't know he was actually in the service."

I glanced at Evie. "What we saw was him talking to his group of men who were in his club for the historical reenactments."

Murray leaned forward, putting his elbows on the table. "But he was addressing them, as if he was their leader?"

Evie and I exchanged looks again.

"Yes," she said. "If that leader is inebriated."

"He was drunk?" Murray's eyes widened.

"Very," muttered Cody. "Believe me, I was up close and personal to all of them after they decided to storm the castle, which happened to be Burlington's son's house."

"I missed that part." Evie flipped her hand. "But I did hear him talking to his men, waving a bottle around, getting more and more sauced by the second."

"At least," said Cody, "when I discovered he had a solid alibi for Burlington's murder, I could let him off the hook for that. But they still all got a citation for drunk driving. No way I could just let that go."

"What's this town coming to?" Murray shook his head.

"Yep." I nodded. "I followed the line of weaving cars, like a parade of meandering turtles."

"I'll have to say," said Murray, "my money had been on that kid Devan."

"Why had you picked him?" asked Evie.

He lifted one shoulder in a shrug. "I think because of his intensity when he'd talked about his girlfriend. Then, when I overheard Johnny Overmeyer telling somebody that he'd witnessed Devan sobbing about her breaking up with him and then adding that Burlington had something to do with that, I really considered him to be guilty."

Murray glanced at me. "Seneca, you talked to those twins the other day, after I told you they'd been yakking about Burlington's murder. Did you learn anything more from them?"

"They had some theories, but nothing conclusive. They're an odd pair, those sisters. I was worried about Flora, the way she was so nervous. I bet she shredded at least a half dozen napkins while I sat with them. But when Nora said they were glad Burlington was dead and that he wanted to have Flora committed, I was stunned. Burlington had a relative who must have had similar actions as Flora, and back then, they didn't know what it was. Probably OCD, or something similar. His relative was stuck in an institution, and they all thought she was a witch."

Murray gasped. "Witch?"

I shivered. "Yeah, can you imagine them thinking that? When Burlington observed Flora in the pharmacy doing something he considered suspicious, he threatened to have her committed. Thank goodness that didn't happen."

I leaned back against my seat. "I'd also wondered about Betty Rollings when she acted so crazy about protecting trees and had a history of chaining herself to them, especially after I learned that Burlington was behind wanting to cut down the trees near her property. But I also have to admit that Karen was on my list for a while, too."

Cody brushed his hand through his hair, leaving a small piece sticking up. "Speaking of Karen, I discovered from her, using a search warrant at the bank, that Burlington had been behind the corporation that had kicked Evie out of her apartment."

Evie's mouth dropped open. "Of course. That makes perfect sense, doesn't it? And it made me look even more guilty as a motive for getting rid of Burlington with the announcement beforehand of him closing down the apartment building."

"Yeah." Cody nodded. "But you were never a suspect in my estimation."

CHAPTER TWENTY-NINE

She smiled. "Thanks, Cody."

"And," he said, "after I arrested Lawrence, he admitted that he found out about Burlington while snooping through his paperwork one day and decided to use the information to frame Evie."

I glanced at Cody's disheveled hair. I wanted to reach up and fix it but knew he'd be embarrassed, so I restrained myself. Instead, I turned to the group. "I'm so glad things worked out for Karen with her job. By the way, Evie, when you talked to her about your loan, did she happen to say who the replacement teller would be for Lawrence?"

"She didn't say who, but I did get the impression they were having a hard time finding the right person."

I rolled my eyes. "That sounds familiar."

"Hey." Murray tapped his finger on the table. "Maybe the bank could hire Norman and Sid to do the job."

I snorted. "With the way they are here just using rakes in the milkweed, I don't even want to think what might happen to everyone's money they'd be in charge of at the bank. And sadly, I still need a permanent assistant."

"Someone is out there," said Cody. "Remember, you didn't know Annie very well before she started working for you. I bet there's somebody you'll like just as well, who will be great at working with you at Majestic Monarchs."

"I hope you're right."

"Of course, I'm right. I'm always right." He grinned.

Evie glanced at her watch. "Oh wow, it's getting late, and I'm beat. Would you guys mind if we start to wind down our evening? I hate to do it, but I still need to clean the café and..."

"We'll help you," I said.

She held up her hand. "No. You all go home. Even you, Murray."

He frowned. "But I can..."

"No, I insist. You made this amazing meal, and I'm so grateful. And Seneca is still recovering from her awful encounter with Lawrence. And Cody saved her life."

From beneath Murray's chair came a loud meow.

"Oh," said Evie, "Sorry, Winifred. Yes, you were a huge help in saving

Seneca, too."

I stood. "If you're sure. But I really don't mind helping you."

She stood too, then hugged me. "I'm sure. Please, go get some rest. I'll see you tomorrow."

"All right. Good night, everyone, and thanks again, Murray."

As I headed toward the door, Cody caught up with me. "Like some company walking home?"

"I literally live right over there, you know." I pointed to the farmhouse. "It's not very far."

"I know. But… after what nearly happened to you with Lawrence, I kind of want to make sure you get home okay."

"Okay." I bumped his side with my shoulder, and he bumped me back, something we'd done since we were kids. How fortunate I was to have him as my friend.

When we reached my door, I opened it so Winifred could run inside to the dry food in her bowl. It wouldn't measure up to what Murray had given her, but it would have to do.

Cody wrapped his arms around me and gave me a quick but firm hug. "I'm so relieved you're all right, Seneca. I thought I'd lost you. And since this was the second time, you'd almost…" He let out a breath. "Well, I'm just so glad you're here."

"I'm glad too. Thank you for saving me. Again."

From inside the closed screen door, Winifred meowed.

"Yes, you too, kitty."

I rolled my eyes at Cody, but we both smiled.

"All right," he said, "now that you're safely home, I'm heading home too." He watched me for a second, then leaned closer. My heart thudded hard. Was he going to kiss me? Had all those people talking about our supposed romantic interlude convinced Cody he should really make it happen?

When his lips landed lightly on my cheek, I let out a sigh. Because I was relieved, I didn't have to face something I wasn't quite ready for, that our friendship might change, or that it might become something that wasn't right for us, forever forcing us apart, no longer close, sweet friends.

But the other side of me was a tiny bit disappointed at what it might have become. At what could have been. But maybe it still would. Someday.

Time would tell.

235

About the Author

Ruth J. Hartman spends her days herding cats and her nights spinning mysterious tales. She, her husband, and their cats love to spend time curled up in their recliners watching old Cary Grant movies. Well, the cats sit in the people's recliners. Not that the cats couldn't get their own furniture. They just choose to shed on someone else's.

Ruth, a left-handed, cat-herding, farmhouse-dwelling writer uses her sense of humor as she writes tales of lovable, klutzy women who seem to find trouble without even trying.

Ruth's husband and best friend, Garry, reads her manuscripts, rolls his eyes at her weird story ideas, and loves her despite her insistence all of her books have at least one cat in them. See updates about her cozy mysteries at Ruthjhartman.com.

SOCIAL MEDIA HANDLES:
  https://www.facebook.com/ruth.j.hartman
  https://www.facebook.com/profile.php?id=100063631596817
  https://www.bookbub.com/profile/ruth-j-hartman

AUTHOR WEBSITE:

Also by Ruth J. Hartman

The Kitty Beret Café Mystery Series

The Bookshop Kitties Mysteries

The Mobile Cat Groomer Mysteries

Ring of Death (A Dorey Cameron Mystery)